"I can be most persuasive." He leaned down to press kisses to the base of her throat. His heated mouth stirred a restless desire to arch her bound breasts.

He lifted his head, and watching her, he cocked his hips in a slow upward stroke of his body against hers. It was a pleasure she could hardly bear. She tried to summon ordinary sensation, but the wicked new pleasure drove out all recollection of familiar delights—the sun on her face, cooling breezes, lilacs in bloom, warm bread, strawberries.

The elusive sensation hovered, fleeting and intense, distilled to a single aching point and vast as a sea in which her other senses drowned. It could not be named or catalogued. She needed to invent a new sense to capture it.

"What did you go to get from March's brothel? This?"

Again she shook her head, keeping her lips firmly closed. She was conscious of the heat in her face and a shameful reflex in her legs to close and hold him there.

"Your parents don't know where you are, do they? But someone does, an aunt, a cousin? Who helped you get to London?"

How had he guessed? Cousin Margaret would be worried sick not to hear from her.

He had that knowing look on his face. "You're not the first fool to run away from home."

Then his gaze settled on her lips, and he lowered his head. His mouth paused above hers.

She told herself it was a threat, a tease. She should turn away, but her lips parted to taste his breath, warm and brandy-scented, and her body strained upward in anticipation.

To Save the Devil

KATE MOORE

BERKLEY SENSATION, NEW YORK

THE BERKLEY PUBLISHING GROUP
Published by the Penguin Group
Penguin Group (USA) Inc.
375 Hudson Street, New York, New York 10014, USA

Penguin Group (Canada), 90 Eglinton Avenue East, Suite 700, Toronto, Ontario M4P 2Y3, Canada
(a division of Pearson Penguin Canada Inc.)
Penguin Books Ltd., 80 Strand, London WC2R 0RL, England
Penguin Group Ireland, 25 St. Stephen's Green, Dublin 2, Ireland (a division of Penguin Books Ltd.)
Penguin Group (Australia), 250 Camberwell Road, Camberwell, Victoria 3124, Australia
(a division of Pearson Australia Group Pty. Ltd.)
Penguin Books India Pvt. Ltd., 11 Community Centre, Panchsheel Park, New Delhi—110 017, India
Penguin Group (NZ), 67 Apollo Drive, Rosedale, North Shore 0632, New Zealand
(a division of Pearson New Zealand Ltd.)
Penguin Books (South Africa) (Pty.) Ltd., 24 Sturdee Avenue, Rosebank, Johannesburg 2196,
South Africa

Penguin Books Ltd., Registered Offices: 80 Strand, London WC2R 0RL, England

TO SAVE THE DEVIL

A Berkley Sensation Book / published by arrangement with the author

PRINTING HISTORY
Berkley Sensation mass-market edition / October 2010

Copyright © 2010 by Kate Moore.
Excerpt from *To Seduce an Angel* by Kate Moore copyright © 2010 by Kate Moore.
Cover art by Phil Heffernan.
Cover design by George Long.
Cover hand lettering by Ron Zinn.
Interior text design by Kristin del Rosario.

ISBN: 978-0-425-23748-9

BERKLEY® SENSATION
Berkley Sensation Books are published by The Berkley Publishing Group,
a division of Penguin Group (USA) Inc.,
375 Hudson Street, New York, New York 10014.
BERKLEY® SENSATION and the "B" design are trademarks of Penguin Group (USA) Inc.

PRINTED IN THE UNITED STATES OF AMERICA

10 9 8 7 6 5 4 3 2 1

For Loren—
my partner in our happily ever after—
with love, K.

I should have been that I am, had the maidenliest star in the firmament twinkled at my bastardizing.

—EDMUND, *KING LEAR*

Chapter One

❧

LONDON, 1820

IT was a bleeding soggy night for a man to leave his bed to buy a virgin. Will Jones looked through the fogged carriage window at the white-columned portico of a discreet town house on Half Moon Street. If Jack Castle's information was good, deflowering virgins was just one of the depravities available inside.

Fistfuls of hard rain rattled the glass. Will nodded to his man Harding to put their plan in motion. He swung open the coach door and stepped down. His foot met wet cobblestones, and a sharp twinge in his ribs stopped him cold. He covered the hitch in his stride with a gentleman's small vanities, tugging white cuffs from the fine wool of his black evening clothes and tilting his hat at a jaunty angle.

The pause allowed him a moment to observe the house closely. He had spent weeks in less-secure prisons. Cleverly painted wood panels covered the upper windows, and two oversized pugilists in footmen's attire stood guard on either side of the door. Still, the place had its vulnerabilities. The top of the carriage met the height of the portico, above which an iron railing connected with others down the block to the corner of Piccadilly, where late evening traffic still passed.

Over his shoulder Will offered his driver a few words in French, shedding his own identity as he became the Vicomte de Villard with a West Indian fortune, an ugly wife, and a habit of collecting erotic prints.

The oversized footmen stared straight ahead as Will raised the door's brass knocker, but he wasn't deceived by their apparent inattention. They'd know him again.

A face as red and pitted as a brick appeared in the peephole.

"Twenty-five guineas." Brick Face had a rasp of a voice that could file metal.

"*Bien sûr.* To attain a great prize, one must expect to invest one's coin." Will shoved the paper notes through the hole.

Inside, Brick Face took Will's cloak, hat, and gloves and grunted an order to wait. The entry hall gave no particular sign of vice, just the well-bred English comforts of a Turkish rug, mahogany console, and tall case clock, but somewhere in London, Archibald March, the murdering maggot who owned the place, was free.

Most Londoners knew March as the city's great

benefactor, a man whose charities reportedly supported widows and orphans, the lame and the blind. Only a handful of people including Will, his brother Xander, and Xander's bride, Cleo, had reason to believe that March was a murderer and a blackmailer who had killed at least three people and kept files on the vices and sins of many more. If the authorities would not bring March down, Will would.

Coarse male laughter erupted from a room somewhere above, and quick steps sounded on the stair.

The next moment the host appeared, and Will decided that the hall was an anteroom of hell after all.

He did not care to shake hands with Guy Leary, a lean, freckle-faced felon with carrot-colored hair and a cold glance that said he was up to any viciousness. That Leary was in charge and not some well-preserved bawd with a plump bosom and an ingratiating air spoke volumes about the place. Will suspected the female employees did not enjoy Leary's style of management.

"What's your pleasure tonight, Monsieur le Vicomte?"

"I understand an auction is about to begin."

Leary glanced at the clock and shook his head. "Sorry, Vicomte. Auctions are by invitation only, to interested parties known to this house. We can offer you other delights, however."

"Allow me to express my interest in participating in your auction." Will put a stack of notes on the console next to him.

"I don't know you."

"You don't know the Vicomte de Villard? I thought

3

my print collection had a certain reputation." He handed Leary a flat package wrapped in brown paper.

With another impatient glance at the clock, Leary tore off the wrapping and regarded the print. Closely.

"How did you come to hear of our auction?" Nothing changed outwardly in the cold face, but Will caught the change in tone.

"A friend took pity on me. I faced a dull evening with my wife, and only my prints to rouse me. The prospect of your virgin lifted my spirits at once. She is the authentic article? One may examine her to be certain?"

"One may not."

"But you do guarantee . . ."

"Do you want in or not?"

Will waved a languid hand. "Please. Lead on."

Leary spun abruptly and led the way up a grand curving staircase.

"Does this exquisite have a name?"

"Helen of Troy."

Will almost choked at the irony. Clearly Leary was a man who'd never had the benefit of a good tutor. A good grinder like old Hodge would have set him straight about naming his virgin after the most famous wanton in history.

At the top of the stairs they entered a red-and-gold salon filled with gentlemen of various ages but a common carnal bent. The air was stale with tobacco and lust. Three young women dressed in cream silk corsets over lawn drawers as thin as tissue circulated among the more completely clad males, keeping every glass brimmed. Their female presence in proper English undress among the fully clothed males gave a carnal kick to the gathering. It also gave new meaning to the practice of dress lodgers, women so wholly owned by their employers they had no clothes to their names. Guy Leary summoned a dark-haired beauty with red pouting lips and empty eyes, who provided Will with a glass of brandy.

Over its rim Will surveyed the mixed lot of pleasure seekers. He recognized two members of Parliament, not of the Reform Party, one octogenarian lord, and where the talk was loudest and bawdiest, one of the Earl of Oxley's other sons, a man with whom he shared a sire but nothing else. His luck held. There were no officers present and no one who knew either Villard or Will Jones. Certainly his Oxley half brother would not recognize the family bastard.

The crowd was the sort he'd known in Paris after Waterloo and before the disappearance of Kit, his youngest brother. Some had lost a sense of the boundaries of civilized men, hooked on debauchery the way a man could be hooked on opium. Others merely came to be titillated. They would go home and pump their wives heartily while images of erotic excess danced in their heads.

For a moment Will felt Villard's identity slip away from him and his old identity as a Bow Street Runner assert itself, but he was not here in an official police capacity. He straightened the diamond stickpin in the folds of his cravat to recover his disguise as Villard, refined connoisseur of decadence, a man superior to ordinary brutes with their vulgar zest for pinching bottoms and ogling breasts.

Chairs and sofas had been arranged to view a stage draped in red velvet curtains at the far end of the room. One of the hulking footmen brought Will a chair as Leary mounted the stage and tapped a glass.

Conversation died, and men sat. The three corset-clad women, nearly indistinguishable in round-limbed, vacant appearance, took positions behind Leary. Most of the room's occupants watched them as Leary explained the auction rules.

Will studied the competition. They'd been invited, so they knew the girl behind the curtain was a virgin, not a professional, and they'd paid a steep fee to participate as he had, so he had to assume that he was up against men with deep pockets and shallow consciences. Still, a lot would depend on the girl herself.

Leary paused. "Gentlemen, what am I bid for a night with Helen of Troy?"

At his signal the women drew back the velvet curtains to reveal a girl with tawny golden hair in a blue-sashed gown of virginal white, lolling on a rose-and-gold-striped sofa, her head resting on one slim arm, dark lashes against flushed cheeks. She had the look of a schoolroom miss who had stayed up too late and just closed her eyes for a moment. Leary would have done better to advertise her as the Sleeping Beauty.

It was hard to tell her age, but at least she was not fifteen as Will had feared. Except for bare feet, unbound hair, and rouged breasts, she looked respectable enough for a ball, innocence and sensuality combined. That wanton innocence hit him with an erotic jolt that could raise a cock stand in a corpse. He reminded himself that in such a place, the girl's appearance could all be a show. She could be a professional after all.

Then her eyes fluttered open, deep brown and instantly panicked. Not a professional, but a trapped, frightened girl. How had she fallen into March's net?

Her attendants helped her to stand. Their efforts had the look of guards restraining a prisoner rather than the Three Graces attending a goddess, but she would have done well for one of those Italian painters. Tall and lithely built, like a young Amazon, she was fighting the influence of some drug. He could see it in her dilated pupils. The narcotic would take hold and make her head sag on her slender neck, or she would shake it off and look frantically about. He wondered that she didn't scream or protest.

Men began shouting. A flurry of bids quickly reduced the competition to a pair of bloods—a ruddy, flat-faced blond and a long-nosed brunet. On their feet, facing one another, the pair swayed from drink. Others in the crowd immediately made side bets on the outcome.

The flat-faced blond gave his opponent a shove. "Bow out, Milsing, you've been sailing on river tick for months."

"I've got twice the blunt you've got, any day, Cowley." Long-nose shoved back.

Cowley staggered, righted himself, and giggled.

"Here's a thought, man." He waved a finger in the air. "We could share her."

There was a general mumble from the crowd, not an actual protest, just a sense of grievance.

Milsing frowned. "Well, we could all buy shares, Cowley, but only one man goes first, you know."

It was time to act. Will Jones would pick up a table or a chair and break it over someone's head, but as Villard, he needed a more subtle approach. He rose slowly and hurled his brandy glass against the mantel. Glass shattered with a satisfying ring. All heads turned his way. The sound seemed to penetrate even the girl's fogged brain. She lifted her chin, and her dark gaze met Will's in a brief moment of lucid consciousness.

That's right, sweetheart, you're leaving with me.

Chapter Two

⧉

WILL controlled an impulse to laugh at the befuddled outrage on the faces of the competition. "Gentlemen, I have yet to make my bid."

"Who the hell are you?" Milsing demanded.

Will bowed. "Villard." The disguise had served him well on several cases while he had been a Runner.

"A damned Frenchie?" Obscene murmurs rippled around him.

"Ah, but I offer English money. Five hundred pounds."

"Five hundred! Damned unsporting no matter what your money is."

"For Helen of Troy? Your pardon, gentlemen, but the lady is priceless."

They turned to stare at the girl as if they'd forgotten her actual presence.

Cowley turned back to Will first. "Look here, this is a closed auction, how did you get in?"

Will turned to Guy Leary with a shrug. All that mattered now was the man's rapaciousness. *"Vraiment.* I arrived late, but so great is my need, you see I am willing to pay."

The girl's head was down again, but he could sense her concentration on his voice.

"Make it a thousand," Leary said.

"Bien sûr." Will didn't blink.

After a moment Leary nodded. "Helen of Troy goes to—Villard." He stepped into the crowd. "Gentlemen, the house thanks you for your participation. We offer other consolations to gratify all who bid." Brick Face seized the girl by the arm, and Guy nodded to the Three Graces, who began refilling glasses.

"Vicomte, we'll settle the bill. Miss Troy will wait for you upstairs."

Will nodded. His gaze was on the girl's arm where Brick Face's beefy grip pinched her flesh. He smiled cordially at the man. "Bruise her, and I'll break your hand."

Another brutish footman led Will up the curving staircase. The route meant he saw little of the house, only its street-facing public rooms. He could guess at the layout of the place, but he saw no location that might hold March's supposed files. Castle had done him a favor giving him information about this auction, but at the moment the girl came first. Her situation trumped

Will's desire to bring March to justice. Besides, Will's escort did not encourage idle exploration of the house.

The room where the girl waited was a flight above the salon, facing the street. A collection of suitably stimulating art and strategically placed mirrors covered its deep coral walls. Over the hearth a still life of gray-speckled gull's eggs in a nest of osiers added the only touch of the natural world. Brick Face standing over the girl did nothing to improve the furnishings.

Will made a quick inventory of what he had to work with. A paneled headboard on the bed at his right met the ceiling in a short overhanging canopy. The bed itself looked sturdy enough for the most athletic of sexual encounters. Red silk cords fastened its dark velvet hangings to the headboard. Across the room from the foot of the bed an iron poker leaned against the hearth. Cords *and* a poker. Things looked to be going Will's way for once.

A bottle of wine and two glasses stood on a table by the door. Will lifted the bottle, uncorked it, and gave the contents a sniff. He turned to Brick Face. "This won't do. We need champagne, don't we, *ma belle?*"

The girl huddled in a chair, gripping its arms. Her gaze shifted from Brick Face to Will.

"Wine is what ye get." Brick Face shrugged his ample shoulders.

"Nonsense." Will waved another note at the Brick. "Take this insipid swill away. We must have champagne. Helen of Troy deserves no less. See what you can do, man, and be quick about it. If you return within ten minutes, I will reward you with another fiver."

After a moment of less-than-rapid thinking, Brick Face took the bottle and backed out of the room.

Will turned to the huddled girl. "Now, *ma belle*, we can begin to become acquainted. You are to be congratulated on your good fortune, I think, to have the Vicomte de Villard for your first lover. I can promise not only pleasure but an education."

By Will's estimate they were twenty vertical feet from escape, thirty from the pavement; not an overly difficult route for a young man, but more challenging for a drugged girl and a battered wreck like himself. He had intended to spend the evening in a healing celebration in his own bed with an accommodating old friend, who could be trusted to please without damaging Will's recently beaten body. *Not to be.*

Positioning himself before an obvious two-way mirror, he pulled off his cravat and removed his jacket with slow deliberation. He strolled to the head of the bed and loosened the cords from the bed hangings, draping them around his neck for later use. The girl's wide, baffled eyes followed him as he shifted lamps and candlesticks, blocked the reverse mirror, and tipped a heavy wardrobe in front of the door. He had perhaps five minutes before Brick Face returned, and the other members of Leary's staff turned from the work of consoling the disappointed lords below to take up their posts at the peepholes.

Time to act. In three swift attacks he pulled apart the bed linens, upended a side chair on the opposite side of the hearth, broke off the rungs at its base with his heel, and took up the poker and the two broken lengths of wood.

The girl's bewildered gaze shifted from him to the room, catching on heavy, solid objects.

He crossed to the pair of windows and flicked back their damask drapery. Just as he'd observed from the street, thick boards covered the glass. He chose the nearest window and jammed the poker between the sill and the base of the covering board and pried. The board came free of the window frame with a piercing screech like a dying bird. Will hoped that Brick Face was still on his errand and that whoever manned the peepholes wasn't in place yet.

He paused briefly, listening for sounds of alarm. When he heard no reaction, he went back to work on the other side of the window until the loosened board hung like a stiff tent flap. With the broken chair rungs, he propped the loose board away from the window frame, and slipped inside the open space to raise the sash. Cold damp air blew up through the open window, but no sounds of alarm came from the footmen on duty below. He waited another minute, then dropped a line to signal Harding.

He turned and found the girl at the foot of the bed with a brass candlestick in her hand. He grinned at her.

"Perfect, sweetheart, let's make a brawl of it." He lunged and she swung at him, hitting the bedpost a jarring blow. He dodged right and swung the overturned chair her way, almost pinning her between its rungs against the foot of the bed.

They stood panting, regarding each other warily. Her eyes were wide now, her limbs trembling with the sudden energy of fear. Will knew how rapidly that would drain away and leave her wilted.

He moved in so that her only escape was toward the window. The draft from the open sash caught her and set her trembling in the thin gown. She glanced at the window, and he was on her, twisting the candlestick out of her grip and binding her wrists with his cravat. He threaded one of the thick cords through the binding around her wrists. Harding must be in place by now.

Suddenly the girl was all fury, writhing and struggling in his arms. He caught an elbow in the ribs that made him suck in a breath before he brought her movement to a halt, holding her tight to his body as if they were in a most licentious waltz.

He pressed his lips to her ear and whispered in his own voice, "In one minute, sweetheart, you and I are going out that window. Fight me then, and you'll break your neck."

Again he felt her confusion, the mind fighting to make sense of him. It was enough to give him the advantage he needed. With a swift waltz turn he whirled her into the space between the loose board and the open window. The cold immediately set her teeth chattering. He caught her under the knees, lifted, and swung her feet over the window ledge.

She arched suddenly and swung her bound arms up over his head. He swore.

"I. Can't. Leave. Yet." Her words came out in a breathy staccato.

"No better time. Don't make another sound."

"I have to get what I came for."

Now he was confused. "What?"

She shook her head, her lips firmly closed.

"The only thing you'll get if you don't go through this window is the unpleasant attentions of half a dozen angry brutes, so whatever it is that you came for, plan to come back later, sweetheart."

There was a banging on the door.

"Now." Will ducked, freeing himself from the loop of her arms, then shoved her feet forward through the window. Her bottom caught on the ledge. He gave her one more nudge, and she dangled from her bonds. Her breath came out in a startled squeak, muted by the storm. Her weight strained his arms for a brief moment, then he felt the cord go slack. *Bless Harding.*

Behind him the door shuddered under a heavy blow.

He climbed through the narrow opening, hanging for a few seconds from the sill, quieting his body for the drop, promising his aching ribs he would not mistreat them again soon, then let himself fall.

H ELEN's heart pounded in her chest. She kept her face pressed to the wall in front of her. The sharp bite of its bricks against her cheek held the dizziness at bay. She dare not look down. Her bound hands could grip nothing. She tried to curl her bare toes into the stone of the narrow, iron-railed ledge. Rain plastered her thin gown to her body. A steadying hand on her right elbow was the one warm, secure point in the nightmare.

She had dangled from the window mere seconds before a white-haired gentleman with a butler-like demeanor had caught her legs and steadied her on the narrow ledge.

In the next instant the madman who had pitched her out the window landed beside her. He simply dropped from above, as noiseless and swift as a shadow passing. In landing he gave a muffled grunt of pain. His handsome features briefly contorted in a wince.

He looked over her head at his accomplice and nodded, no words, no sound.

They clung, an unlikely frieze along the ledge. Above the storm she could hear the rattle of a carriage in the street. The next moment it stopped somewhere below them, the horses blowing and stomping, harness jingling.

Voices came from below.

Her madman turned and swung his leg over the iron railing and stepped off the ledge. Helen felt a scream die in her throat. Then she was lifted into his arms, and he brought her down flat, sprawled under him on a wet rocking surface, a carriage roof. It sagged under their weight. His accomplice stepped over them and dropped onto the box next to the driver. The driver cracked his whip, and the carriage sprang forward.

Two shots rang out. Glass shattered behind them. There were angry yells and pursuing footsteps soon lost in the clatter of wheels over the cobbles. Helen and her madman swayed across the roof with the coach's motion, but he kept her anchored to his side with an iron arm around her waist. With her wrists bound she was helpless to save herself. A terrifying turn at the end of the narrow street took them into Piccadilly. Their pace did not slow until they entered a darker quarter of the city. The carriage halted briefly. The white-haired man helped Helen descend via the box into the coach's black interior. He draped a carriage blanket around her shoulders. In the next minute her kidnapper entered and settled opposite her, his pale face the only bit of him visible in the gloom, his dark hair and eyes part of the gloom itself. The carriage resumed its journey.

"You're not a Frenchman, are you?"

"London bred, through and through." He pushed damp black hair away from his face.

"Not Vicomte de Villard?"

"No."

Her head was still dizzy. Her brain was a mad ballroom of whirling thoughts. She wanted them to slow down so that she could order them, maybe into a stately quadrille instead of a galloping waltz. The stranger opposite her had been one person in the salon, and now he was someone else entirely. He seemed to be in some pain in spite of his strength and his remarkable leaps. "Are you called Hades by any chance?"

"Nothing so exalted or so damned. Did you think I was taking you to hell?"

"A maiden seized and carried off in a black coach? It has that Hades-Persephone look about it."

"What's your name?"

"Helen of Troy." The name had come spontaneously to her lips when she'd fallen into Guy Leary's hands. In that moment she had still believed in her plan to gain employment as a maid and search the house.

"You cost nearly as much."

So her madman knew more Greek mythology than the thugs at the brothel. "I didn't ask for your assistance."

"If ever fair maiden needed rescuing, you did." The words were not a compliment.

"I can repay you."

"I doubt it. I laid out some serious coin for the pleasure of your company."

The words made her conscious of the luxurious interior of the carriage.

"I'm not without resources." She had no intention of telling this mad stranger her real position in the world.

"You were for sale in a brothel."

"I told you I went there to get . . ."

"Something you don't wish to name."

"Exactly." Everything she had done had been perfectly reasonable. Only Guy Leary had been unreasonable. Now she would have to begin again. She supposed her madman's use of the word *rescue* was encouraging. He probably meant to restore her to her family or to the authorities, so she had only to assure him that she was capable of taking care of herself.

"Did you think you would just ask them to give you this something?"

The hint of male mockery in the voice stung. "No, of course not. I planned to steal it."

"Pardon me. Before or after someone raped you?"

The well-sprung carriage rolled on as she digested that comment. There was no mistaking the word. Her head throbbed, and she held herself taut against the shivers that threatened. She had believed he was preparing to rape her himself. Instead he'd dropped her out of that window. She couldn't really see him well, and the mystery of him deepened, his plain speaking at odds with the elegant evening clothes, his purchase of her at odds with a rescue.

"You're not a gentleman, either, are you?"

"Not in the least."

She held out her bound wrists. "Are you going to untie me?"

"Are you planning a return to the brothel?"

"I must."

He shrugged. "Suit yourself."

The coach came to a halt. Her madman leaned forward abruptly and bound his handkerchief around her eyes.

Chapter Three

ॐ

WILL tugged his prize virgin down from the coach. She stumbled on the carriage step and fell heavily into his arms. His ribs might complain, but no other part of him made any objection. Silky hair brushed his cheek, and firm, round breasts met his chest, breasts he would see in dreams for weeks. His interrupted plans for the evening came back to taunt him. He was ushering a delectable female into his quarters with no possibility of taking her to bed.

His conscience noted that she was a wet, cold female, near naked in the soaked gown. He needed to get her warm and dry and free of the drug's hold, and take himself out of reach.

He set her on her feet on the pavement and led her by

her bound wrists through the brief maze of lanes that led to his own door. Once his neighborhood had been London's finest, the haunt of lords and ladies, ambassadors and poets. Now its ways were vile and filthy and home to the disreputable and the abandoned. He had acquired his unusual apartments through an earlier case in which he'd cleared the house of a ring of counterfeiters.

He had an arrangement with the local blind man to guard the door. As Will entered the passage, Zebediah's black mastiff detached himself from the shadows and shoved his large head against the girl's ribs.

"Do you have a pony?" she asked in a thin voice.

"Helen, meet Argos, our local blind man's dog."

"Dog?"

"Mastiff. Let him sniff you. He'll know you next time you call on me." He unlocked the hidden door and led her up the two flights of stairs to the outermost room of his linked apartments. He settled her in an antique tapestried chair by the fire and removed the blindfold.

Everything in the room was just as he left it. He stirred up the fire where jugs of water stood waiting to be warmed for the bath. A great copper tub stood next to a bench piled with fragrant towels. He lit a branch of candles on the cabinet by the bed. Ah, he did enjoy that bed.

"Are we still in London?" she asked, looking at the bed.

"In its depths. You're safe here for the moment." He put a kettle on the hob for tea. She would need warming and something to counteract the drug's effects. He took hold of the chair arms and leaned over her. "What did they give you to drink in the brothel?"

"Some chocolate."

"Breathe on me."

"What?"

"Let me smell your breath."

She pressed back in the chair. "You're not serious."

"I am. I'll be able to tell what drug they gave you."

"Oh." She stopped straining away from him. After a moment, she opened her mouth like a singer and exhaled.

He almost groaned as the huff of warm, sweet breath reached him. "Opium and *satirio*."

"What is that?"

"A wild orchid, something to make you most receptive to a man's attentions. Drink as much tea as you can. And eat. You'll find bread and cheese by the bed."

She glanced at it again. "Are you perhaps a sultan?"

He laughed as he spooned leaves into a pot. "No sultan."

He knelt and took her hands in his, chafing them lightly. "I take it that it was not your plan to end up as a prize auction item this evening."

"Of course not."

He laughed at the look of offended intelligence in those brown eyes. "What went wrong?"

"Guy Leary. He was not . . . I did not expect to have to deal with him."

"Whatever your business there, send a man to deal with Leary."

"I can't." Her face was solemn. "I have to go back."

He pulled her to her feet and dragged her over to stand in front of a cheval glass by the enormous bed. "Then I suggest that you change and wash the paint off your breasts before you attempt to pass unnoticed through London's streets."

Their eyes met in the glass, hers shocked and wide, his frankly hungry, with no concealing vicomte to hide behind. He pulled the cords from her wrists, tossed her a towel, and turned away.

ONE moment he was there. Then he was not. Helen was left staring at the wavering image in the glass, which surely was not her father's daughter, not her mother's savior, not herself. The image confounded her. She, who had unthinkingly admired her quiet dignity in her own glass countless times as she left the house, had never seen this woman, had never imagined her.

The damp gown clung to her like the drapery on an alabaster statue. She wore no corset, only a thin chemise that concealed nothing. Her cheeks were flushed. Above the rounded swell of her belly, her nipples jutted out, red as cherries. The triangle at the juncture of her legs stood out darkly from her pale skin. Her body throbbed there.

The towel hung from her numb hand. Her father's deep voice echoed in her brain. *Frailty, thy name is woman*. It was his favorite line in all of Shakespeare. Helen hated Shakespeare for penning it.

She tossed the towel at the glass. It shuddered, and

the image wavered. Her breasts quivered, too, from the motion of her arm, an odd sensation that tied her to the woman in the mirror, the woman she was not. The woman in the mirror could do nothing, go nowhere in London. Her madman knew that. He had simply walked away, making no effort to stop her from leaving. He didn't need to. A glance in the mirror would stop her.

I am not you, she told the woman in the glass. She turned away from the image and snatched another towel from the bench. Her madman was gone, but she did not know for how long. With tingling hands she pulled the gown over her shoulders and rubbed the towel across her breasts.

The mild coarseness of the cloth abraded them and sent jolts of sensation snaking down her belly to the throbbing place between her thighs. She rubbed harder. Streaks of red stained the towel, but her breasts still wore their cherry hue.

She stopped, drew a shuddering breath, and looked about the room again. It was an antique apartment, a gentleman's bedroom from an earlier age, where a man in dishabille would entertain his guests in their panniers and powdered wigs, their velvet frock coats and buckled shoes.

There had to be something at hand with which to restore her appearance. Her gaze found a cake of soap in a dish by the tub. She snatched it up. It smelled of lavender, familiar and ordinary, like the soap she and her mother made each summer. She crossed to the hearth and plunged the fragrant soap in the water pail nearest the coals. The water felt warm to her cold skin. She lathered the soap and spread it on her breasts, and sucked in her breath from the slick contact of her own hands. Steeling herself against another wave of sensation, she scrubbed until the towel contained most of the stain. Her breasts were sore and, though still rosy-tinted, not so vivid in hue. Her gown was sopping and useless.

A wave of dizziness rocked her. Where had her own clothes gone, her layers, her corset and drawers, her stockings and garters, her petticoat and fichu? She had chosen a plain brown wool gown for her plan. She had felt so herself in it, a modest, levelheaded woman of decent birth and means, the sort to whom no man would ever offer insult. She had a hazy memory of three women undressing her as if she were a doll.

She staggered light-headed across the room and threw open a large clothespress. A man's clothes filled it. Shirts, waistcoats, and jackets hung in neat array, fine cravats pressed and ready, shoes and boots lined up beneath them. She pulled open the drawers and found folded undergarments and stockings.

For a moment she stared dumbly at the clothes, as if they had no meaning, a fragment written in a strange tongue. Then she snatched a cravat and wound the long rectangle of linen tightly around her chest, covering and flattening her breasts. At once she felt more herself, plain and contained. She raked her fingers through her hair and coiled it in a knot at her nape.

The teakettle whistled by the fire. She rushed over to it lest the sound should bring him back. With a towel about her hand she lifted the kettle from the hob and filled the pot he'd left for her. By the bed she found the tray of bread and cheese and nuts and figs.

She sank into a high-backed, nail-studded chair by the fire, another relic of that earlier age, and made herself eat and drink. Each bite was an effort. She had no idea of the hour, still night but close to day. She kept nodding off when what she needed was a clear head and a new strategy.

The question was how to get back inside the brothel without ending up as an item on the bill of fare. She could not pretend to be a housemaid in search of employment as she had two days earlier. That plan had failed, but she had learned some things nevertheless. To avoid Leary she would need a new way to gain admission to the place.

Her head dropped, and she jerked back to wakefulness and pushed out of the chair on shaking legs. She wrapped the second towel around her shoulders and made herself walk around the strange apartment. Its wide, old parquetry was worn, but the rugs were soft under her feet.

Her madman claimed they were in the heart of London. Its *depths* he had said. The bed was not English at all with its fat posts like straight, young palm trees, its tangerine damask hangings and blue silken coverlet and pillows. She saw now what she had not recognized earlier: that he had prepared for a guest. The tray of refreshments bore two glasses, two plates. There had been two towels on the bench. Candles lit the way to the bed.

Had he left some other woman to cross London in the storm to buy Helen and free her? But how could he have known how her plan had gone awry? Nothing he had done made sense. He was not the vicomte, so who was he? She had not asked his name, and he had not offered it. Her head spun with the effort to answer a sudden rush of questions until a single question took over. Where was he?

She saw only the paneled, pedimented door through which they had entered. They had climbed two flights of stairs, and she would have heard him descend them. But he had walked away toward the far wall. She stared at its paneling, dark with age, worn, and intricate, with raised molding around each of the squares. A few paintings of London—boats on the river, the park, a boxing match—hung here and there, but there was no door. There must be more to the house, but she could not see how the room around her connected with others, unless one went out again through the main door.

Still, she had perhaps only minutes to find something with which to cover herself. She went back to the closets and opened the second one. A mixture of smells as varied as London wafted out—ale and smoke, vinegar and fish. These clothes were entirely different, tattered and colorful, theatrical even, purples and checks, green and red velvets, clothes for a gypsy at a carnival, nothing a gentleman would wear. The whole closet was a costume warehouse.

Staring at its contents a new plan came to her. She would become a man. He had told her to send a man, but she could be that man. She had disappeared once into Helen of Troy. Now she would disappear again.

She began to pull items from their hooks, looking for the plainest pieces: a shirt, a jacket, a wool waistcoat for warmth, some breeches, a cap, all in grays and browns so that she might pass unnoticed. She made herself recall the youth who delivered books from Hatchards to her father. That boy would be her model.

She almost gave up over the matter of boots. It took three pairs of stockings to make a pair of her madman's boots fit her feet. When at last she checked the image in the mirror, she made a creditable young man, except for one thing. She returned to the hearth, took up the cheese knife from the tray, and went to work to complete her transformation.

Chapter Four

❧

MORNING light of ruthless clarity woke him. Even the upward drift of his eyelids told him that other parts of his body meant to protest the previous night's adventure. Harding hovered somewhere in the outer apartment, stirring pots, but the girl made no sound. No surprise there. One aftereffect of the drug was bound to be extreme fatigue.

"Coffee, sir?" Harding came through the wall into Will's inner chamber.

"Our guest still sleeping?"

"Gone, sir."

"Gone?" Will swung himself upright. Where could she go barefoot and looking like a Cyprian? He stood, ignoring sharp objections from a dozen parts of his anatomy.

"She left a note."

"A note?" He was through the door, taking in the details of the room. On the bench was a discarded towel vivid with red stains. The useless gown lay in a heap on the floor. His closet doors stood open. On the bed were a jacket and shirt.

"Clever baggage." Harding stood at his elbow.

"Not if she's headed for bleeding Half Moon Street again." Will scanned the room and saw that she'd eaten. That showed some sense. Then he stopped. The second towel lay on the hearthstones; in its folds were long, tawny gold locks of hair, that sweet mass in which he had briefly buried his face the night before. He picked up one of the long curls and saw the cheese knife. It had been a butchery to chop off her hair with such an instrument. It meant she was determined to pursue her end, whatever it was. "Where's the note?"

Harding handed Will the note and a cup of dark brew. The note said simply: *I will repay you.*

For a woman she was terse. The writing was a fine, trained lady's hand. She'd been to school or had a governess. He already knew she was well read in the Greeks. He had to applaud the instinct to give nothing away, but she didn't know how every choice she'd made while he slept—*nobly apart from her on a blasted cot*—would allow him to trace her.

He finished the coffee and turned to examine the riffled closet until he could see its former contents in his mind. Carefully he built his picture of the youth she had become.

He checked his inventory with Harding. "What's missing, Harding?"

"A pair of plain boots, three pair of stockings, a shirt, a neckcloth, one gray flannel waistcoat, a russet jacket, and dark brown trousers."

"There's something else." Will pointed to an empty hook.

"A brown cord cap, sir."

He could feel Harding on the verge of saying more. "And?"

"A pair of silver candlesticks." Harding held the discarded tapers in his hand.

"Bleeding thorough, isn't she?" Will had expected her to curl into an exhausted and humiliated ball in his bed. She'd been shocked at her appearance in the glass. The stained towel was further evidence of her embarrassment. She'd ruthlessly undone Leary's effort to turn her into a wanton. And he was the devil's own because the thought of her rubbing the cochineal off her breasts while he slept in the next room roused his yard, not his noble sentiments.

Harding's granite face revealed nothing of his thoughts. There was not much need of conversation between them. They'd been together since Sergeant Harding's regiment had been decimated in an engagement along the Bidassoa River and Wellington had recruited the two of them as spies.

"Keep an eye on the papers for any notices of missing wards or daughters."

"You think she's a runaway, sir?"

Will nodded. She meant to go back to Half Moon Street. There was something in that brothel that she was desperate to get her hands on. *March's files?* He turned the thought over in his mind. He himself wondered whether March kept them there. Could Helen of Troy have ended up in one of those files? He looked at her note again. He was in full agreement with the sentiment it expressed.

Oh, you will repay me, sweetheart. He would wager anyone that he knew the city better than she. Even if she managed to get some coins for the stolen candlesticks, it would take her most of the day to get back to Half Moon Street, and when she did, he'd be there to meet his missing virgin.

HELEN dawdled along Clare Street. The busy market street had proved the best so far for her purpose. People went about their business without paying her any attention. The rain had cleared, carts and wagons rolled through mud. The streets exhaled the metallic scent of wet stone. Her rescuer's boots might never be the same. She banished the thought of him again. She would repay him eventually.

Boys moved freely about the market, some on errands, some with hands suspiciously in their pockets. She was one of the few in boots, and she wished she had stolen gloves. The cold made her hands stiff and clumsy.

In her other life she had hardly noticed London's boys, but now she tried to match the slouch and swagger of them, and she kept her cap pulled low. It seemed wise to hunch her shoulders and keep moving. The candlesticks in her pockets knocked heavily against her hips with her stride, and she did not see any shop where she might sell them.

Shops advertised their wares in signs and hung merchandise from hooks or jumbled it in open bins along the pavement, but not one invited customers to trade old goods for new, though Helen knew such trade was a major industry in London. She had to make a try sooner or later. She was hungry, and her new plan required a modest investment in goods, something she could claim to deliver to the house on Half Moon Street.

She turned up a lesser street, winding north, and passed a likely shop. A sign above the door read MESSRS. WEEMS AND HIGGET, SILVERSMITHS, and through the dusty window she could see old salvers with tarnish in the grooves of their design and blackening teapots in need of a good polishing. A boy coming out of a warehouse opposite gave her a sharp look, but she circled back as the proprietor of the silversmith's bundled a woman's purchase in brown paper. He seemed a cheerful sort of gentleman with white whiskers and a green-striped waistcoat. The woman left and the shopkeeper took up a broom. Helen decided to try her luck.

"Sir, I wonder if you could help me? I'm new come to London to make my way in the world."

"Off with you, boy. I've no positions here." The shopkeeper plied his broom without giving Helen so much as a glance.

"Oh, I don't need a position, sir. I've got a legacy."

"A legacy, boy. Ain't you grand, then?"

"My grandmother's candlesticks, sir. She told me to sell them to get my start in a new life." Now the shop-keeper stopped, leaned upon his broom, and studied her.

"New come to London, ye say?"

"From Oxford, sir." Helen did her best to slouch like the boys she'd watched all day.

"And why should yer grandmother's legacy lead ye to my shop?"

"It appears that you deal in silver, sir. Could you kindly tell me where I might sell a pair of silver candlesticks?"

"Silver candlesticks? From Oxford? Do ye have them about ye?"

"I do, sir."

"Show me." The shopkeeper leaned his broom against the doorframe.

Helen pulled a candlestick from her pocket and handed it to the man. He hefted it in his palm and turned it over to look at the base.

"Yer grandmother in Oxford, boy? Then why does it say Rudges of Drury Lane, London?" He tapped the base of the candlestick.

Helen instinctively stepped back at the man's accusing tone.

"Sir me, will ye! Thief!" His voice turned heads all along the street. "I have a thief here." He held the gleaming candlestick over his head.

Helen felt herself the object of hard stares. She wanted

to say *no*, to insist on her innocence, but the words wouldn't come. She stepped back and collided with a boy at her elbow, the boy who had stared at her, rough and ruddy with strong, white teeth in a cheeky grin.

"Grab yer stick and run, mate, or Weems'll have the coppers on ye in a wink."

Helen snatched the candlestick and shoved it back in her pocket as Weems hollered again, picking up his broom.

"Follow me," the boy urged. He darted into the street. Helen hesitated only a heartbeat.

The boy was remarkably quick and daring. He stuck to the street, weaving in and out of carts and wagons, letting traffic create obstacles for their pursuers. Shouts seemed to come at them from all sides. Hands snatched at her cap and jacket. The candlesticks hit her hip bone with bruising force.

Still the cry "thief" followed them, as if the chill wind carried it.

"A few turns more," the boy called. Her sides ached, blue spots danced before her eyes, and her muscles stung from the effort. She had no knowledge of where he led, only that he seemed capable of eluding pursuit.

On a street filled with hawkers, a man with a knife-sharpening cart blocked their path. The boy ran straight at the cart. The man stepped back as if at a signal, and they raced past him through a doorless opening in a derelict house and out the rear into a court with a half dozen openings. They dashed down one, and the boy slowed at last. They leaned for a moment against a wall of blackened bricks.

"Yer a green one, aren't ye?"

Helen gasped for breath, her limbs shaking. She nodded. He had accepted her as a boy.

"Yer first 'hot beef,' weren't it?"

Helen thought it safe to nod.

"Wot's yer name?"

"Troy." It was the only syllable she could manage.

"Nate Wilde. Where ye lodgin' then, Troy?"

"Nowhere until I sell the candlesticks."

"Easy enough if ye know a good man. Come along, then. Let's do it right this time."

The place Nate Wilde showed her had a side entrance off another court. Its heavy door stood ajar with a row of iron bolts sticking out from the inner side. Inside, sturdy wooden bins, like troughs for kneading dough, held piles of trinkets, one for rings, another for brooches, a third for silver watches, and still another for snuff boxes. One wall was devoted to fiddles and bows, and a vast army of chess pieces marched down a long, narrow table. The weight of those small losses, gifts and pleasures given up for cash, piled up in such abandon, made Helen inexplicably sad.

The proprietor was nothing like Mr. Weems. He was long and lean, his velvet coat patched and worn, his nose sharp, and his eyes heavy-lidded. He leaned over a thick book, pen in hand.

"Never tell me you are up the spout, young Wilde," he said, making an entry in the book.

"Not me, Mr. Dry. My friend 'ere."

Dry put down the pen and swung his hooded gaze to Helen. "Let's see the goods."

Helen produced her candlesticks. They outshone everything in the shop.

"What name shall I say?"

"Troy."

He wrote in the book. "Your own property, of course?"

"Legacy from my grandmother, sir."

She could see that Dry no more believed her than Weems had, but his bland gaze didn't waver. "And your direction?"

"'E's with me," Wilde said. "Just put down Bredsell's school."

Again Dry wrote in his book. "Four shillings."

"Eight," said Wilde.

One of Dry's black brows rose in a tall arch like a cat's back. "Well then, shall we say six, for a new customer?"

Helen nodded. Dry made the correction in his book.

When she and Nate Wilde were outside again, he advised her on where to stow her blunt so as not to lose it in London.

"You 'ave a position, ye say?"

"I do." It was not strictly a lie. In her other life, she had a position. "I start making deliveries tomorrow. I only need lodgings tonight."

"Stay at the school with us. Ye'll save yer blunt."

Helen hesitated. Her plan did require money, and she didn't know precisely where she was. She could not be more than two miles from her objective, but her feet hurt. Her companion walked with a jaunty stride, as if their earlier escape had not taxed his energies at all.

Helen was conscious of a crop of blisters where the over-large boots rubbed her feet in spite of the three pairs of stockings.

"There's cake," her companion offered.

"Cake?" It seemed an odd inducement.

Nate Wilde stopped, his hands on his hips, and looked her up and down. "Listen, Troy, yer in no case to go about on yer own. Ye don't know a decent fence from a copper's tool. Ye can't run to save yer life. A drunk barber chopped yer 'air. Yer greener than grass, so ye'd best stick with me."

Helen started to protest, stopped, and laughed. He was right, and he offered her an identity she would be wise to use. "My blind grandmother cut my hair."

Wilde's grin approved. "Blind, is she? 'At's why she never saw ye makin' off with her candlesticks."

W ILL left Half Moon Street sometime after two, his body stiff and aching from the cold. Either he or Harding had watched the rear of the house most of the day. Helen's disguise gave her few options for gaining entry to March's well-guarded brothel. In her place Will knew what he would do—enter in the guise of making a delivery and leave a window open for a later visit.

He had observed six deliveries to the house. There would be plenty of wine, coal, ale, and oysters for the guests, all delivered by established local tradesmen with no new apprentice among them. No one had left a window ajar, and the large individual at the back door had been an unmoving presence all evening. Only his breath moved, a frosty exhalation in the bitter air. If hell could freeze, it would have.

When another came to relieve the man at the rear door, Will moved in to have a chat with the new man. Not an agreeable fellow but willing enough to talk with a knife to his throat. His account of the night's usual business made it clear that Helen had not returned.

Where was she?

He dismissed the question. She could have an accomplice. She could have lodgings. If she had an ounce of sense, she had returned to her family. But his instinct, and two missing candlesticks, told him she was acting alone. And that pile of ruined hair told him she wouldn't quit. Whatever drove her to risk entering March's nasty little pleasure palace with such disastrous results, she would do it again. So why hadn't she?

Not his concern. Surely, a man was not obliged to rescue a woman more than once. After that she had to act with enough sense to avoid the near occasion of rape. He had done his part. At least she had been wise enough to escape him, and she knew what a true villain Leary was. Will could go home to bed, his conscience clear of sins against her. Thinking of bed unfortunately stirred a host of impressions. His wayward imagination had already placed her in his bed, her ripe, untouched body arching up to him, those glorious breasts his for the taking.

It didn't improve his humor, when in the hack on

Piccadilly, Harding merely said, "I'm sure she left a trail a blind man could follow."

A small grating noise woke Helen. Her ears strained to catch and place the sound in the cold dark room.

She hadn't meant to fall asleep at all but to make her escape. Nate Wilde's freedom had misled her about the school. The other boys marched, sat, stood, ate, and slept as directed by a large gruff person named Coates, who wielded a leather strap. He scarcely glanced at Helen but instantly disposed of her.

"'E sits where oi say 'e sits. 'E sleeps where oi say 'e sleeps. 'E's boy number ten, now, 'e is."

At the long supper table and in the prayers and preparation for bed that followed, she had escaped detection as a female, but she had no intention of standing cap in hand for the scrutiny of the masters in broad daylight. The boys were young and small, and she had not yet caught their accent or their manner. She was bound to be exposed. She felt for her money and found it still tucked into the band of linen around her chest.

She lay in the last bed in a row of ten on one side of an attic sleeping room. The roof sloped sharply up over them with a window at the outer end and stairs at the inner. Two dormer windows in the roof itself on either side of the room let in faint light.

The sound came again, something being dragged or pushed across the floor, and she turned her head to locate it. A shadow flickered at the base of one of the windows. A small boy's head appeared outlined by the faint light. She could see him now, balancing precariously on a stool, stretching to reach the window latch.

Helen swung her feet to the floor and winced as her blistered feet took her weight. She kept her stockings on both for the cold and because they were bloodied and stuck to her skin. She crossed to the little boy and twisted a hand in his nightshirt for a firm grip on him. He felt like a piece of ice.

"What are you doing?" she whispered.

The boy turned, dark eyes round and large in his pale, solemn face, fair hair sticking up like unraked hay in a field.

"Can ye open the window?" he asked.

"It's too cold."

The little one shook his head. "Boy is coming from the sky to take me."

Helen was lost. The little one spoke with calm certainty about what was impossible. "One of the boys is outside?"

"Boy."

Helen tried again to make sense of the little one's words. "A boy is on the roof?"

The little one nodded. "Boy walks on the sky."

"The sky?"

He nodded. "This is a bad place."

Helen had come to the same conclusion. She sympathized with the little one's desire to leave, but walking on the sky did not seem a good escape. "Let me try."

She reached up and tested the latch. "Locked," she

told her companion. "Let's get you back to bed for now. We'll have to find another way to get you to Boy." She'd gone through a window three stories above pavement, and it was an overrated experience in her opinion, and not one for little boys to contemplate.

The little one didn't move. "Can't sleep. Oi want Boy." He sounded bereft.

"What's your name?"

He seemed to have to think about the question.

"Boy number four."

"Your true name," Helen insisted.

"Robin."

"I'm Troy, Robin. Come with me." Helen started to take him by the hand, but he jumped into her arms. His icy hands clung around her neck. She pushed the stool away from the window and carried her new friend to her bed, tucking him in beside her.

His small person pressed against her, and she sucked in a breath at the contact with his icy feet.

"You can come with us when Boy comes," he told her.

Chapter Five

❧

IN the morning a few inquiries to his neighbors put
Will on Helen's trail. It led north and west from his
own unsavory neighborhood into the heart of the dark
rookery where the long search for his missing brother
Kit had at last led them in October. It was home territory
to the boys loosed from the Reverend Bredsell's supposed charity school on Bread Street. In these crowded
streets young felons perfected all the arts of lifting their
neighbors' goods from their neighbors' pockets.

By noon Will was listening to Mr. Weems's com-
plaints about the immorality of modern youth. Weems
was full of righteous indignation at a young man's brazen
attempt to pass off stolen goods to a reputable merchant.
It was with no surprise that Will recognized toothy Nate

Wilde as the accomplice in the story. Wilde was the star pupil of Bredsell's school, a lad whose talents ran from thievery to spying and worse.

From Weems's establishment Will went straight to the known receivers and fences on Saffron Hill. It didn't take long to find Benjamin Dry.

For two pounds Will was able to purchase his own candlesticks, and for another pound he could inspect Dry's thick book. Troy, as she now called herself, had named Bredsell's school as her residence. If ever a woman had a knack for jumping from the frying pan into the fire, it was his virgin.

Bread Street, when he reached it, was a changed place. Months earlier when their search for Kit had narrowed on the crooked old street, it had been one of those places in London where neither ordinary citizens nor officers of the law could safely go. The main occupations of the inhabitants had been idling, drinking, brawling, and bashing in the heads of passersby.

Now idleness had apparently been outlawed. The brewery yard was a hive of activity with men constructing new vats to replace those that the unfortunate Dick Cullen had sabotaged. A skeletal framework for huge new fermenting tanks rose above the crumbled walls where ten thousand gallons of porter had flooded the street.

The flood had been Archibald March's plan. Through his ties to the Home Secretary March had arranged the arrest of Will's older brother Xander. And while Will and Xander had been evading the law, March had kidnapped

Xander's bride, Cleo, and hidden her in a cellar at the foot of Bread Street.

At the time they had all believed that March acted simply to keep Cleo's fortune for himself, as her uncle and trustee. But even then Will had suspected there was more to it. To him the flood looked like a desperate strategy to stop their search for Kit.

It had failed. If anything the flood had made it easier for Xander to begin his project of bringing gas lighting to Bread Street. Now Xander came every day, and among his workers were men listening to the talk around them. Any hint of Kit's whereabouts would be reported to Xander at once.

Down the center of the street ran the ditch that would hold the gas main, three feet wide and already thirty yards long or more and growing. A small army of men swung picks, wielded shovels, and pushed carts of dirt and stone. Xander's burned signs advertising work and wages had been replaced, and a line of men stood outside his makeshift office in the court. Hawkers circulated with trays of ginger cakes, jacket potatoes, and oranges.

Will spotted his brother in the midst of a group consulting a surveyor's map, and was struck at once by the change in him. Xander had now been married nearly four months. Apparently, sleeping with the woman you loved could make a man believe in the impossible, like saving Bread Street. His brother's energy was palpable.

With the same dark hair and severe symmetry of features, Xan and Will looked enough alike to be mistaken one for the other, the Jones bastards. Only Will's eyes were darker, and Xan was the taller of the two by an inch or more. And there was something in those broad shoulders of Xan's that told the world he remained unbowed under its contempt.

Will caught up with him as he left the little group. "The bleeding Thames is frozen. You couldn't wait for spring?"

It was just like Xander to move forward on his single-minded quest as if he thought that they could find Kit under the paving stones. Cold as it was, men were shirtless and sweating as they swung their picks.

"Hard ground makes a satisfying target." Xander gave him a searching glance.

"Wages seem to agree with Bread Street."

"It's no paradise, but they keep coming to work. I took your advice. We keep the tools locked up, and Cleo bribes everyone who signs on with potatoes and candles."

Will nodded.

Xander's expression sobered. "Nate Wilde is about."

"He has a habit of showing up in March's wake, doesn't he?" Nate Wilde was their remaining lead in the search for Kit. The two informers, Dick Cullen and Mother Greenslade, who had brought them to Bread Street, had died in the flood. Will knew that when your sources went missing or turned up dead, it meant you were getting close to something nasty.

"Wilde's just the lad I came to find." Will made a few further changes to his appearance and began to work the street. Nate Wilde would be wherever people pressed together in a crowd and were unlikely to notice a bump or a tap or a sudden lightening of their pockets.

Wilde was good at disappearing, becoming part of the scene itself, except when he flashed that toothy grin of his. Cleo's brother Charlie simply referred to Wilde as "Teeth," an apt enough term.

Will found him among the carpenters, coopers, and masons working at the brewery. It made sense. These were journeymen with their own tools, and a plane or a chisel was a regular pawnshop item, dispensed with when a man was out of work and reclaimed with the next job.

Will collared Wilde as he slipped out of the brewery yard with a bulge in his jacket.

"Whose is it?" Will asked his writhing victim.

A string of curses was the reply, so Will applied more pressure to the boy's arm. There was a gasp and then silence for half a minute.

"Fat fellow there. See, 'is jacket won't close."

Will force-marched Wilde across the yard. "My son owes ye an apology, sir."

"'Ere's yer plane, sir." Wilde produced the object with his free hand.

The startled fellow took it. "Ought to 'ave 'im taken up."

"Or beaten," said Will cheerfully. "I won't spare the rod, mate." He dragged Wilde out of the yard, through a broken fence into a high-walled court filled with rubbish, and pinned him to an upturned barrow to have a chat.

"'Ey, 'at's my best jacket ye put yer knife through."

"You're making mistakes you can't afford, Wilde."

"Ye got it in for me is all."

"Your sins'd shock the devil."

The boy squirmed, but the knife held him pinned. "Well, wot do ye care?"

Will shrugged. He could see himself in the boy, a survivor, always weighing the odds, distrustful, belligerent. "End up drowned by March like Dick Cullen and Mother Greenslade if you want. Suits me."

The boy's expression sobered, no teeth showed at all. "They narked."

"They trusted March and Bredsell."

"An 'oo's a bloke supposed to trust—yew, copper?"

Will shook his head. The boy was headed for a bad end—thieving, spying for March, recruiting for Bredsell. Will knew something about bad ends. He didn't wish them on boys, even toughs like Wilde. "You have something I want, and it's something you don't want."

Immediately a sharp bargaining gleam lit the boy's eye. He stopped twisting against the knife. "Ye want ta deal? What's it worth to ye?"

"What's it worth to you to stay out of jail?"

The boy stuck out his chin. "Yew can't prove a thing."

"I've two candlesticks in my pocket that'll buy you a one-way passage to Botany Bay."

"'Ey, Oi'm not yer thief. That was Troy."

Will waited for Wilde to see that he'd sold out his friend at once. Maybe he and Wilde weren't entirely alike. "It's Troy I want, and Troy you don't want. He'll bring every Runner in London down on you."

A suspicious look crossed Wilde's face, but to Will the boy suddenly seemed younger. It was clear that he had no idea of what he really had in Troy. "'E's green as the grass in May."

"A dozen West End swells want him for a major swindle, and you know Bredsell won't thank you for bringing the police to the school."

"So, yer in it for the reward?"

"Get me Troy before supper tonight and you'll get your share."

"'Ow much?"

Will named a sum and a place to deliver Troy. He pulled his knife out to release the boy.

"'E's a bad 'un, eh?"

"The devil's own favorite fiend."

H ELEN'S nose ran from the cold. She had her chin down and her frozen hands tucked under her arms, concentrating on putting one foot in front of the other down a dark street, which Nate Wilde promised had a lodging house where a room could be got for the night. What happened next happened so fast, she had no chance to avoid the trap.

A hack door opened directly in front of her. Her shin scraped against the step as she was hauled inside. She landed in the devil's lap, twisting and swinging her elbows. Her cap fell off and her chin collided with his hard head. His hands worked fast and left her wrapped like a mummy in a blanket that smelled of horses. He settled her next to him and passed Wilde a wad of bank notes.

Helen glared at Wilde. She had trusted him. When

he'd offered a way out of the school, she'd jumped at the chance.

Wilde stuffed the bank notes in his jacket. "Keep clear of Weems, Troy."

"Turncoat." The door closed and the cab rocked into motion.

"Don't blame Wilde, sweetheart. The inducement I offered was too much for a man of sense to refuse."

"Money."

"You owe me." He held her chin in his warm palm and applied a clean, soft linen handkerchief to her nose.

"I told you I would repay you. It's necessary to my plan that I take on the appearance of someone without resources, but I assure you I have . . . friends in high places."

"You'll pardon me if I'm not satisfied with these assurances from someone who makes it a habit of landing in situations which, I'm guessing, would appall those high-placed friends of yours."

"Where are you taking me this time?" She twisted her face away from his hand. Once again she had no clear sense of where she was, and she probably had less than a quarter of an hour to convince him to let her go.

"Going about London alone, you've been headed only one place all along—a man's bed." His voice was grim. "Mine."

The word was an unmistakable claim. His voice had the timbre she'd first heard in the brothel. She turned to judge the intent in those dark eyes. "You won't . . . rape me." She made herself say the word.

"I won't read you Fordyce's sermons on *The Character and Conduct of the Female Sex*."

Flickering shadows in the interior of the hack revealed only fragments of his appearance, the hard-edged profile, the gleam in his dark eyes. She had not properly understood him in the brothel. She had believed him preparing to bed her, and his languid air as a Frenchman had made her think she could overpower him and escape. But outside the brothel, the fastidious vicomte did not exist.

"I don't know who you are. Yesterday you wore a cravat and silks, today a Belcher neckerchief and corduroy."

"Neighborhoods change. Depravity . . . remains the same."

"Do you have a name?"

His grin flashed briefly in the dark. "Will Jones. Descended on both sides from a distinguished line of fornicators back to the Conqueror himself."

"You didn't have to hunt me down. I told you I would repay you."

"Was that going to be before or after your arrest for stealing and fencing the goods?"

"I know exactly where those candlesticks are."

"I doubt it."

She took a calming breath. "You are interfering with my plan."

"Which was going so well."

"There were setbacks, I grant you." Since she'd come to London she'd lost three days. Her mother was three days closer to disaster.

"Setbacks, sweetheart? First Leary, then Wilde—both quite willing to sell you, though to Leary's credit, he had a much higher appreciation of your value. How long did you expect to pass as a boy in a boys' school?"

"I was only going to stay the night." Her missteps accumulated moment by wearying moment.

"What kept you today then?"

She wasn't going to tell him about Robin. The little boy had followed her about the school all day, and leaving him behind with his vain hope that a phantom hero would come over the rooftops to save him struck her as the one true crime she'd committed. Stealing from the devil didn't count. "Did you come after me for the candlesticks or the clothes?"

"Ah, Helen, for all your experience in Troy, how little you know of men." There was a teasing note in his voice.

"There was only one man, you know, Paris, endlessly Paris, and a woman can hardly judge other men by such a man. Really the rest of the time, I was among the Trojan women. Imagine a room full of women, fifty looms and tongues going at once, and the old queen's stern eye on us every minute."

"Good at weaving, were you?" He laughed. The hack came to a halt. Leaning close he told her, "You undid my first efforts on your behalf, and when I do a thing, I like it to stay done."

"Please, don't trouble yourself further on my account. I'm sure you have other business to attend to."

"I do, Helen, but you see, as I go about *my* business, you keep turning up in suspicious places." Will extracted his prisoner, unwound her from the fragrant blanket, paid the hack driver, and led her through the usual passageways to his door. "Home," he announced.

"I'll be leaving in the morning."

"You are an ungrateful baggage, you know. You were unable to get yourself out of either the brothel or the boys school without my aid and my money."

"With which you are quite free for a man from your neighborhood."

Argos in the shadows thumped his tale in welcome. "Argos knows you already." Will made her sit two stairs above him on the second flight of stairs.

"What are you doing?"

"Removing my ruined boots from your feet. Harding will take it ill if you track mud on the rugs."

"Harding?"

He could hear the weariness in her voice. He doubted she'd slept much in three days. "My man. You met him on the ledge at the brothel. A good man in a tight spot."

"You've been in tight spots with him before?"

"Dozens." The stockings she'd stolen from him stuck to her feet in dark coins of dried blood. *Bleeding determined chit.* He swung her over his shoulder and carried her through the door.

She lay where he put her on the bed and her eyes fell closed. "I warn you, whatever you mean to do to me, I'll be asleep."

"Oh, I doubt that."

Her eyes opened at once as he secured her left arm to a bedpost with a silken scarf. A red streak marked her wrist where he had dangled her from the brothel window two nights before.

"Do you mean to torture me?"

"Definitely."

Her eyes widened, and he offered her a wicked grin. "We'll deal with your clothes later, unless there are any items you'd care to remove."

"No, thank you."

That made him chuckle. "What a well-bred young felon you are, Helen."

He tied her other hand to the base of the carved headboard and propped her up against blue silken pillows. Her ruined hair framed her face in uneven gold-streaked rays. The white shirt gaped at her open collar, and he realized that she'd bound one of his neckcloths around her breasts. Her limbs lay slack on the silk counterpane. "Legally, those are my clothes. Did you know that a woman can be transported for stealing a nightshirt?"

"You're a font of comforting information."

He glanced at her feet and turned to stir the fire. When her eyes drifted shut again, he stood over her briefly. "It's answers I want from you, Helen of Troy." The shallow rise and fall of her flattened chest was her only response. He passed into his inner room for the means to treat her blisters.

Helen woke to a gentle tugging at her feet. "Is this the torture?"

He sat on the bed, a basin nestled in his lap, holding her left foot. "Sadly no bastinados about."

Her pale, naked foot resting in his warm, strong hands

sent shocking vibrations pealing up her leg. Sleepiness vanished in sensuous alertness. Even her bound breasts responded to his touch with sharp pricks of tingling awareness. He washed her foot in warm water, tended the blisters, and wrapped the foot in a clean cloth. He repeated his care of her other foot, giving no sign of noticing her reaction.

His touch, while not gentle, was careful and competent, and at odds with the fierce concentration on his face. It was her first chance to look closely at him. His dark brows met in a furrow above a nose that must once have been straight perfection, but that now had a slight bend midway. His upper lip, too, was marred, not quite meeting the lower on the left side. His intense gaze, his shadowed jaw, and his wild jet hair made her think of the mad things he did—breaking furniture, dropping out of windows, clinging to the roof of a careening coach, so at odds with this homely act of bandaging her wounded feet.

She controlled a strange impulse to compliment him. "You aren't like other gentlemen."

"But then I'm not a gentleman." He spoke carelessly, but Helen understood that it was no light matter, his banishment from good society to this den of faded splendor. He took away the basin and towels and stood outlined by the fire now, shadowy and aloof in its flicker.

"You don't like yourself much." She had listened to voices all her life, learning to catch a speaker's sense of himself.

He laughed off her observation. "I'm in good company then."

He went round the bed to the opposite side, tossing a pile of penny pamphlets on the coverlet. They fluttered down next to her, and she saw that they were like the religious tracts her father read. She remembered Will Jones' threat to read Fordyce to her—not that she needed that text to tell her how her world would condemn her conduct of the last three days.

She had earned all her father's bad names for womankind—wayward, wanton, wicked, strumpet, harlot, whore.

Standing beside the bed watching her, Will Jones shrugged out of his jacket and pulled off his neckcloth, undoing his collar so that it fell open. The intimacy of the act, his comfort in doing it before her, his reflection in the gilded mirrors made the pit of her stomach drop like a bucket in a well. "What are you doing?"

"I've made you comfortable. Now it's my turn."

He regarded her steadily. The open shirt exposed the strong column of his throat. A gray wool waistcoat with thin red stripes hugged his ribs and made the breadth of his shoulders and narrowness of his waist and hips plain. His charcoal cord trousers bunched across his loins, cupping that part of him that she could not even name to herself.

He removed his boots and sat to remove his stockings. Catching her watching him again, he held up one bare foot for her inspection. "Not cloven. In case you were wondering. Brandy?"

She shook her head. He poured himself a glass, took a long swallow, and set the drink on the table. Then he made a nest of pillows beside hers and settled himself on the bed, stretching out his long limbs, crossing his elegant feet. For a moment he simply stared at her legs. Helen held herself perfectly still under his scrutiny.

A woman must not make too great a display of her person. A woman must not unmask her beauty to the common gaze. Her legs, so uninteresting to herself, so useful, practical, ordinary, seemed to absorb him wholly.

He took a deep breath and withdrew his gaze. "Now, you can explain why you remain so determined to invade March's nasty little pleasure palace, or I can read to you."

"Read to me? That's the torture?"

"Unorthodox, I know." He picked up a handful of pamphlets. *"The Virgin's Night in a Brothel: Lord Thrustmore meets Miss Yeeld."* His dark brows slanted up with a look of inquiry. *"Or would you prefer—Boys' School Archive: The Pleasure Principle.* Or *A Visit to the Temple of Hymen: Lady Pokingham's Boudoir."*

She stared at him. "You're making those up."

He showed her the title page of the pamphlet in his hand. "Your long sojourn in Troy has apparently made you unaware of what London has to offer, produced right here in the neighborhood, a penny apiece. You can divulge the dreadful secret that's led you to a life of crime, or I read."

She stared at the dark paneled ceiling. "My purpose in going to that place must remain my secret."

"Well then." He swallowed more brandy and opened one of the pamphlets in his lap. The others slid into the narrow valley between their legs.

Chapter One

Miss Miranda Yeeld enters the service of Venus.

    Miranda Yeeld, newcomer to London, waits in a silk wrapper in a dainty room for a gentleman to initiate her in the service of Venus. Advised by Nan and Poll, she has cleaned and sweetened her person. Apprehensive of pleasing her first gentleman, she checks her reflection in the glass and straightens the curls under her cap. A dozen instructions flit through her pretty head. She can't remember what she is to do first, but she squares her shoulders. She will seek instruction from her guest himself.

    The door opens and young Lord Thrustmore enters, a fine gentleman with a cockaded tricorn and flowing lace at his throat and wrists, gay blade hanging at his side, and fitted blue coat. His ruddy, handsome face and fair golden curls are just what Miranda dreamed of.

    "Am I to be your first, then, fair Miranda?"

    Shyly she nods.

Helen jammed her elbows into the pillows and pushed herself upright. He paused immediately. She stilled and he resumed.

She told herself the words did not affect her, but the rough timbre of his voice made her conscious of her body and his, stretched out in the bed. The striking contrast in their naked feet, his arched and strong, hers narrow, pale, and bandaged, fascinated her.

Will Jones stopped reading to look at her again. "Anything you want to tell me? Like how it is that in two days you've been inside two unsavory establishments connected to Archibald March?"

She shook her head. She recognized the name. She had met Mr. March at some gathering or other, a lean man with almost poetic good looks. He was one of the great promoters of charity work in London. Both her parents admired his efforts, but Helen had not detected any warmth in him. The boys' school might be one of his causes, but she could not believe that he had anything to do with the house on Half Moon Street. "The bed really is splendid, worthy of a pharaoh. And this room must have been magnificent when Henry Tudor was king."

"Queen Anne." He gave her one of his sharp glances and took up the book again.

Lord Thrustmore doffs his hat and removes his sword. He sits in a large upholstered chair at the foot of the bed and invites Miranda to sit on him so that they may become acquainted.

"How did you know about the auction?"

"A friend of mine among the officers of the law in our wicked old city."

He had friends among the police. The idea made her pulse skip. As wholly improbable as it seemed, it made her situation worse, much worse. What she must prevent was any information about her mother's reckless bank drafts to her lover ever reaching the police. There was nothing she could tell anyone connected with the law. "Why did you go?"

"The question is—why were you for sale?"

"I've explained."

"No. You haven't." He picked up the pamphlet again.

Lord Thrustmore turns Miranda on his lap so that he can admire the fine swell of her bosom. He invites her to help him loosen the linen at his throat. She smiles, happy to oblige him. It is just the cue she needs. His warm hand slides up and down above her knee over the dainty garter. His strong thumb brushes her inner thigh.

"Would you believe that I had information that something of value to me had come quite by mischance into the possession of persons at that address?"

A cynical lift of his brow was all the answer he gave.

"It's true. A letter came from that very address." She had to be careful not to reveal too much.

"When?"

"Just after Twelfth Night."

He didn't answer at once. "And you instantly hatched a plan to walk into a notorious brothel to retrieve your missing possession?"

"The address seemed perfectly respectable."

It was hard to look at him then. She had never had a conversation with a man that made her conscious of her body and his, of nearness and something more, some feeling that united them.

"It must have been an awkward moment for you, Helen, when you realized the nature of the place."

It had been a moment of realizing her own sheer idiocy. She had known such moments all her life, her skin on fire with a blush. Her disguise as a misdirected maidservant answering a request for employment had worked perfectly to get her in the door. She had not expected Guy Leary or the two large men who'd carried her off. Only later did she learn that the house had two kinds of employees—large men and unclothed women. Still she had hoped in spite of her predicament to find a way to search for her mother's stolen letters. She had spent the day in a plain room at the back of an upper floor listening to footsteps and voices, getting a sense of the inhabitants and the arrangement of the rooms. She had been so hungry by that late hour that when the women had offered chocolate, she'd accepted, never dreaming the drink would contain a drug.

"Are you going to turn me over to the authorities?" Word of those letters must not reach her father.

"Not when you are intent on a second plan that won't work any better than the first."

"You think you know my plan?"

"Don't I? You've made yourself into an errand boy so that you can show up at Leary's back door on the pretext of making a delivery. You'll leave a window open a crack and return later to break in."

"Will it work?"

"No. Your life in Troy has made you a bit soft, Helen, ignorant of men like Leary and March and the lesser malevolences that trail in their wake." He lifted the pamphlet again.

Miranda tosses his lordship's linen aside, and he invites her to unbutton his waistcoat. As she works the tiny buttons, he unties the ribbons on her lacy wrap. They race to see who can finish first. Miranda wins and spreads the wings of his lordship's waistcoat wide. His lordship opens her wrap and slides it down her arms to pool in silken folds around her hips. He admires each lovely globe and strokes and teases until the dark nubbins stand to soldierly attention. Miranda breathes in husky pants and arches into his lordship's eager hands.

Helen made herself yawn, stretching her mouth wide, ending on a long, gusty exhalation. She was so tired. She should be sound asleep by now. But his voice kept her on edge. It had an element she had not heard in the conversations of the earnest powerful men around her father.

He laughed. "You find Lord Thrustmore tame stuff after romping in bed with Paris all those years?"

"Paris was extraordinarily single-minded, you know. I think Aphrodite stole his wits in their bargain."

"Paris had wits?"

"And cunning and charm to spare. He knew just what to say to persuade a woman into his bed."

"He was rather stuck on one woman, wasn't he?"

"Just my luck."

"The curse of beauty."

"It does make one vain."

"Right. You're so vain, you butchered your hair to get back to that brothel. Makes a man wonder what you're so bleeding desperate to retrieve." He tucked a lock of her hair behind her ear, and his fingers slid down her neck. The sensation lingered and spread, a compound of languor and excitement, more intoxicating than the drugged chocolate she'd been offered in the brothel. She turned to him to protest. His dark gaze burned. "Do you want to tell me about it?"

She shook her head, and he picked up the pamphlet again. Helen pressed her lips together and studied the ceiling. She counted the number of squares in the paneling. *Twenty along the wall to her left. Four to the left of the fireplace. Eight to the right.*

Still her tormentor read on. When Lord Thrustmore had Miranda naked, when she had removed his boots and stockings and shirt, when he had turned her in his lap so that she knelt facing him, Helen was not sleepy at all. She felt distinctly uncomfortable. Her body ached and wept in surprisingly personal places.

The ache perplexed her. It was like a lump in one's throat, an ache of longing, not entirely a physical sensation that could be confined to its place in the body.

"Had enough?"

"I can't tell you a thing."

In a swift move he pinned her under him. Their thighs and bellies met. Their pulses pounded. "Heated, Helen? Restless? Aching? We can stop this right now if you tell me what I want to know."

She looked directly into those pitiless dark eyes and made no appeal. "No."

With one knee he pushed her legs apart and settled between them, pressing that most male part of himself against the place that ached and wept. Her legs felt the unfamiliar stretch to accommodate him, but the throbbing place welcomed the press of his body.

He held himself above her, braced on his arms. His voice turned coaxing. "You cost me a night of pleasure in this very bed. You could repay me."

She shook her head.

"I can be most persuasive." He leaned down to press kisses to the base of her throat. His heated mouth stirred in her a restless desire to arch her bound breasts.

He lifted his head, and watching her, he cocked his hips in a slow upward stroke of his body against hers. It was a pleasure she could hardly bear. She tried to summon ordinary sensation, but the wicked new pleasure drove out all recollection of familiar delights—the sun on her face, cooling breezes, lilacs in bloom, warm bread, strawberries.

The elusive sensation hovered, fleeting and intense, distilled to a single aching point and vast as a sea in which her other senses drowned. It could not be named or catalogued. She needed to invent a new sense to capture it.

"What did you go to get from March's brothel? This?"

Again she shook her head, keeping her lips firmly

closed. She was conscious of the heat in her face and a shameful reflex in her legs to close and hold him there.

"Your parents don't know where you are, do they? But someone does, an aunt, a cousin? Who helped you get to London?"

How had he guessed? Cousin Margaret would be worried sick not to hear from her.

He had that knowing look on his face. "You're not the first fool to run away from home."

Then his gaze settled on her lips, and he lowered his head. His mouth paused above hers. She told herself it was a threat, a tease. She should turn away, but her lips parted to taste his breath, warm and brandy-scented, and her body strained upward in anticipation.

Her eyes fell closed. Desire for his kiss held her suspended in the moment. It was coming. She waited. In the silence she heard a door open, and above her Will Jones froze. She opened her eyes to see the teasing lights in his go dark. He didn't move or turn toward the newcomer, but he seemed to forget Helen's existence.

A long moment passed.

"I thought I might find you . . . here. Harding let me in." The deep male voice was laced with sarcasm.

"As you see, Xan, I'm engaged."

"Not, apparently, in the search for our brother."

"Pressing business keeps me from it at the moment. How did your search happen to bring you here?"

The other man said nothing as she and Will Jones lay with their hearts beating against each other.

"Mother's returned from Paris. I came to ask you to stop by Hill Street in the morning, if it's convenient."

"A family reunion?" Will Jones lowered himself to lie heavily on her, the warm scratch of his cheek against hers. His heart had slowed until it hardly beat against her breast.

"Just so. I'll see myself out."

The door closed. In a flash Jones rolled off her and came to his feet, his back to her. A string of oaths came from him. She closed her eyes and clamped her legs together. She could hear him swearing and moving in rapid strides. Then there was silence.

Humiliation washed over her, a hot, stinging tide of a blush. Her body shook, and her pulse throbbed. Her breasts strained against their linen binding. The ache at her center felt huge, consuming. She didn't need the gauzy dress or the image in the mirror to reproach her for weakness. Her breasts, covered, flattened, bound tight to her body, had betrayed her. And he walked away.

A door opened, and she opened her eyes. He strode toward her wearing a hat and a greatcoat. Without a word he cut her bonds with a knife. He slapped a wad of bank notes in her open palm.

"This time don't steal the candlesticks."

Chapter Six

〜

H E was gone. Her body spasmed in a shameless plea for him to stay. Her heated cheeks stung.

She closed her fist on the bank notes in her palm. *Ridiculous to feel disappointed.* She was free. She needed a coat and footwear. The pair of wardrobes standing against the far wall might as well be on the shore of France. She looked at them from the warm, soft bed, her senses humming, while her body lay as lively as a sack of oats on the stable floor. If she didn't move, she'd likely sleep for a week. With a wrenching effort she sat up and swung her bandaged feet over the edge of the bed. Gingerly she lowered her heels to the floor and hobbled to the fire. The antique chair with its high back and carved wooden arms recalled Lord Thrustmore and

Miss Yeeld, so she huddled on a bench instead and concentrated on her anger against Will Jones. It was there like an ember she could coax into a good blaze.

He was caustic and cold. There was nothing of the gentleman in his manner or his manners. He didn't care what people thought of him and didn't think well of himself. He lived in a kind of exile, like Lucifer himself. *Better to reign in hell than serve in heaven.*

To get information out of her, he had used her body against her. Her shameless body had responded enthusiastically to the bawdy story and to his nearness, his voice, the press of his length against hers. Most humiliating of all, to him it was a game in which he had all the advantage.

But he had shielded her from his brother's view. The dry contempt in his brother's voice had fallen on him alone. And he had rescued her from rape and bandaged her feet. Helen was willing to wager that his arrogant brother made Will Jones feel he had failed, though she could not imagine how. With his clever mind and reckless daring, it seemed impossible that he should fail.

She stopped herself. She would not allow a ridiculous sympathy for the devil to confuse or distract her. She was in London because her mother's foolish gift to a man had involved them in disaster.

Her mother would be sleepless, too, at this hour. She was often awake through the night and unwilling in those dark hours to call her maid.

It had all begun when Helen had come upon her mother on that January afternoon after one of Jane's regular visits from her physician. Jane had been weeping, as Helen had never seen her mother weep. Helen had been alarmed, fearing that her mother's poor health had taken a turn for the worse, but the story that spilled out was not about Jane's health but her past.

Almost a quarter of a century earlier, before her marriage, Jane had had a lover, a wild, reckless young man of education but no fortune, who had gone off to the colonies and returned no richer, too late to claim her. Jane had not seen or heard from him in all the years since that bitter parting.

Jane begged Helen to understand how she had come to exchange letters with her former lover now returned to England and to send him two generous drafts on her bank for the sake of that memory. Jane had not heard from him again. Instead she gave Helen a chilling letter she had received explaining that her money had been used to promote treason. The writer included Jane's own words and those of her lover and the exact amount of each draft.

What had seemed discretion in a married woman writing to a former love now read like conspiracy. The unnamed person requested that Jane send another large draft to the address on Half Moon Street by Valentine's or the letters would be put in the hands of the Home Secretary himself.

Helen's first wild thought had been that her mother had done no wrong. She had nothing to fear from such an exposure even if her money had fallen into the hands of radicals. A second thought followed immediately. Her father must never hear of this. He must not gain knowledge with which to reproach his wife forever.

Nothing in the shocking story fit Helen's knowledge of her mother. The mother she had always known sat for hours in her chair with colorful silken yarns in her lap. The smaller the cushion, the more color her mother seemed to stitch into it. The mother she had always known submitted daily to her father's careless rebukes about the running of the household. *I suppose there was no good fish to be had today. I noticed that my notes have been misplaced again.* The mother she had always known insisted on Helen's daily walks and made her report each evening on how far she had gone and by what paths, and what she had seen—moorhens or rooks or gorse or primroses—each color had to be described.

It was to amuse her mother that Helen had first told stories of Troy. In time she had developed voices for all of the principal characters. To imagine herself the famous stolen queen had made her Greek lessons bearable. To be wanton, wicked Helen, Helen, who neither swooned nor wept, relieved the drudgery of those lessons. None of the other female characters offered the same escape. Helen was at the center of the story, wicked and defiant of all that dutiful, faithful wives were meant to be, and she got away with it. No man cowed her, not Menelaus or Paris or Deiphobus, speared in the end by Odysseus. So as her tutor had explained inflections and drilled her on Greek vocables, Helen had held herself in queenly aloofness.

In time the fantasy had given her a way to handle

her first suitors, those earnest young men in awe of her father with their eyes more often on him than on her. As Helen she found it easy to ward off impassioned but insincere speeches.

Being Helen seemed to make no impression on Will Jones, however. He thought her plan for gaining access to the house on Half Moon Street would fail. He had given her money only because he believed she would not succeed. There had to be a way. She had only until Valentine's to find her mother's letters and thwart her blackmailer.

Her mother had promised to do nothing until that day. She had simply squeezed Helen's hand and reminded her to do her daily walk wherever she was, and they had agreed to tell her father that she was visiting cousin Margaret in London. Helen looked at her bandaged feet. At least she had done her daily walk.

She stood and swayed dizzily. Black spots danced before her eyes, and she reached for the wall to steady herself. She leaned against the paneling and began to edge her way around the room to those wardrobes of his. She wondered if he had any slippers.

She limped along, leaning her hand against the wall. Halfway around the room, when her sliding palm caught on one of the raised panels, and as she gripped it to keep her balance, a catch gave, and the apparently solid wall swung away from her. She turned and stared into another room wholly unlike the one in which she stood.

To step through the threshold was to switch centuries again, back to the present. The room was a sort of office such as a barrister or a bailiff might have. The walls were a smooth pale yellow, and below the white wainscot were long low shelves lined with books.

The furniture was plain and worn, a cot in one corner covered with a rug, a pair of serviceable brown armchairs by the banked fire. In the corner opposite the hearth was a neat desk, and above it a large engraved map of London stuck with pins, each with a small flag of paper attached. Next to the desk a glass-fronted oak cabinet was filled with weapons, and above it a corkboard was covered with fragments of notices from the London papers and sketches of low characters from handbills.

On top of the cabinet were scales, and instruments she could not name, and a pair of manacles. She leaned against a table in the center of the room. Her heart pounded as if she had run up a flight of stairs. Who was he really? The languid vicomte, the madman who leapt from windows, the reader of Lord Thrustmore's amorous adventures, or some secret officer of the law?

She steadied herself. The room before her revealed his mind—sharp, careful, and tenacious, and she saw what she had not imagined before. He could help her. If instead of fighting him, she could enlist his aid, she stood a better chance of getting those letters.

Her heart slowed its tempo. She pushed away from the table and hobbled over to examine the map. Most of the pins were clustered on a single street, and as she peered closely, she saw that it was Bread Street where the school stood. Six pins with black-bordered flags marked its length. Each had a name and the letter *d*. She shuddered. Other pins marked with red-bordered flags simply read *March*. There was a red-bordered flag on the corner where the school stood and another several doors down next to two black-bordered flags. There was a pattern to it all, and she stepped back to see the whole. It was like a military map of a campaign with pins for each point where the enemy had his forces. There was no doubt who that enemy was. Pins for March appeared at her mother's bank and the Bow Street police office. At the west end of town both the red- and black-bordered flags stood side by side again on Half Moon Street at the site of the brothel. Apparently Will Jones connected March with death.

She turned her attention to the notices on the corkboard.

WILL welcomed the cold and fog. He needed the bite of it to cool the riot in his veins. He had let the game get away from him and hadn't gained a bit of useful information. *Never trust the one-eyed rat's intelligence report.* The adage was as true now as it had been when Tinsley was teaching Will the spy business. He still did not know who his Helen was or why she wanted to get into March's nasty little establishment.

He hadn't intended an actual seduction. He only meant to embarrass her into revealing her plans. But desire made him forget who he was, who she was, and why he had her tied to his bed. Everything about her but her mad charade as Helen of Troy suggested that she came from the proper, guarded world of blue-blooded English virgins whose idea of sex, at least until their husbands disillusioned them, was a peck in the dark and a poke under a linen tent of a nightgown. But she had responded, and he had lapped up every virginal sigh, every faint inclination of her body to his, like cream.

Only Xander's voice had stopped him from taking the game too far. Trust Xander to remind Will that Kit remained missing because he, Will, had not followed their plan. On the night March had taken Xander's bride and arranged an accident to drown her, Will had gone in pursuit of March, not Cleo. Will did not think Xander could forgive him for it.

Or for not truly believing that Kit was alive after three years. That had been his biggest failing. They had proof now—only Will had not been there to see it or to help Xander recover Kit.

The recollection of that one failure opened the door in his mind that let them all come crowding round, a howling chorus of his misdeeds from the time he'd left home at sixteen to join the army. He fled along the empty streets, a darker shadow in the fog. What he needed was a coal heaver, some fellow the size of a minor monument with a left fist like an anvil, to barrel into Will's path and knock him into oblivion.

He had crossed Piccadilly when he realized that London's coal heavers were sensibly snug in their own beds. His ramble led him to St. James's with its gaming hells and its clubs, where men of much less sense than the average coal heaver were still abroad wagering their fortunes on the next turn of a card. When he found himself face-to-face with March's club, he decided to curb his unruly conscience and make his mind submit to reason.

From the shadows opposite, he looked into the upper rooms, where the cardplayers were still at their games, waiters passing among them. Time to unlock this particular room of the past. The choices he'd made that night had cost him his position as a Runner and nearly cost Xan and Cleo's lives. The choices he'd made that night meant that Kit was still out there in the dark.

First he made himself remember the room—the high-vaulted ceiling, the carpet pattern of wide burgundy stripes of a swirling design, the deep upholstered chairs.

The cocky sense of confidence he'd felt that evening as he sat in March's chair came over him again. He'd been sure that he had the upper hand, that he could expose March for a hypocrite and a felon, that March would panic and reveal a detail they needed to find both the missing Cleo and Kit.

He forced his mind to go slowly. March had started at seeing him, mistaking him for Xander. Then March had glanced at the clock. What time had it been? Will waited, summoning the details, the clock face, the number of chimes, the quarter hour before five. Now they all knew the significance of that glance. March had planned an accident to drown Cleo and Xander and his other enemies on Bread Street. Will's former partner, Jack Castle, had attended the inquest into the deaths of those who had drowned that night. The magistrates ruled the deaths accidental in spite of the evidence of sabotage, a sign that March was still protected by his powerful friend, the Home Secretary.

Will should have recognized March's look in that moment for what it was, a gambler betraying his hand. But Will had been intent on his own goal, so intent that he hadn't at first sensed anyone standing behind him. What had happened next had been a cold voice speaking.

March, your sordid interview is disturbing the members. I suggest you see this man out.

He hadn't turned, but he would know that icy contemptuous voice anywhere. He made himself remember all of it—March's face with its shifting expression, the first blow across his back, staggering, tossing the glass in his hand, catching the waiter's arm, and shattering a mirror before those irate lords summoned enough courage to jump him. The chill voice had spoken once more. *Put the trash out, gentlemen.*

Will let the whole scene play out in his head, holding on to that look on March's face until he understood it.

Ice Voice was a man March feared. Who was he, and why did March fear him? To ask the questions was to see March's apparent disappearance in a new light. March was not hiding from the authorities. There was no official search for him because no one believed the Home Secretary's good friend Archibald March had committed a crime. March was hiding because he feared someone powerful. Ice Voice was a likely candidate. Somewhere in London was a man who had a hold on March.

It was a cheering thought. At least one other citizen of London, a powerful ruthless one at that, saw through March's great benefactor act. It would be helpful to know who owned that cold voice, and Will was sure he could find out with a bit of investigation.

The club door opened and two members sauntered out. Servants scurried to supply the men's coats and hats. A waiting carriage pulled up, and footmen hastened to open its door. Will turned toward home.

He found his great outer chamber empty when he returned near dawn. The penny pamphlets lay in a heap on the rumpled bed. The candlesticks stood in place on the mantel. She'd left without disturbing a thing. *Very wise.* This time he'd not follow her. He had no claim on her. He wished her luck. Maybe now that he had a lead, he would bring down March before she found a way back into that brothel.

He tossed aside his hat and greatcoat and took a last look at the big bed. *Later*, he promised himself. He sprung open the door to his inner apartment; better to sleep in the narrow field bed in his office with no reminder of Helen of Troy. Tomorrow he would find the identity of Ice Voice.

The fire was a banked glow in the hearth. He needed no additional light. With unconscious and efficient routine he shed his boots and clothes and set aside his pocket watch, weapons, and money. He could catch at least two hours of sleep before Harding came up the stairs and started banging things about in the outer room and before he had to face the prospect of an affecting family reunion.

He found his bed occupied.

For a moment he simply stood in his linen smalls, no barrier to lust, his senses overcome with the soft, warm mound of an invitingly female form. He could retreat to his outer room and sleep in his great bed. But before the thought could direct his feet, he took hold of the counterpane and ripped it off her. She started up into a sitting position. At least she was dressed.

"Bleeding hell. Do you have no sense of self-preservation?"

"You're back. Good."

"How did you get in here?"

"I pressed the panel on the wall." Her gaze took in his undress. "Why do you care so much where March is?"

"Helen, you do not invade a man's bed, and then start a chat with him. Even Goldilocks had the sense to run when the three bears returned."

"I thought the other bed was your bed, but who is March, really?"

"Now you've heard of him?"

"Everyone's heard of his charitable works, but you aren't interested in his famed kindness to the unfortunate."

He didn't comment on what she was revealing about herself. The room was too dark for him to see her face clearly, just the gleam in those wide, dark eyes. "He's a maw worm. He keeps files on hundreds of men, with information to embarrass or ruin them."

"For money? I thought he was rich."

"Let's say he inspires donations."

"But how does he get that sort of private information about . . ?"

"Victims? For years he's had access to a major bank."

"Evershot's."

Will held himself very still. She said it with such certainty. He had to laugh at himself. Under his erotic torture she'd revealed nothing, and here she gave up information like a condemned man narking on every crony he had.

All Will had to do apparently was stand nearly naked in her presence. She seemed not to notice. "Yes, Evershot's Bank. And should that source fail to yield compromising information, there's always the house on Half Moon Street where he can invite gentlemen to debase themselves and then forever after remind them of their sins."

"That very nearly explains your map." She stretched, damn her. "What do the red flags mean?"

"That March owns that piece of property."

"He doesn't own the bank."

"No, but he has had influence over Samuel Evershot for years."

She seemed to consider that in silence.

"And what is the meaning of this article about March?" She held out a paper clutched in her hand. "I found it tacked to the wall."

He remembered it, a scrap of gossip from the *Chronicle* about March's absence from London, written in a teasing style speculating where the Great Benefactor had gone. According to the writer, March was not to be seen in his usual haunts at his club nor was he present at any dinners. Hostesses needing a single gentleman to make up their numbers were apparently in dismay. March's former wards, Lord Woford and Cleopatra Jones, nee Spencer, were under the protection of the notorious Sir Alexander Jones. The wretched of London would surely perish in this current bitter cold without March to inspire almsgiving in us all. Will had kept the piece because the date of the paper indicated when March's absence had become known.

"No one in London seems to know where March is at the moment. He's left his former home and not appeared in society since November."

"You want to destroy March, don't you?"

"I want him to face justice."

"So we could work together."

"Work together? While you lie to me and conceal both your identity and your purpose?"

"We don't have to share everything. Just a common enemy, a common goal."

"And what would you, with your vast experience of Troy and staggering ignorance of London, have to offer this partnership? You've never used a weapon, you have a habit of ending up in unpleasant traps, you've never had sex or been kissed even, have you? You are, as Nate Wilde would say, greener than grass in May."

She regarded him in silence.

"I can get into that school, and I'm a bleeding good mimic."

He had to laugh. She had, for one sentence, sounded exactly like him.

"You're cold."

"A block of ice." A good thing, too, since his poor confused private parts had shrunk into the warmth of his body instead of jutting out like an eighteen-pounder on the deck of a frigate aimed at her. "I can't help you, Helen."

"You can, you know, but you don't think you need my help." She swung her bandaged feet to the floor and started to rise. "Thank you anyway; I will manage on my own."

Hell. She still thought she could head straight back to Half Moon Street to take on Leary. He pushed her down with a hand on her shoulder as she reached up and shoved a warm palm against his belly. Her hand slid down and away, brushing over his thigh, and his cock woke instantly.

"You need a better plan for dealing with Leary. And a haircut. In the morning you can talk to Harding about both." He turned and headed for his own bed. "Meanwhile, be my guest. You need a place to stay the night. Consider this your personal dormitory for wayward women."

"I'll be on my way in the morning."

"If you can find your way out." He stopped at the secret door. "Good night, Helen."

On the other side of the closed door, he saluted his conscience for a noble night's work saving silly virgins from their own folly. That other, more insistent part of his person stirred, reminding him that his baser instincts had simply saved her for himself.

Chapter Seven

❧

N ATE Wilde knew his part in the meeting going on in Bredsell's library. He was to look humble and eager to do whatever job they gave him next. He wasn't to look too interested in the details of the talk between Bredsell and March. He wasn't supposed to notice that neither man was pleased this morning or that their voices had a sharp edge. He leaned back against the wall, his hands in his pockets, his eyes on his boots, his ears open.

It was early for such a meeting, so Nate judged the problem to be a big one, like the enormous, red-faced man standing in the middle of the room. His name was Noakes, and he worked at March's fancy bawdyhouse in the toffy part of town. Nate knew about such places, of course, where the women were clean and pretty and did the deed in beds soft as clouds. And he had gone to the house on Half Moon Street a half dozen times lately on errands for Mr. March himself. There was a library there, too.

"Tell us again, Noakes, what happened to the girl." March leaned back in a green velvet wing chair by Bredsell's fire.

"Frenchie paid for 'er."

"His name?"

"Bee-comp bee-lard." Noakes spoke carefully like a child reciting his letters.

"Do we have anything on the man, Bredsell?"

Bredsell shook his head. He sat forward in the mate to March's chair. No one invited Noakes to sit, and the big man shifted from side to side on his feet.

"How much did she fetch?"

Noakes considered. "'Undred quid." He was lying and March and Bredsell knew it, but Noakes was too thick to know they knew it.

"And then, Noakes?"

"I took 'em up to the usual room."

"Did you leave them?"

Noakes nodded, puzzled at the interruption of his story. "'E wanted champagne. Told me ta 'urry it up. But when oi came back, 'e 'ad the door locked. An' when we broke the door in, they was gone."

"Out the window you said?"

"'E popped the boards clean off."

"And flew away?"

Noakes accepted the idea with a confused mumble of assent.

It got quiet in the room. Mr. March could get quiet like that, a thinking kind of quiet. It could make a bloke sweat. Nate could hear Noakes sweating. March's thinking would not be good for Noakes, but it meant some kind of job for Nate.

His main job for weeks had been running errands to and from the house on Half Moon Street, ever since the beer flood wiped out two narks and three Bread Streeters not sharp enough to heed the warning. It was not Nate Wilde's fault they hadn't run when they should've.

The flood had changed Bread Street in ways that Bredsell and March didn't like. Now that toff Xander Jones was a hero on Bread Street. He said anyone who wanted work could have it with his East London Gas Company that was going to light the street. Even boys. Every day he was there, a tall toff in his fine coats, hiring and giving out wages and hot jacket potatoes and beer. A bloke could get tired just watching him. The word on the street was that he would find work for anyone and his blind dog.

That kind of backbreaking work was not for Nate Wilde. He liked carrying messages. It took smarts to remember what he was to say and what the other fellow said or how he looked. No other boy from the school worked directly for Mr. March. But if March and Bredsell had to call it quits and run, Nate was prepared. He kept two stashes, one on his person, and one in Clement Danes church, where the sexton would never find it.

Noakes yawned.

March frowned, his hands tapping the arms of his chair. "Bredsell, someone knows more about my establishment than I care to have known."

"A randy Frenchman made off with a little whore, for whom he paid top dollar. Leary is another matter, I grant you, regrettably untrustworthy. But this vicomte stealing a girl doesn't hurt your operation. You're leaving for France soon enough, aren't you?"

"You aren't trying to hurry my departure, are you, Bredsell?"

"Of course not." The two men exchanged a look of distrust. Nate could see that things between them weren't right.

"Nevertheless, Bredsell, the security of the place has been breached."

"I tell you it's Xander Jones you should worry about, not Leary or the Frenchman. Jones is here every day, and I don't want him or any of his gas company people talking to my boys."

"The boys aren't talking to anyone, and Jones can tear up every stone of Bread Street, and he won't find a thing."

"You're sure of that?"

A look of annoyance crossed March's face. "If the boy's not dead, he must have been taken from London long ago."

"But Cullen and Greenslade saw him alive."

"Well, they are no longer a problem, are they?"

Bredsell looked like he would argue and stopped.

March turned to Nate. "Wilde, my boy, I have a job for you."

Nate came away from the wall. "Yes, sir, Mr. March."

WILL found Helen sitting on a stool by the fire in his inner room, her shoulders draped with a towel while Harding cut her hair. Harding, professional as ever, snipped those deep gold strands with unmoved efficiency while Will's mouth went dry at the thought of running his hands through that hair.

He stopped in front of her. It was his first look at her in daylight. It didn't help his clarity of mind that she looked him over with a slow sweep of those brown eyes. In the morning light he could see gold and violet in the irises.

Her eyes widened at his appearance. He had dressed with some care for this first meeting with his mother in three years. "You are someone new every day."

"Only on the outside. Did Harding like your plan for entering the Half Moon Street house?"

"No. But he says that using sweeps might work. No one pays attention to sweeps while they go about their business."

Will turned to his man. "Sweeps, Harding?"

"An exceptionally well-guarded bawdy house, sir. Makes one wonder."

It was true. March had a lot of hired muscle keeping the place sealed up.

Will could see his virgin thinking. "Harding, what

do you suppose they keep inside that requires such a guard?"

"That, miss, is the question." Harding stepped back to look at what he'd managed to do with the cropped remnants of her hair. It now fell in thick waves that framed her face and brushed her ears while longer strands hugged her nape. "Ye'll do, miss."

Schoolboys wore such cuts, but she didn't look like any schoolboy Will had ever known. True, there were boys who possessed a certain prettiness, but something in their air or manner made them grubby boys, something that Helen lacked. He'd make sure she wore a cap.

"Your valued object must require the heavy guard."

"Don't jest. My purpose is no light matter, and your interference may . . . ruin good people."

Harding took the towel from around her shoulders and shook the loose locks into the fire. He offered Will a long strip of linen. "The young 'gentleman' needs a neckcloth."

Will stepped forward and lifted Helen's chin with his fingers. Just that, his fingers touching the softness there, sent a carnal jolt through him. He wanted to rub his thumb over her lips. He began to wind the linen around her throat. If he wanted to stop her from another disastrous attempt to breach March's den, he had to find out who she really was. Maybe he could turn her over to his mother or to his sister-in-law, Cleo Jones. It wouldn't do to tell her that plan, but he would keep the possibility in mind.

He stepped back from her. All he saw was female—

smooth skin, sweet lips, and black eyelashes so thick and heavy they'd tip a grocer's scale.

"Let's see if you can really pass yourself off as a boy. We'll take a hack to my mother's house."

Nothing Helen said in the hack met with Will Jones's approval. She'd had a much easier time talking with stone-faced Harding. The older man had a way of asking questions that revealed difficulties without making her feel like a dolt. Will Jones simply gave her an impatient flick of a glance at each suggestion, as if she were a dull scholar, which she was not.

Still she had resolved not to let him affect her as he had in the bed, and it was easier to keep that resolution under his withering sarcasm. So far today she'd only been in danger once when he had stalked into his inner room dressed only in his linen smalls, lean and mean but scarred and bruised. He'd opened shutters she had not observed, and so she had seen his body plainly in the morning light.

"Admit it. You don't like any plan in which I return to that house."

"Recalling our first meeting there makes me doubt your tactical brilliance."

"I saw you exchange looks with Harding. You have information you aren't sharing."

He might think he concealed things from her, but she now understood that the place from which the threat to her mother came was owned by London's great benefactor, Archibald March. March, who moved in her parents' circle of acquaintances, apparently had shocking access to private dealings at her mother's bank. If March had sent her mother that letter, then she and Will Jones had a common enemy.

As the hack slowed, Will Jones pulled her to him by her neckcloth, his face just inches from hers. "Your rape or murder won't keep anyone from ruin, and there are persons in that house capable of either or both."

They were stopped on Hill Street in front of a substantial brown brick town house. Cold and fog swirled about them, and the house looked warm, inviting, and fashionable. "*Your* mother lives here?"

"Sophie Rhys-Jones. You've not heard of her in Troy, but in London she's a notorious courtesan. With each of her noble lovers, she's produced a bastard—the Sons of Sin. I told you I was descended from a long line of wickedness." He leapt down from the hack. "What shall we call you? Troy what?"

"Tibbs." It was her mother's maid's name. Of course he didn't offer to help her after him. She was a youth.

"You've an hour to prove you can pass as a boy. Keep your voice low."

"Like this?" She mimicked Harding's gruff tone. *"That, miss, is the question."*

Will Jones gave her his sardonic-devil look. "No need to overdo it."

A silent, horse-faced servant answered the door, took their coats, and led them up a curving elegant stair to a pretty blue-and-white drawing room. When the servant announced them to the five persons in the room, Helen saw the test Will Jones had set for her. If she failed or if he revealed her femaleness to them, they would be even more inclined than he was to discover her true identity and return her to cousin Margaret or worse, to her father's house.

A woman in black silk rose from a curving blue velvet sofa with a gold-tasseled fringe. She gave a delighted cry and floated toward them, a rustle of silk and fragrant air, and Helen forgot her situation.

This was Aphrodite herself, the goddess in one of her many guises. Here she had raven hair and a complexion of pearls and roses in a heart-shaped face dominated by the most expressive dark eyes Helen had ever seen. Helen could not say her age. She had Aphrodite's compelling power in full measure. If she pricked her finger on an embroidery needle, every man in the room would rush to her side as if a gaping wound had opened.

The dark beauty went directly to Will Jones. "My son." Tears streamed down her flawless cheeks without making her large dark eyes any less brilliant.

"Mamma," he said through tight lips, and allowed the beauty to fold him in her silken embrace. He accepted her touch and her affectionate gaze. But Helen could see in his stiff, unbending posture how he resisted the goddess herself, love.

Like Helen, the four others in the room watched the awkward embrace until a stiff, elegant version of Will Jones stepped forward to end it. He had a frown as intimidating as his voice. "Mamma, his ribs are still recovering."

The beautiful woman in black released Will Jones, wiping the tears from her face with the back of one hand. A tall, slim gentleman, with close-cropped silver hair and a military cut to his moustache, who watched the goddess with a besotted gaze, offered her a handkerchief, and she gave him a tremulous smile. "Luc," she said, "my son Will."

The gentleman introduced himself in the accent of a Frenchman as "Major Montclare of His Majesty's guard."

Will Jones immediately addressed the other man in French. There was a rapid exchange through which each seemed to take the other's measure. When they stopped, Will Jones laughed and offered the major his hand.

Will Jones drew Helen forward with a hand on her shoulder. "You must excuse me, Mamma, for bringing young Tibbs, here, with me. We are working on a case." Clearly, Will Jones was practiced at offending his family.

The man who looked to be a colder, more proper version of Will frowned severely. He was Sir Alexander Jones. The gangly boy with a head of wild brown hair, who gawked openly, proved to be Charlie Spencer, the brother of a young woman not much older than Helen with remarkable green eyes and the rounded contours of pregnancy. Her frank green gaze met Helen's, and Helen knew her femininity had been detected.

She glanced at the door. She had no chance of fleeing if the green-eyed woman revealed the truth. She turned out to be Lady Cleo Jones, who with an arch look at Helen, suggested that Charlie, her brother, the boy with the hair, take Master Tibbs aside with a plate of cakes and some hot chocolate.

Settled with Charlie in a pair of chairs by the window overlooking the street, Helen observed him closely to see what to do with her legs. His stuck out from his body like fishing poles dangling over a stream. She arranged her limbs in a less sprawling posture and divided her attention between her companion and the group gathered in the center of the room. At first the voices belonged to Sir Alexander and his mother.

Her own companion's undemanding conversation allowed her to catch the drift of Sir Alexander's story. He was explaining how a long search for their missing younger brother Kit had led to the discovery but not the recovery of the boy.

"He is alive; that's all that matters," Sophie insisted in a low, throaty voice. "What do we do now, Xander?"

As Xander made a quiet, firm reply, Charlie leaned toward Helen and whispered, "They are talking about the third brother, Kit Jones, the one who's been missing for over three years. Xander and Cleo found him alive in October on Bread Street. Try a lemon cake."

Helen broke a small cake into four pieces.

Charlie went on. "There was a beer flood on Bread Street when the brewery's vats broke. Xander and Cleo escaped to the roof, and they saw Kit standing with a gang of boys on the opposite roof. They couldn't get to him, of course, because of the beer."

"A gang of boys on a roof?" It was like Robin's story. She had dismissed the little boy's talk as a wishful fancy, but the school stood across Bread Street from the brewery, so perhaps Robin had seen boys on the rooftops and imagined some rescue would come from them. "You're not in school, are you?" Charlie asked.

Helen shook her head.

Charlie went on to say that he had just started the winter term. It was all Greek and Latin for him, no adventures, but some maths, he hoped. He was fond of maths, and he had Xander's promise that he could see the gasworks Xander had built, if he did well. Did she know that Xander had been knighted for saving the prince regent's life, and that now he was lighting the streets of London?

Across the room Xander was explaining how they believed Kit had escaped his captor over a year earlier. "Mamma, we think Kit has lived by his wits on the streets since a year ago November."

"But he's still just a boy."

"Our information suggests he's somewhere in the neighborhood of Bread Street. That's why . . ."

"But how can he live? Does he have a room, warm clothes, food?" The low voice rose to an anxious pitch.

"I suspect he . . . scavenges and does odd work." Helen sneaked a peek at Sophie Rhys-Jones. She looked horrified but still beautiful. Helen could only look at her in brief glances, while the besotted major could hardly look away. She could imagine the effect on his brain. This time Sophie's voice was a cry of complaint. "But why does he not return to us?"

The brothers looked at one another, alike and not

alike, the older one proper and commanding, the younger, reckless and dangerous. Helen felt as if she had overturned her mother's embroidery frame to expose the web of threads connecting the bits of the design. Bright threads of feeling crisscrossed the room in her mind, connecting mother and son, lover and lover, the fabric stretched tight by the crisis.

Xander spoke at last. "He may not believe we want him back."

"How could he think such a thing!" Sophie was plainly outraged.

"Or he might fear that whoever was behind his kidnapping will strike again at someone else in the family." Will Jones leaned forward. "The two people who saw him alive last year and informed us where he might be are now dead."

Sophie gasped, and the major took her hand, but Will didn't stop, his intense gaze fixed on his mother.

"Murdered, Mamma. So Xan rightly urges caution. Someone in London doesn't want us to find Kit alive."

Sophie raised her chin. "If the man who took him is dead, whom does he fear?"

Xander spoke again. "Very likely the person who took Kit was hired by someone else. That's the mystery, Mamma. Who wanted Kit to disappear?"

This time there was an even longer pause before Sophie spoke. "Who would want a son of mine to disappear?"

Will spoke. "We suspect a man named Archibald March was involved in some way."

Sophie's confusion at the name was apparent. She looked at Cleo Jones. "Archibald March is your uncle, isn't he? He's the man who had Will beaten at that club." She shuddered, and the major squeezed her shoulder.

"March was there, but another man at the club actually ordered the beating."

"Who?" It was cleverly concealed, Helen thought, but Sophie had hesitated before the natural question just an instant too long for complete ignorance, and she did not meet her son's gaze.

"I don't know his name, only his voice. Ice Voice is someone with a great deal of power, and March likes power. He has close ties to the Home Office and to Evershot's Bank, your bank, Mamma. Could March have discovered something about our family through the bank?"

The brilliant dark eyes flashed. "Only that we are solvent. What do we do now? Do we put a notice in the papers? Do we hire men to search Bread Street?"

"No. Xan will continue his work on Bread Street, and I will find Ice Voice, the man behind March."

Sophie's beautiful mouth crumpled. "But this is no plan at all. I've waited three years. You tell me Kit is alive. I return to London. You tell me he chooses not to come home where he is loved. You tell me I must sit and do nothing."

"Yes, Mamma." Both sons answered at once.

It was Xander's voice Helen heard next. "We have one more lead, a young thief named Nate Wilde. Will saw him the other day."

"Can we talk to this boy today? What can he tell us?" Sophie asked.

Will Jones glanced at Helen. She gave no sign in response to hearing Wilde's name, but it made her rethink Will Jones's actions. He had found and taken Helen twice not out of kindness of course, she knew that. He wasn't kind, but he was even more indifferent than she had supposed. He had taken her from places owned by his enemy March. That was to her advantage. Because she had been inside the brothel and inside the school, she might convince Will Jones that she had something to offer him in his war on March. They might act as partners yet. She could not let him see her mother's letters, but she could use his help to search for them in that brothel.

"Look, Troy, something's happening in the street." Charlie's voice recalled her to him.

She looked out the window.

Outside, a man was loping along the fog-shrouded street shouting. As people heard him, they stopped and huddled together. Some of the gentlemen removed their hats at the shouting man's news. He ran on.

The door to the drawing room opened, and the solemn, horse-faced servant stood there. Everyone turned to him.

"The king died at Windsor last night," he said.

Chapter Eight

❧

WILL set off from the house on Hill Street at a brisk pace. An hour in the bosom of one's family was just the thing to make a man know himself and his history.

Nothing had changed. His mother wore black and shed buckets of tears. It was what he remembered most from those last months of his boyhood, her bouts of weeping and one mad day of locking all the bright gowns away in closets. Nothing he tried had helped to stop the tears. Even when she clung to him, sobbing and he promised . . . He didn't remember those extravagant promises.

The only thing that stopped the flood of tears was the baby Kit. His mother's maid, Janet, would lay the bundled infant in Sophie's lap, and the tears would stop.

Will had marveled at the enchanted babe, who, doing nothing, possessed powers that Will obviously lacked. He decided to leave home, not for Oxford where Xander was, but for the army.

It had taken three years to get away. And his first step had been a piece of youthful folly he still regretted—going to his father to beg for money. The recollection had the power to rankle even now.

Impersonating a footman, he had managed to get inside his father's club. The Earl of Oxley had barely looked up from his drink, even when Will had identified himself. The dissolute face had shocked Will, the mottled veins on the nose and the deep pouches under the eyes.

"You want to touch me up for money? You've been bought and paid for many times over, boy. Your mother freely opened her thighs, which hardly obliges me to open my wallet. The jade had enough off of me to fund a kingdom."

Will hit him, breaking the earl's nose, he thought, Xander's instruction paying off. Only a youthful burst of speed enabled him to escape arrest. He never went home. He had understood then that he wasn't meant to be. He was an accident of the worst sort. He had cost his mother her protector. She had been seduced and abandoned again because of him. He was marching with his regiment in Horsham by the end of the week.

Now he was twenty-nine. He must be getting too old for folly, for he was cold, cross, and still felt the effects of the beating he'd taken in October.

He marched Helen past the house on Half Moon Street

to show her in the gloom of a foggy day how blasted impossible it was to gain access to the place. Then he took her to the White Bear Inn in Piccadilly. He would try once more to convince her to share her secret and let men like him handle March and his ilk.

The inn bustled with the usual coaching traffic and with news of the old king's death. Rumor had it that the new king had taken to his bed out of fear or a suspicion that his embarrassing estranged wife would return and insist on taking the throne beside him. Will had little faith in prince, Parliament, or cabinet, but Wellington could hold the country together.

He settled Helen in a corner with a plate of blue-veined cheese, some rough bread, and a warming cup of punch. Around them people toasted the old king and the new king and predicted economic chaos and new prosperity with equal vigor.

He took a swig of ale and watched the girl pick at her food. He hadn't exposed her as a woman to his family as he'd intended. He'd forgotten that part of his plan. From the moment Sophie Rhys-Jones had embraced him, he hadn't been thinking clearly. And as their talk continued, every instinct had screamed that his dear mamma was withholding information. She knew something about Kit's disappearance that she wasn't telling. Fine, he had two women lying to him.

Helen looked up at him over her mug of punch. "I admit I don't see a way in. That doesn't change my situation. If I don't get what I came for, people . . . good, kind, helpless people, will suffer unbearably."

"You mean the sort that usually suffers." It was clear that she was a hopeless believer in the good. He dropped the sarcasm. "You can't prevent it. Let me turn you over to the authorities. Let it be their problem. Jack Castle's a good man, an honest Runner."

Instant alarm flared in those deep brown eyes, so seemingly guileless. She shook her head. "No. No Runners. Just you."

"Not me, sweetheart. Your cause is hopeless if you think I can help. Besides, I'm not inclined to help a woman who lies to me."

"If we were partners, would you help me? I know things that can help you." She watched him closely.

"I doubt you know anything of any use in London." He tipped his mug back again and watched her weigh her strategy.

"I think I may know who your Ice Voice is."

He went very still. "You bleeding better not jest."

She pressed her lips together watching him. Then she spoke. From the sweet, ripe mouth came the cold, haughty tones he remembered. She was very good. It chilled him how good she was. But if she knew that voice, who the hell was she? She had already as much as admitted that she knew March. "Who is he?"

"Your word that you'll help me. And I must be the only one who sees the object I'm looking for."

"Think, Helen. If you are discovered in this adventure, you will no longer be marriageable even if your father's a duke."

She shrugged and offered him a wry smile. "Marriage is one of the worst fates that can befall a woman."

"It's the usual fate, in any case, and don't think the world is kind to a woman without a male protector. If we work together, you follow my rules."

"*Your* rules?"

"*My* rules. In the end you'll be alive, and you'll still be a virgin."

She nodded. "Your word." She stuck out her hand across the table.

He reached for it. "Who is he?"

She withdrew her hand and leaned toward him across the scarred table, suddenly conscious of the comings and goings of waiters and patrons. "The Duke of Wenlocke."

Will glared at the girl in front of him. She had buckets of cheek. He lost himself briefly in some language she ought not to hear. Wenlocke. Wenlocke, who had more power than the regent, now king. Wenlocke was Kit's grandfather. It was his noble son, the Marquess of Daventry, who had fathered Kit, left for India, and died at Assaye. *Hell.* If the girl was right, Sophie knew something about Wenlocke she had not told her other sons.

He studied the girl. "If you know the Duke of Wenlocke, you move in exalted circles."

She crumbled a bit of cheese. "It's an uncommon voice. You recognized it, and you only heard it once."

He grabbed her wrist and stilled her hand. "Who are you?"

She didn't flinch. "Somebody's daughter. Nobody. Helen of Troy. It's not important who I am."

He released her. "I ought to turn you over to Jack Castle anyway."

"You swore."

"Bleeding hell."

F OG and bells owned the city. The old king had reigned longer than any other in English history, and invisible spires rang his knell from every corner of London. The frosty air quaked like a jelly with their ringing.

Kit Jones wasn't thinking of the mad old king, who had been locked away for years. He moved alone and unseen along familiar pathways of slate and shingle, looking for Robin. The boy had gone missing the week before when the younger members of their band took turns in the line where Cleo Jones handed out jacket potatoes to families of workers on the great ditch Xander was digging in Bread Street.

Collecting potatoes had been Lark's idea. To Kit it had seemed a dangerous exposure of their group, but in the end the pinched faces of the boys had been too much for him. He had stayed away, and let Lark lead the band. Everyone had eaten well that night, but they'd lost Robin. When he had not turned up in any of the usual places, Lark suggested that the school had got hold of him.

The approach to Upper Bread Street lay over a block of adjoining tenements and shops, the tallest of them a five-story warehouse. He scaled the icy peak of a gable and slid down its other side, and then ran hunched over behind the open parapets of three flat-roofed buildings ascending in height like steps. Ice crunched under his boots, chimney pots billowed their hot, ashy breath around him, and he ducked and veered to miss the occasional clothesline stretched like a crystal wire in the frigid gloom. At the end of the block of buildings the sharp peak of another gable jutted up between him and the school. He climbed its far slope and lay flat across the tiles to look down into the walled yard of Bredsell's school. The cold pressed down on him, heavy in the still air.

He settled himself to wait and to study the scene. The masters would turn the boys out into the yard for half an hour before supper, and he hoped to spot Robin in the crowd.

The school stood on a corner, inaccessible on two sides to roof walkers because of the width of the streets. A flat-roofed brick building, four stories tall, it had two attic gables with sleeping quarters for the boys. From each of the long attics a pair of dormers protruded. If Robin was inside, they'd have to go in through one of those dormers and out the main doors. That was the problem. Robin could not walk the length of the wall enclosing the yard.

Below Kit the streets looked deserted, but he knew that empty look for an illusion. On Bread Street danger could come from any direction. It knotted his stomach to see Xander return with his bride each day.

Kit had made a mistake in showing himself to them

on the day of the flood. He had been watching the house, watching Xander's wife, trying to judge whether he might give her a message for his family, and then March had taken her. Kit did not know how Xander had found her, only that Xander was fearless. He had thrown himself against the door of the public house and plunged into the darkness as the flood roared down on them.

Kit had stood on the roof opposite, boys clinging to his coat, unable to tell whether the shaking in his limbs was the building under him or his own fear. Even when he saw Xander come through the window and pull the girl out behind him, Kit had been unable to move.

He knew he'd been foolish to show himself when those who wanted him dead would kill anyone connected to him. Now he'd brought them all to Bread Street. And Xander seemed oblivious to the danger. He strode up and down the street among the roughest of men, inspecting the ditch they were digging for his gas line. All the while Kit knew that anyone, anyone, the most ordinary-looking of men could be hired to kill Xan.

Harris had been that kind of man, ordinary in appearance. For a moment just thinking of him, Kit's body shook where he lay against the icy slate. He waited for the shudders to pass.

In the first days of his captivity he had believed Xander would find him. He knew they were in London not two miles from home. He had only to hold on and not offend his captor. To speak at all set Harris off. The big man would seize Kit by the throat and shake him, shouting in his face the whole while. *There is no search.*

No one is looking for you. Who wants a bastard? No one. Every parish gives them away. No one wants you. Except dead. Do you know how much those swells paid me? But Timothy Harris is no murderer.

Harris had chained Kit from the start and moved them if anyone took an interest. At first Kit had found hope from those acts in spite of the endless monologue of warnings from Harris. *Don't think to escape. Don't think you can go back to your family. They don't want you, and they'll end up dead if you go back.*

It took weeks to lose that hope, to realize that Harris spoke the truth. No one would come. He forgot the sound of his own voice.

When Harris died, Kit went up to avoid capture. He had no plan, but from the roof of the tenement, London lay before him; the sheer openness of the view, the absence of walls, had made him dizzy. That day he had been cold, hungry, and afraid to move quickly. He had picked his way across a row of rooftops to find himself stymied by an impassible gulf of a street. Retracing his path, he'd found a gap he could leap. He threw himself over it, and passed on away from Bread Street. He soon learned where a chimney leaked heat or where an overhang provided shelter or where an unlatched opening admitted him to a warehouse attic. And where an iron pipe led down a wall to a safe street.

He had been free for months before he thought to go near his old home. He told himself he would just take a look. He would bring no danger to Hill Street. He just wanted to know that Mamma and Xander were well and safe and that his old life continued untouched in spite of Harris's threats. He'd been astonished to find the house lit up like a blazing stage. There was no sign of his mamma, only Xander and a handful of servants.

Shortly after that visit, he had begun to collect a family of his own. Lark was the first, a boy of ten who had escaped Bredsell's school. Now there were seven of them. They knew the tides, and the wagon routes to every market in London. Whatever fell or floated in the wake of London commerce was fair game, theirs for the taking. They could grab what they needed and disappear to one of their rooftop sanctuaries.

In spite of his resolve, his old life lay in wait for him, the way a Bread Street cosh carrier lay in wait for a victim. So he had fallen into the habit of visiting his mother's house at night when he'd settled his band in a pocket where a steeply sloped roof met a flat one and a row of crumbling chimneys leaked heat. The Hill Street house was a puzzle to him. It was his home and not his home. He was not the boy Harris had taken. Walls now meant something different to him than they did to his family.

The bells fell silent. Below him a door opened in the brick face of the school building, and boys filed silently into the yard. They formed a circle, each boy an arm's length from the boy in front or in back, heads bent. The shuffle of their feet whispered on the stones. From above all the boys looked young and small. Kit found a dark patch on the brick wall and set himself to watch each head as it passed the mark. He needed Robin to know they would come for him.

From the roof of a shop on Bethnal Green Road, Kit had seen the boy sitting beside his dead mother. Standing over the child, two of the watch had argued over who had to take the boy. Both claimed the child was not the responsibility of his parish. No one touched the child or the body. Kit had taken a loose brick and heaved it into the midst of a passing herd of cattle being driven to market. In the milling confusion that followed, he had simply taken the boy by the hand and led him away. They had stopped in a church for warmth and said a prayer for the dead woman.

Below Kit in the school yard it took three shuffling passes of the boys before one stood out in the silent gray parade, a boy who tilted his head to the left to cast a glance upward as he passed along the wall of the building under Kit. Kit picked out a pebble-size bit of broken roof tile and waited. As Robin came around again, Kit tossed. The tiny piece landed and the boy looked up, his round red cheeks unmistakable even in the gloom. Kit rose, his finger on his lips, then dropped back behind the concealing gable. He and the band had a rescue to plan.

CLEO Jones stood in her husband's dressing room, her back to him, lifting her chestnut hair away from her neck so that Xander might undo the row of looped fastenings on the back of a pale green gown, for which he'd recently seen the bill.

"What do you call this fetching color?"

"Pistachio."

Xander was not deceived by his wife's apparent docility. They had quarreled with some heat a quarter of an hour earlier about Will's bringing a woman disguised as a boy to their family meeting. Xander had been furious when Cleo pointed out Troy Tibbs's gender. Xander had no doubt where Will's companion had spent the previous night.

Bringing a doxy from his bed to a family meeting about Kit's fate proved Will was capable of every kind of selfish, decadent, unthinking folly. Cleo, however, had defended Will's act as the first sign of hope for him that she'd seen. She claimed he was obviously looking out for the girl. When she walked out of their bedroom, Xander was left trying to understand how the quarrel differed from their past confrontations.

Now he slipped one hand around his wife's gently rounded middle above her ribs to hold her steady, and began to release the loops along her spine. They had not yet been married five months, but things had deepened between them.

She sighed. "I wonder that you married me after all once you had the money for your gasworks."

Xander smiled. He recognized the tone. As he worked the loops, the pale green silk fell away. He kissed her once on the white slope of her shoulder where the muscle tended to knot when she worried. "I had no choice."

She exhaled a scornful puff of air. "You did, of course. I see it now even if I did not then. Henry Norwood could easily have got you out of our marriage in the consistory court. That was your plan, and Henry is very clever."

Xander had undone all the fastenings of the bodice. Only his hand pressed under and between her breasts held the top of the gown in place. He began to work the strings of her stays, worn loosely in her pregnancy. He felt considerably better about the quarrel already. It was different, he decided, because they could be more open with each other and because there was an underlying assumption about how it would end, here, in their bedroom.

"You are forgetting that the matter had already been decided. In the bank the first day we met. I thought you understood that."

"I thought I did, but I had not then met your mother. Your mother's beauty changes everything. With such a mother how could you end up married to me?"

"I believe I was not thinking of my mother at the time." Xander felt his mouth widen in that grin his wife could so easily provoke.

She twisted out of his hold and turned to face him, keeping her sagging bodice in place with her hands, her collarbone and the tops of her breasts exposed. "You know very well that her beauty is stunning. I see now where you and your brothers get that look you have. It's a peerage of beauty. She's royalty, the queen of beauty, and you are the princes. The rest of us are mere commoners."

Fortunately, Xander knew what to do when his wife's unruly tongue betrayed her unease. He reached out and pressed his fingers to her lips. She stilled and a little tremor shook her. He waited until the green eyes were focused on him. "Men think differently about their mothers. No matter what that poor Greek fellow did who ended by poking out his eyes. My mother locked me in closets. You, I believe, opened all the closets." He let the words sink into his wife's troubled brain before he took his hand away from her mouth. She looked at him in a way that wiped out all other concerns. "To bed. Now."

Hours later in the warm, dark envelope of their sheets, she stirred and spoke again. One could not distract Cleo Jones for long. "The thing is that the girl with your brother has your mother's kind of beauty, the compelling kind."

"I hadn't noticed." He lay on his back with his wife's head nestled in the curve of his arm.

"Will can't resist her, you see. He thinks he can, but he's not in control of the situation at all."

Xander smiled up into the lofty darkness of the ceiling high above him. There was his wife understanding the people in his life, once again, and proving him wrong. A quiet laugh shook him. It was glorious to be wrong, utterly, hopefully, satisfyingly wrong. Will Jones had met his match.

Chapter Nine

❧

I T must be near midnight. They'd been at it for hours and still had no plan. Helen felt as if Jones had tied her head to an anvil and hammered or pried every faint recollection of the brothel's rooms and layout from her brain. She had been asked to recall each corner of Leary's office. Was there a cabinet, a desk, a closed case for books, a wardrobe, a closet? *Think, think*, he had ordered relentlessly, standing over her, shedding his jacket and his cravat, loosening the button of his collar, running his hand through that thick jet hair while Harding sat at the table rendering her wisps of memory into neat black lines and sketches indicating rooms and doors and staircases.

Besides the ground floor, there were three upper

floors and a basement. The basement would have more than a dozen rooms. In an ordinary house these would be devoted to cooking, laundering, storing ale, coal, and wine, and providing living space for servants. If Helen did get into the house, she would have to know where to look to find her mother's letters, or she would never succeed in recovering them. The black lines of Harding's drawings blurred before her eyes.

They pulled down the rate books from Jones's bookshelves and poured over house plans. The city of London had a strict building code that allowed for little variation in the design of row houses. March's brothel would be much like its neighbors. Only the details of the center of the house, where an architect could vary the design, still eluded them.

As the Vicomte de Villard, Jones had entered a front hall, passed up a grand stair to a salon, and then ascended the grand stair one more story to where two bedrooms faced the street. He had never penetrated the rear of the house. Helen had entered through the servants' entrance below the street and gone up a closed servants' stair to Leary's office. After her disastrous interview with him, she'd been led further up the same servants' stair and hustled along a passage to a rear bedroom. Later her brain had been so fogged that she couldn't be sure of anything she'd seen on her way to the grand salon. But Jones pressed her anyway.

"A closed passage? How many doors? On the left or the right?"

"I can't remember."

"Close your eyes. Stand." He yanked her out of her chair by her arm. "You were barefoot, *sweetheart*. What was the carpet like?"

Sweetheart. The word, low and rough, like his touch, gave her a sudden feeling of dislocation as if she were back in that time and place. She had been unsteady on her feet, her head thick, intent on trying to escape her captors. She felt the low, stiff pile of the carpet prick her unusually sensitive feet. She had spun out of their hands and tried to run, but she had staggered clumsily into a rail and folded over it, looking down into black nothingness, her heart pounding, her stomach threatening to heave. She had been relieved when they pulled her back from that edge. She shuddered as the memory floated back up into her consciousness. "There's a well, a wide, dark well with bands of stone. It goes down forever. I looked over a rail, and they pulled me back."

Jones let her go. He leaned over the table, studying the drawings again. He pointed to the empty center of the drawings for the ground floor and each of the next two stories.

"Here, Harding, there's a two- or maybe three-story room that's open on the top floor." Jones tapped the center of the drawings.

Harding sketched in a rough addition. "It has to be open then, here and here." Harding pointed. "Not a likely place for storing secrets, sir."

Jones' frown deepened. "I doubt March uses his basement for those precious files. Helen saw nothing in Leary's office that could hold those files if they are as extensive as we think. I think that mystery room is our target."

Harding nodded. "Could be a hide-in-plain-sight strategy."

Jones clapped a hand on the other man's shoulder. "Let's call it a night. Thanks, man."

"Anything else, sir?" Harding rose. He glanced at Helen.

She sank back into her chair, tired and wobbly on her feet.

Jones shook his head. "Just sleep. Tomorrow we scout."

"Scout?" It came out like a squeak of protest, not the reasoned objection Helen wanted to make.

"Every successful mission relies on scouting, right, Harding?" A glance passed between the two men.

Harding nodded solemnly. "Scouting's the thing, miss. A mission's a disaster without it."

Helen looked from one to the other. Will Jones stared at the drawings. "You're humoring me. You don't wish to act."

He turned on her. "How many men are in that house? Are they armed? Do they have lookouts? Passwords? Who comes and goes? When? Does Leary ever leave?"

She stiffened her spine and held her ground. "So we sit in the cold and do nothing?"

"We act when we have answers."

She knew that implacable male tone.

"Harding will take the first watch on Half Moon Street while we scout the nearest public house. Someone is bound to talk among the locals."

"How long do we *scout* rather than act?"

"Two days should do it." He nodded to Harding, who turned to leave.

Helen could hear him in the outer room, moving about, attending to the fire. If Harding was a servant, he was not like any in her father's household. In a moment she heard him close the door. She and Will Jones were alone. They'd been alone the night before. The same awareness of him rose up as soon as Harding left, as if the very air in the room had been altered. She slanted another glance at him, his hands, his throat, the silk waistcoat that hugged his ribs, his wild black hair.

She'd known from the moment she'd heard his voice in the brothel that he was dangerous in a different way from the other men in the room. They had been careless and stupid with drink and easily manipulated by Leary. He had been a match for Leary. She'd known it instinctively. He had squared off against Leary. He had meant to have his way.

He studied the drawings on the table as if she did not exist. That was the difficulty. He had agreed to help her, but it was plain he did not believe she could help him. He would rather be done with her, and he could turn her over to the authorities at any hour. She had to get all the help she could from him, so that she could act alone. She would get those letters and disappear back into her own life. Her mother's good name and her heart depended on them.

She watched him puzzle over the incomplete drawings. No possibility seemed to escape his notice. Deceiving him would not be easy, but it was necessary. Failure would harm her mother in incalculable ways, while deception would hardly harm Will Jones, not in the ways his body had been hurt before, nor even in the ways she had seen that his family could wound him. He thought he had no need of her. He would take anything he had learned from her and go back to the brothel for his own purposes. She would do the same.

Her knowledge of Wenlocke's arctic voice had been the one advantage she had in this game they played. How could she forget that voice? She had never heard another voice like it. Wenlocke was one of the few men in whose company her father was ever silent. One slight pronouncement of Wenlocke's would be remembered for weeks, treated as profound. Helen had not often been in the duke's company, but she had been struck by his loftiness, his perfect indifference to those beneath him. The ancient gods themselves were less indifferent to mortals than the great duke was.

"I don't like it." Will Jones spoke to himself, not to her. It would be like him to leave her behind and act alone. He couldn't know, and she couldn't tell him, that what she wanted in that brothel was nothing less than her life.

If her mother's letters brought any public inquiry or trial, any scandal, her father would not allow her mother to remain in their home. She would be cast out. Even without any public talk, even if he allowed her to remain with them, her father's knowledge of those letters would condemn her mother to a life of withering scorn. Either way she thought her mother would have to flee, and without her mother, her father's house would be . . . a tomb.

Will Jones pushed away from the table with only a brief glance her way, returning his books to the neat and orderly arrangement in which he kept this inner room. "You asked for my help, and you agreed to my rules. We start early, so you'd best sleep now. You can take the bed in here. I'll get you a nightshirt." He turned away. It was a dismissal.

"I'd prefer the other bed." If she gave him a chance, he'd lock her in again as he had the night she'd discovered this room. She had yet to discover what triggered the hidden door from this side.

His gaze swung back to her, annoyed. "Well, I'm not giving up *my* bed for you."

"It's huge. You'll never know I'm there."

A low laugh escaped him. He tilted his head back with a glance at the ceiling. "After all those years with Paris, and his brother, too, wasn't it?"

"Only after Paris died." Helen felt herself blush.

"For a wanton, you have a remarkably unformed understanding of sharing a bed with a man. I think I may have to read to you again, to further your education." He passed through the secret door to the outer apartment.

She was up and after him instantly. She could not let him lock her in again. "Hah. I'm sure I could give you lessons. You are no Paris, you know."

"An idiot so lost in love he destroyed his city and his family. No, I'm no Paris." He stopped dead, and she collided against his back with her nose pressed between his shoulder blades. She inhaled sharply and regretted it, as she seemed to breathe him. She had an odd desire to stay like that, pressed against him.

But he stiffened instantly. She pushed away, righting herself, surprised at a spurt of pleasure at the mere contact with him, with his solidity of flesh and bone.

He turned. The dark gaze held hers. Her pulse inexplicably quickened. She shouldn't bait him. His person was rigid with tension. She held herself perfectly still, wary of provoking a sudden act. His hand shot out and snared her waist and pulled her securely against him. "I have this handy instrument that tells me where you are. If that bed stretched from here to France, I'd know exactly where you were in it at all times."

For a moment he simply held her clasped to his body, letting her feel the full, strong shape of him pressed against her hip. She knew what it was, the male breeding instrument. She was not wholly ignorant. Then he released her, and she stumbled back a little, catching herself against the doorframe.

"Choose your bed wisely."

She had chosen it. If it was dangerous to sleep next to him, she would still chance it. She could not afford to let her mother's letters fall into the hands of anyone who would hand them over to the police.

He turned away and crossed the room. From the clothespress he tossed her a nightshirt; its folds fell open as it fluttered to her feet. She scooped it up and turned to the bed, laying it over the edge.

He stood rooted to his side of the room. "Put the damned nightshirt over your head."

She shrugged and took up the garment. The nightshirt was made for his much larger frame. When she slipped it over her head, it hung to her ankles. Under its concealing folds she removed her waistcoat and shirt and unwound the linen that bound her breasts. Her body shuddered at the contact with his shirt as if he himself were touching her, and the boldness of her actions made her throat too dry for speech, but she knew better than to back down.

His gaze on her burned hotter than his profanity. "Some Helen of Troy you are."

"Helen did not display her charms to just anyone."

"To her blasted lover, she did."

"You are not my lover."

"Just the poor sap you are proposing to share a bed with."

"You're the one proposing to read Lord Thrustmore's adventures."

An odd broken laugh escaped him. "Two can play this game, Helen."

While her fingers still fumbled with the fastenings of her unfamiliar male garb, he simply shed his clothes, until he stood in linen smalls, the part of him that was most male proudly lifting the linen. He was long and lean from his shoulders to his hips, the skin taut over ribs and muscles, and puckered with scars in several places.

Her stomach did a queer little flip, and her breath

grew tight in her chest. She let her breeches slip to the floor and stepped out of them. She poked her arms out of the nightshirt sleeves and rolled the overlong cuffs up over her wrists, every move careful and deliberate, containing the flutter of awareness within her.

He blistered her ears with oaths, turned away, and picked up the stack of pamphlets by the bed. Helen scrambled up and slipped under the blue silk coverlet and sheets while he looked through the little booklets. The bed, soft and smooth, made her sigh. Idly he chose a pamphlet and tossed it up on the bed. As if she weren't there, he arranged his pillows against the carved headboard and climbed in beside her, taking up the little book and turning its pages.

"Where were we?"

"I don't remember." She pulled the covers up firmly around her chin.

"Liar." His eyes skimmed one of the pages. "I think Lord Thrustmore is about to make love to Miranda's breasts."

"Oh. Well, if you must read, carry on. Don't mind me. I'm sure I can sleep through anything." She closed her eyes and willed sleep to come. *Fast.*

The little pages rustled in his hands. "Did Paris make love to your breasts, Helen?" His voice was a low, dry whisper that banished sleep instantly.

"We locked in love. Often."

He laughed a low wicked laugh. "I think you haven't a clue what it means to lock in love. Want me to show you?"

"No, thank you. Sleep is what I need, and you, too, if we must scout early in the morning."

"Wise, as ever."

Will snuffed the candles and slid down into the bed beside her. She lay at least three feet from him, but he could feel her presence, the whisper of the silk coverlet when her breath shifted it, the scent of her, a sweetness that defied the soot and stink of London. He should not have glanced at even one page of Thrustmore, but the modest undressing she had done in his presence had him full and aching. She had unbound her breasts, and his memory of them from the first night, round and with reddened areolas, was enough to put his private parts on permanent sentry duty. He had not lied to her that he would know where she was in the great bed.

With little effort he could pin her beneath him and explore those breasts with his hands and mouth. Maybe if he did, it would shock some sense into her and she would go back to her safe life and let men like him and Jack Castle go after the Marches of the world. Who did she think she could save by risking her sweet self in that brothel?

She shifted again in the dark, a restless movement of her legs that told him she was as on edge as he was. All that was wicked and low in him rejoiced.

"Where does Harding sleep?"

"He has rooms on the floor below, and he's a sound sleeper."

She made no answer, and he guessed she, too, was struggling with sexual awareness.

"You and Harding were in the war together."

"We were."

And when British bodies choked the Bidassoa River because intelligence had been late and wrong and Wellington had been looking for new spies, Will had been young enough and mad enough to volunteer for the work. Sergeant Harding, whose mates mostly stared skyward with unseeing eyes, had gone with him. They had proved to be a good team until Waterloo cured them both of further desire for warfare.

It was good to think of war and Harding and not breasts and sweet, sweet Helen.

"I like him."

"He's a bit starchy."

"He's kind."

"I won't tell him you said so. Why Helen of Troy?" he asked. Her disguise suddenly seemed so incongruous.

Again he waited for a reply she might not give.

"Helen doesn't weep, and she doesn't swoon. Everyone thinks the worst of her, but she doesn't crumble. She doesn't let them wound her."

He had to admit he liked her answer. It surprised him, but it made sense of everything he'd seen in her. "She ends up with no friends but Paris."

"Better Paris than Menelaus or any of those famous suitors."

"Paris was an armor-polishing coward."

"He was a good architect, you know. He had excellent taste."

"That's what you want in a man? Good taste?"

"No. Do you want me to tell you?"

That should put an end to his lustful fantasies. No doubt she had some paragon of noble virtue in mind. "Tell me."

He felt her turn to face him, rearranging the pillows and shifting the bedclothes, so that sheets slid across his body, and her warm scent reached him.

"I want a man who sees me and knows me and wants me. For all his faults, Paris really did see me. You think I was wanted by all those other men, those famous suitors of mine, but it wasn't true—they just wanted things that came with me—a kingdom or victory or treasure. Nobody wanted me except Paris."

"What if I want you, Helen, just you, just your sweet self? Can you resist me?" Stupid question he realized.

She made a quiet movement, a rolling onto her back away from him.

"You don't want me. You want March."

"A smart answer."

Chapter Ten

꿍

WHERE do you suppose he's gone? A man can't just disappear." Lord Palgrave's voice rose above the low murmur of late morning conversation in the club, and he recalled himself to speak in more measured tones. Though he and Sir Walter Ruddock were alone in their corner of the room, it was a sober day of national mourning. A man would be wise to take stock of where he stood in the world. With Prinny about to be crowned, political winds were shifting. "His message says by the first. Damned inconvenient, don't you know."

Sir Walter nodded. He perfectly understood Palgrave's position. The two men had recently discovered a connection through March's messenger. "Evershot was sly as a fox about it, but I don't think March has touched a penny from his bank since October. Haven't seen him anywhere in town for months."

"Do you suspect foul play?" Lord Palgrave actually glanced around the club as if he thought a murderer might be lurking in a corner of the coffee room.

"You mean that fellow who tried to attack March right here?" Ruddock shook his carefully arranged locks. "More likely someone refused to be bled a moment longer."

"But when did you last hear from him?"

Sir Walter didn't have to think twice. "Saw that damned toothy boy of his not two days ago."

Lord Palgrave's face fell. "The thing is one does not want to fail in an obligation, but deuce take it, if one were free . . ."

His Grace, the Duke of Wenlocke, folded his paper and rose from his chair. He stood over the two club members, a tall man with a stony aspect. His disfavor could sink a fellow completely in society. His coldness was the stuff of legend in the club. No member made the joke inside the club, but outside the club, it was said that the end was near not when hell froze but when the Duke of Wenlocke thawed.

"Your Grace, so sorry to disturb," Palgrave mumbled.

Wenlocke did not acknowledge either man. "You have messages from March?"

"Your Grace, we are in private conversation."

Wenlocke simply extended an open palm. "Mr. March is no longer in the business of collecting on any obligations."

"You've seen him?" Sir Walter inquired and realized

at once that he'd overstepped. One did not take liberties with Wenlocke.

"You mistake me, Ruddock." The hand remained extended, unmistakable in its demand.

Ruddock reached in an inner pocket for the note he'd received through March's messenger. He placed it in the duke's hand. To refuse Wenlocke would be social suicide.

Palgrave glanced at his friend and followed suit.

The duke tore the two messages in half and tossed them on the flames of the nearby fire. "I prefer that you not send any further remittances to Mr. March."

The two men turned astonished faces up to him. Wenlocke's expression did not encourage questions.

"I say, Your Grace, these are private matters."

One of Wenlocke's iron brows rose a fraction. "Really, Ruddock, if you think your visits to Half Moon Street will not reach the scandal sheets and, Palgrave, if you think your daughter's precipitous trip to the continent will not become public knowledge, you are mistaken."

Leslie Atherton Granville, the Duke of Wenlocke, returned to his own chair on the other side of the room. The two friends found nothing further to say to one another but buried their faces in the paper.

Wenlocke preserved that outer air of arctic disdain he had learned as a young man when he first came into his title. He had outlived the closest companions of his youth and his only son. Now he had outlived the mad old king. He found himself surrounded, even at his club, by weaklings and nonentities, like Palgrave and Ruddock, men of inferior birth and character.

Even the defeat of Napoleon and the restoration of monarchies everywhere could not stem the democratic tide. The prospect of the next George's reign was wearisome. George IV would do nothing to restore his countrymen's faith in the superiority of ancient blood.

Little remained for him to do in life, but he meant to do it. He would crush Archibald March, and he would insure that his dukedom passed intact to hands worthy to receive it, not to the misbegotten offspring of that whore of Hill Street.

K EEP your back to the door and your face in the shadows at all times. Let me do all the talking."

Helen nodded.

They hunched in the cold a few doors from a public house in a lane not far from Half Moon Street. Grooms, stable boys, and footmen frequented the place as well as draymen and tinkers. For over a quarter of an hour they had circled the black doors. Now they waited for Harding to come out and give a signal.

Will Jones gave her a quick sharp scrutiny. He had not spoken to her since morning except to insist that she look the part of a boy, approving her oversized cap and making her wear a scratchy brown woolen scarf knotted around her neck. Now he pulled the bill of her cap lower across her brow and poked a curl under her ear up into the cap. The touch of his warm, wool-gloved fingers against her neck sent a little quiver through her.

He had a knack, she realized, of transforming himself

into someone else. It was not just a change of clothes but an ability to shift his walk, his posture, his gestures, even his face. He could make his intense dark eyes almost expressionless as if he'd gone away somewhere inside himself. He had not shaved this day, and dark stubble blurred the sharp planes of his face. He looked like any one of hundreds of dark-clad workingmen who moved about the streets of London and stopped for a pint when they could.

Harding emerged and headed toward them. As they passed, Harding and Will Jones exchanged a silent signal unreadable to Helen.

Will Jones pushed open one of the pub's heavy black doors and led the way inside. Most of the light came from a roaring fire in a large open fireplace, its rough stone edge painted dark green. Jones indicated a bench, and Helen slid along its length. He ordered at the bar, where a dozen men leaned in conversation and settled beside her with his back to the wall.

The room was full of voices, mostly good-humored and rough. The place smelled of ale and warm, wet wool. Nothing seemed sinister in the jests or the company, and no one glanced at Helen. She set herself to pick out individual voices. She'd been doing it ever since her childhood, sitting silent in the midst of the gentlemen's talk around her father and his associates, catching speakers' tics to share later with her mother. She listened for pitch and tone, for the staccato tempos of anger or urgency and the smoothly oiled roll of pompous men. The only voices she could remember from the brothel belonged to Leary and Brick Face, and she would know either voice if she heard it. Brick Face she could imagine in such a place, Leary, not so much.

When her punch came, she huddled over the steaming drink, inhaling its spicy vapor. Next to her Will Jones made himself nearly invisible in the gloom, his head lowered over a pot of ale. But she knew he was sharply alert. When he was near, she could not shut off an awareness of his body. Maybe it was because they had slept together in that grand bed of his that she had somehow become attuned to his nearness. In the morning, he had left her abruptly, and she had not seen him until both were dressed.

Talk went round the public house about horses and some great lord's temperamental chef until a newcomer entered, greeted by all. "Mr. Castle, what're ye having, sir?" called the proprietor.

A stiffening in Will Jones's posture told her that the man was known to him. In a flash she remembered. Castle was the name of the Bow Street Runner he wanted to turn her over to. Instantly she slid to the right, but Jones's hand landed on her thigh, pinning her in place as the man approached their table.

"Who's the miscreant, Jones?"

"Castle, what brings you here?" The warm strong hand on her thigh kept her anchored in place and sent distracting sensations shooting along her nerves.

"Milady's stolen dog." Helen felt Castle's gaze on her, but she kept her head down. He turned to the crowd, and called out, "Three shillings for any fellow who knows anything about a King Charles spaniel belongs to Lady Bellingham."

In the babble of noise that greeted the offer a loud voice blamed the French. "It's Frenchies wot steals the dogs and sells 'em abroad, they do."

Jack Castle swung a chair around, straddled it, and faced Helen and Will. He put down a blunt black stick bearing the golden emblem of the crown. Will Jones glanced at the stick and then away.

"No offense, la—" Castle said with a glance at her. He stopped and looked from Helen to Will and back. "Out of the frying pan into the fire, lass. Are you sure you're safe with this devil here?"

Helen nodded. The hand on her thigh squeezed once but did not move away. Its warmth burned into her leg.

Jack Castle took a long pull on his drink, frowning his disapproval. He drank his ale, but Helen could tell that like Will Jones, Castle mainly had his ear tuned to the talk in the room.

"So you're after dognappers, Jack? Sounds like just the work to advance a man on the force."

Jack Castle looked up with a quirk of a grin. He had a long, lean face topped by a mop of brown curls that barely concealed ears like pitcher handles. "Ah, but it is Lady Bellingham's dog, ye see. I expect to be well rewarded for my efforts. What brings you back to this neighborhood, Jones?"

"March."

"You think he's in the house on Half Moon Street?"

"He has to be somewhere."

"The continent, I'll wager."

"The proprietor here tells Harding that fellows from

March's bawdy house are a tight-lipped lot. You'd think they were guarding state secrets."

Jack Castle's face turned wary and closed. He contemplated his ale, no longer listening to the talk around them.

"The Home Office wouldn't be interested in the place, now would it, Jack?"

Helen felt the blood drain from her cheeks. Certain phrases in the letter to her mother came to mind, phrases accusing her mother of supplying arms to treasonous men. *The madman who had taken her mother's money had done something to make the government suspect a plot.*

"Just dognappers at the moment." Castle's dismissal of the question rang false.

Will Jones's voice turned mocking. "Bleeding inconvenient time for a plot, wouldn't you say? Has Bow Street sent anyone into the house to look about?"

"You know I can't tell you that, Jones. You didn't see anything the other night, did you?"

Helen felt Will Jones stiffen. His tone when he spoke again was light, indifferent, that of a man who had lost interest in the conversation. He did not look at Castle.

"Just the usual depravity, no signs of treason. I did wonder at the heavy guard. Two men at each door at all times."

"That strikes me, too," Castle admitted. "But March seems to have vanished."

"I doubt it. Unless he has funds elsewhere. He can't get a farthing out of Evershot's Bank any longer."

"Then he's still squeezing his pigeons."

"How else can he live, or escape."

"Devil of a thing to prove about a man with friends in high places." Castle stood and took up his stick. Will Jones seemed not to notice. "Let me know if I can do you a good turn."

"I will, Jack."

When the door closed behind Castle, Will Jones lifted his hand from Helen's thigh. "March's lackeys won't be hanging out here with Bow Street nosing about."

"How do you know Mr. Castle?"

"Used to work with him."

"You were a Runner, too?"

"Drink up. It'll warm you. We're about to relieve Harding."

When they stepped into the street, the cold took hold immediately, stinging Helen's nose and cheeks. Her eyes watered. She dashed the tears away with the back of her hand and lengthened her stride to catch up with Will Jones.

Harding's post was a vacant carriage stall down a narrow turning off Shepherd Market. They could see the comings and goings to the back entrance of the house on Half Moon Street. Will Jones handed her a pitchfork and took one himself.

They bent over their forks to poke at stray bits of hay whenever someone passed. The place smelled of horse and rotting hay, and Helen wrinkled her nose when her fork turned up an eye-watering clump that reeked of ammonia. She paused a moment to lean on the handle of her fork.

"I suppose you had maids to do any real work in Troy, Helen?"

"Three handmaidens—Andraste, Alkippe, and Phylo—always at my side."

He had to give her credit; she never let the mask drop. He doubted he had ever done better as a spy. "So your only work was the loom?"

"You misjudge the loom if you think there was no work involved."

"No stink however."

"Nothing so humble as a stable, but you see me pitching in." The words came out through chattering teeth.

"Come here, you're frozen. Lean against me."

"I'm a boy."

He gave her that sardonic look of his and leaned her pitchfork against the wall. He pulled her back with him and lowered them both to a pile of relatively inoffensive straw, tucking her between his outstretched legs and wrapping his arms around her. "Don't get above yourself. You are a most unconvincing male. Castle spotted you at once."

"I blame you for any failure of my disguise. You are the master of it."

He laughed. "London must be quite a comedown for you."

"It is not the city of the wide ways and the heights from which to overlook the whole plain as far as the sea. But Troy had its tedium, which London has not."

"Troy, tedious?"

"Oh yes. The endless royal processions, the inescapable

ceremony. Men in robes do give speeches from on high. And always the walls. One might look at the sea forever and never go to the shore."

"Am I supposed to pity poor Helen?"

"Never."

For hours until her limbs stiffened, no one came or went to arouse the least suspicion, and then Nate Wilde sauntered into view around the turning.

Of course, Will Jones saw him first. He was up and free of Helen in an instant. As soon as Wilde entered the gate in the rear wall of the garden, Will Jones made a quick dash and leapt for the iron rails at the top of the wall where a bare plane tree stood. In a flash he hauled himself up to see through its branches.

She could see the gleam in his eye when he returned to the stable.

"Maybe you're my lucky charm, Helen."

"I'm your partner."

"Harding's my partner. You're . . ." He grinned at her. ". . . An appendage, but possibly a useful one. We'll follow Wilde when he leaves. I'd like to have a chat with him where you can hear his accent again."

"Do you think he's our way in to the brothel?"

They waited nearly an hour before Wilde came back into the lane, his hands stuffed in his pockets, a figure muffled in a jacket, scarf, and cap. His pace was brisk and steady as he headed east across London. Helen could see that Will Jones was excellent at following. She followed his lead. He threaded his way through traffic so that his individual moves never separated him from the

London scene. The day passed from late afternoon shadows to the gloom of night as they followed the youth.

Will Jones's concentration on Wilde never wavered. They lost their quarry briefly in the Strand and only spotted him again where the traffic split around St. Clement Danes. Wilde banged through the gate in the iron fence and entered the little church. Will Jones sped up, and they slipped in behind their quarry as the bells rang the quarter hour.

Helen stopped dead in the back of the nave. She had come before to this loveliest of churches with its dark wood pews and paneling and the soaring white arches of its upper story. The loveliness of the small church and its sacred purpose were at odds with everything she had done for days. The very hour made her feel a pang for her old life.

At her side Jones whispered, "I don't see our quarry. I'm going to try the crypt." He disappeared down the rough spiral stairs to the lower region of the church.

A sexton began to light candles for vespers, her mother's favorite service. She closed her eyes for a moment and promised her mother again that she would not fail, then turned from the lovely nave to follow Will Jones.

She pressed her hand to the rough sides of the steep spiral staircase, picking her way down its turning pie-wedge steps. At the bottom, squat pillars held up a vault of low pointed arches heavy with brick, not the soaring white curves of the church itself. Helen moved from pillar to pillar until she was close enough to catch the conversation. The boy had stopped halfway up the crypt where a few candles glowed faintly in an iron candle stand. In a niche in the old brick wall was a white stone coffin with an effigy of some sleeping knight on the lid. Wilde slipped his hand under the stone sarcophagus, pulled out a purse, added something to it, and shoved it back into place. Will Jones moved into place behind the boy.

"Very wise. I wouldn't trust my blunt near March or Bredsell, either."

Wilde started at Will Jones's words and flung himself forward, but Jones had him snagged, and hauled him to a kneeler and shoved him down on it. "Time to confess your sins, Wilde."

"Oi tyke messages is all. No 'arm in 'at."

"Messages that kill people."

"Oi ain't killed nobody."

Helen crept closer to stand behind another of the fat pillars holding up the rough vault.

"Dick Cullen, Mother Greenslade, and the unfortunate Dobbs family. You're lucky so few died in that flood."

She could see Wilde shake his head, but he couldn't shake Will Jones's grip. The boy was going nowhere. Instead Jones lifted him and searched his pockets. The boy flailed at the man, his blows falling unheeded on Jones's shoulders and head.

Jones pulled a packet of letters bound with a cord and a folded wad of bills from the boy's pockets and let him go. A sullen, mulish look took over the boy's face, none of his toothy grin showed. His eyes never left his lost possessions.

"It won't do to go back to March without these items, now will it, Wilde?"

"There's other jobs. Oi can tyke care of meself." He shoved his hands in his pockets.

"Without your stash under the saint's sarcophagus, you'll be in the dock at the Bow Street Office inside of a week and bound for Botany Bay in a month. It might be your salvation."

"Oi got nothing to sye to you, copper."

"I think you do. I think you can tell me where March is."

"Yer dreamin'."

"Am I?" Will Jones strolled over to the candle stand. He undid the cord binding the pile of letters together, opened a letter and held it to the flickering light. Someone's letters, someone like Helen's mother who had trusted that her private correspondence would remain private. Helen did not recognize the stationery as her mother's distinctive lilac pressed paper, but she knew that those letters mattered to someone.

Wilde started to swear. The stream of oaths was shocking.

"Maybe you want to start by telling me all about your afternoon in the house on Half Moon Street, and when we're done with that, you can tell me about Bredsell's school."

"Told ya. Oi'm a messenger is all. Oi carry wot they tells me to carry."

"Letters and money and what else?"

"None of yer business, copper."

"Tell me about the house on Half Moon Street. Who lets you in? Who gave you these papers and the money? Where are the papers kept? Who tells you what to say, what to ask for? When do you go next?"

"Oi ain't no nark."

"But you want your possessions back, don't you, Wilde?"

The boy's face said he did. The little flames flickered in their tin holders. Voices drifted down the staircase as people entered the church for vespers.

"Mr. March is educatin' me. 'E has me sit in his grand library and read 'is books. Lots of books."

"You've got to do better than that, Wilde, if you want the papers back. Here's another way. There's a boy I'm looking for. Maybe you know him. Tall, fair, keeps a gang of younger boys with him."

"'E's dead. March killed 'im in the beer flood."

"You're lying, Wilde. His body never turned up."

The boy shrugged.

"Try again, Wilde."

"Oi don't 'ave nothin' to do with 'im. 'E's on his own that one. 'E's not a Bread Streeter."

"But you've seen him?"

"Wot's it to ye?"

"What's it to you? A quid?" Jones held one of Wilde's paper notes over a flickering flame. "Your choice, Wilde."

Again the boy erupted in colorful oaths.

Jones lowered the note to the edge of the flame. The paper quivered in its heat.

"Leave it, copper. Ye don't want March thinking the boy's alive."

"March has plans to kill him?"

"'Eard 'im talking of it to Bredsell."

"Where did you hear that particular conversation?"

Wilde said nothing. His eyes darted around the crypt, looking for some escape. Helen pressed her back to the fat pillar.

"Bredsell's office."

"Good work, Wilde."

She dared to look again. Jones actually grinned at the boy. He reached under the stone sarcophagus and retrieved the boy's purse. "Now you have a choice—your stash or March's letters and his money."

The boy stared at the purse in Jones's hand. "Yer goin' be the death of me, copper."

Jones tossed him the wad and the letters. "On second thought, I'll keep your stash. It'll be much safer with me. If you decide to leave March, you can find me."

Helen slid further round the back of her pillar as Wilde slipped past, swearing under his breath.

Will Jones came to her side. "Do you think you can do Wilde's voice?"

"Yer goin' be the death of me, copper."

He grinned at her. "I hope not, Helen."

Chapter Eleven

❧

T HEY returned to Will Jones's rooms by a maze of quick turnings, which Helen knew she would not remember by daylight. In spite of the cold and the national mood of mourning, the doors of the nearest taproom swung freely, and laughter and light spilled into the street. Across from the crescent moon sign that marked the hidden door to Jones's apartments, a pair of vividly painted women leaned out an upper window of a bawdy house watching the patrons of the taproom as they came and went. The women spotted Will Jones at once.

"Will Jones, where've ye been, ye mad devil? Those ribs of yours 'ealed yet?"

"Willie love, 'oo's the new pigeon with you?"

"Bring 'im over. Let Nell set 'im straight."

"'Alf -price for beginners."

"Evening, ladies, thanks for the offer. Wait till this one gets some hair on his chin first."

"Don't keep away now, Will Jones. Ye'll ne'er 'eal alone in that grand bed of yours."

He opened the mysterious door that seemed not to be a door at all.

"Where's the dog?" Helen asked. It was not the burning question on her mind, but it was the one she allowed herself. She had no reason to be annoyed by the coarse cheeky voices of the women. There was nothing offensive in their friendly boldness. It did not matter to her if he had read Lord Thrustmore's story to one or all of them or arranged his bath and his grand sultan's bed for their delight. She tried to shake off the thought. It wasn't a thought for Helen of Troy, but she almost missed his answer about the dog.

"Zebediah must still be up on Oxford Street. That's his main lay."

They passed up the stairs through the outer apartment and the paneled wall into his inner room. Helen followed him, watching as he put Nate Wilde's stash in a drawer of his tall cabinet. She remained intrigued by the neat order of his inner room with its cabinets and maps and shelves of books. Harding was nowhere in sight. Will Jones stirred the fire to life and strode off, telling her she could have five minutes' privacy. Helen knew better than to linger. She shed her outer garments and made use of the privy she'd discovered when he brought her back from the school.

When she emerged, he was standing by the fire, his face in the shadows. She saw at a glance the impatience of his stance, one elbow jutting out, knuckles resting against the arrogant cock of his hip. All day he had been bundled as she had in layers of wool and leather. Now he was pared down to the lean taut form of him. A worn gray wool vest lacking two buttons hugged his ribs over a plain cotton shirt open at the throat.

She was used to male arrogance of course. All males were arrogant. They looked down their noses at women, gave orders, assumed obedience. But the familiar arrogance of her father and his associates came with trimmings, with position and title, with incense, robes, and lace, and lofty heights to speak from. Here was an imperiousness of mere person. She knew Will Jones would be arrogant naked, and the thought brought a rush of heat to her cheeks.

It was safer to look at the table set for two with a bottle of wine, a plate of cheese and bread, a dish of oranges, and a covered platter of something that smelled deliciously like roast hen. Her stomach made an immediate and undignified grumble. He hardly seemed to notice the food.

He frowned at her, and she understood why. Her chopped hair had not seen a brush or a comb. It was electric from contact with her woolen cap. She'd had no bath since the brothel. He probably wanted to keep his distance.

"Eat," he invited.

She sat while he brought a brand from the fire to light

the candles. The question she could no longer contain slipped out. "What happened to your ribs?"

It stopped him. His hand over a candle in a plain brass holder on the table made just such a pause as a faulty clock hand might make before ticking off the next second.

"Someone kicked them." He finished his task and sat opposite her.

She stared, uncomprehending. "How?"

"Like you kick a dog." He poured the wine, his hand perfectly steady.

She controlled a shudder as she worked out what he meant. She, who listened for tone in every voice, heard the self-dislike in his. "I never kick a dog."

He lifted his glass to her, and she raised hers. "To London, Helen, where dogs are kicked every day."

"In Troy, of course, the royal dogs were always well treated." She drank. The dark wine was fruity and rich like nothing she'd been permitted to sip before. She felt it immediately, a warm wave of sensation, loosening her limbs. She put down the glass. She needed to be practical. "You think the police are investigating the house on Half Moon Street."

"It's likely. Castle's a rising man on the force. He's *not* after dognappers." He lifted the cover on the platter to reveal a pair of game hens roasted brown. He speared one and put it on her plate.

"When do you think they'll act?"

He didn't answer at once but cut into the bird on his plate. "You're not going back in there."

"That's for me to decide. Whatever else is going on there doesn't change what I need to do or the persons counting on me to do it."

"My rules, remember." He said it quietly. "That was our agreement."

She didn't answer but cut her meat and resolutely ate. She would be foolish not to. She would need strength and nerve to go against him. She could mimic Wilde's voice now. Maybe his accent would get her in the door. Could she lie her way past Leary's underlings? Could she get to that mysterious room marked on Harding's drawings? Would the letters be locked away? How would she get out? The questions consumed her.

For an eternity it seemed they did not speak. The scrape of cutlery against china, the hiss and pop of the fire, the rustle of their clothes sounded unnaturally loud in her ears.

He put down his fork first. "You're a noisy thinker, Helen. You don't have a plan worth a damn, and trust me, you don't want to be inside March's place when the police show up."

"I'll come up with something."

"I have a better idea. Why don't you tell me what it is you're so keen to recover from March. I'm guessing a letter or letters—something March got hold of through Evershot's Bank."

Will watched her closely. She picked an orange off the plate without giving any sign he'd guessed her secret. If he was right, and he'd wager a pony he was, he had to give her credit for not showing her hand. Instead she broke the pebbled surface of the fruit with her nail, releasing its bittersweet scent.

"We could act tomorrow, early when most of the house is asleep. Leary has to sleep sometime, doesn't he?"

"I take it you don't want the police to get there before you do."

"Will they arrest March?"

She had him there. He took an orange from the plate. Whatever suspicions Bow Street had, the Home Secretary was a crony of March's. The two had undoubtedly traded information, and the Home Secretary would be cautious about having March investigated. If Will wanted March brought to justice, he was going to have to do it. He knew that, had known it for some time.

She was watching him with an upward gaze of those dark eyes from beneath those two-pound lashes.

"We could pay off an errand boy," she said, "and I could make his delivery for him. Harding must have noted which merchants make deliveries."

"And then?"

"I leave a window open. Harding creates a distraction. You enter."

"And we go where?"

"Straight to Leary's office. Anything important would not be trusted to the others."

He did like the girl's intelligence. "And how much time would we have before they came for us?"

"What I'm looking for is distinct. I'll know it the minute I see it."

"And if we meet Leary before you find that distinctive stationery?"

A tiny wave of annoyance passed over her face. "We could take weapons."

"Never go anywhere in London unarmed, I say." He slid a dagger from his sleeve and laid it on the table. "Are you prepared to kill someone to recover your letters?"

Her eyes widened briefly at the blade and the question. After a minute she met his gaze and answered. "No."

"Good to know. I'll sleep better knowing you're not going to slit anyone's throat to get your . . . letters back."

"You're so sure of yourself."

"March has been trading in people's secrets for some time. It seems likely that he's got hold of a secret that matters to you."

"So, will the plan work?"

"No." She had given him an idea, however. He thought he had a way to solve her problem without risk to her. He, too, had been thinking as they ate. Allowing her to go back to the place seemed a particularly bad idea, but his reluctance puzzled him. Sacks, carnage, rape, he had seen it all. How many lives had he failed to save? A delayed report, faulty information, lost documents. Too many to count. His concern over the fate of one stray virgin was laughable.

Certainly no one else was concerned about her. He'd had Harding search the papers for notices. Nothing. Will figured she didn't have a male in her household to fight this particular battle for her, so she had run away to fight it on her own. An entirely female household wasn't likely either given her frequent uncharitable references to men in authority.

He watched her take a delicate bite of orange between those lips and felt the thing he'd been denying all day leap to life inside him.

He still didn't know who she was. Everything he had learned about her said she wasn't for him, an educated virgin of upper-crust English society. But he would have her.

He would start with that mouth, wide and lush with its sweet, jutting lower lip that disappeared into tight corners, because she didn't smile readily. He would have those lips open and clinging to his. He would lose himself in her sweetness. He knew it for a bad idea at once. He wanted her body. Kisses were only the preliminary skirmish in the encounter, a softening up of the enemy before a full attack.

Her character was as much a mystery as her circumstances. She hadn't been educated at school around other girls, or she would not lose herself so completely in the role of Helen. He understood how disguise worked, how it kept one from quaking in one's boots in the face of the enemy. She was good at it, which meant she'd had practice. Only once had he seen that mask slip.

Her beauty must have attracted suitors, but her gift for mimicry told him she had spent time unnoticed in company. That was the puzzle. In what company would rich beauty such as hers go unnoticed? Around the Duke of Wenlocke maybe, and if Helen had crossed paths with the powerful duke it probably meant they had a family connection. She was definitely above Will's touch.

Unlike Xander, Will had never sought the beds of titled ladies. He had always preferred working girls.

The trouble was his cock thought Helen was his. A steady pulse in his veins beat *mine*.

She wasn't indifferent to him. He had felt every second of her frank perusal of him before dinner. He had seen the furrow between her brows, the puzzlement of an inexperienced woman trying to work out what was happening between them, and he had seen her flush with consciousness of her own carnal interest in a man.

He could make her want him. It wouldn't be fair, it wouldn't be decent, it wouldn't be honorable, but he was long past caring about fairness, decency, and honor. He had rescued her from Leary. She was his.

He refilled her wineglass. "Tell me again about Paris's lovemaking."

She sat across from him, pulling apart sections of another orange, stripping off the white lacy membrane, a fastidious queen, his Helen. She slid a measuring glance his way.

"You like to mock him. Were you a good soldier?"

"A good soldier? Foul-mouthed, irreverent, implacable in battle, able to keep myself alive until some higher up asked me to die? No. I was a better spy."

He thought to shock her, but her gaze didn't waver. She shook her head. "Tell me one thing you've done to deserve Harding's good opinion."

"Harding's good opinion?"

"Yes, Harding thinks highly of you. He would follow you into any battle, would he not?"

"He would." He had to admit she had him there.

"I know. So tell me why? You must be able to name some good that you have done in the last, what, seven years or more?"

He took a deep swallow of wine. She was entirely too satisfied with herself for turning the conversation around.

"You've stumped me, sweetheart."

She gave a little sniff. "Never."

In the end he had to tell her three well-edited stories before her lids closed and her hand fell open on the table around a crescent of orange. Maybe she'd escaped him after all. He reached across the table, plucked the orange piece from her open palm, and popped it into his mouth.

He wondered if the tutor who had taught her so much of the Greeks had ventured into any works beyond Homer. He certainly remembered those lessons with Hodge. Will had joined the tutor's sessions with Xander early on, determined to catch up, not to let his older brother outstrip him in knowledge. Now it was a habit of Hodge's he remembered. *My dear boys*, Hodge would say, removing the eyeglasses from his nose, and Xan and Will would know that he was about to share with them one of the juicier aspects of the great epics.

Will stood and circled the table and gazed down at her. Her feet were crossed at the ankles so that her knees opened in a perfect V of invitation. Not her intention, but his mouth went dry and his cock pulsed to a hard stand. He hoisted her up out of the chair onto her feet. She leaned against him like a drowsy child easily steered toward bed. In the doorway between the rooms she woke more fully with a graceless jerk that caught his ribs a sound blow from her elbow. He sucked in a harsh breath, staggering back against the jamb.

She righted herself, clinging to his shoulder, looking up with startled eyes, her free hand pressed to his side. "Your ribs."

He started to make a light reply and lost himself in her eyes, deep pools of regret for the minor hurt she'd inflicted.

"Mistake, Helen. Never show sympathy for the devil."

He tilted her face up to meet his and gathered her into him, his hand wide over the small of her back, fixing her in place against him, his whole frame vibrating with just that contact. He lowered his face to hers.

He meant to go slowly, to teach her how mouths could cling, explore, and yield, but she tasted like Spain, like wine and spice and oranges, like a city opening its gates to the victor, and he plunged in, taking sighs like prisoners.

He raked his hand up her back to bring her closer, to crush her against him, and felt the tight band of linen confining her breasts. He wanted those breasts, remembered the lush feel of them against his chest that first night.

She wore male garments like his own, a waistcoat and cotton shirt over wool breeches. Her hand still pressed helplessly against his ribs. He freed the button at her wrist and reached down to tug her shirt from her breeches. He touched the smooth skin of her back inside the shirt, and his mind went blank. He slid his palm up inside her garments to feel along the edge of the linen binding, so tight it bit into her skin.

He turned her in his arms, one hand across her belly, holding her pressed against him, the other hand working the buttons of her waistcoat. The garment fell open, and he scooped her up in his arms and carried her to the bed. He lowered her to the coverlet and trapped her between his thighs as he pulled off her waistcoat and shirt.

She stared dazed at his chest as he smoothed his hands over her bare shoulders and down her arms. Her silken flesh had a creamy translucence. He spotted the knot in the linen binding below her left breast and with shaking fingers undid it and unwound the cloth. She watched his face, intent. He felt exposed as he uncovered her breasts, impossible to conceal desire, no mask available.

A deep red crease marred her skin above and below her breasts, the breasts he remembered, so round and lush with sweet pale pink peaks. He drew his hands up her sides over her ribs to cup each mound and draw his thumbs over the tips, and she arched into his hands, her head falling back, her hands gripping his arms, holding him there, lost in sensation.

Some buried virtue, some ghost of old Hodge's moral lessons, rose up and rattled its chains and wailed that Will ought to warn her. She was too inexperienced to know her body's weakness as he knew it and would use it against her. He lifted his face.

For a moment again he was back in the study with Hodge and Xander, Hodge reminding them that they were men of reason. Monsters, he told them, devour virgins chained to rocks. Men should stick to a nice roast capon and seek a partner, not a sacrifice, in bed.

He banished the inconvenient memory. "Helen, I'm going to make love to your breasts."

She looked at him, dizzy from wine and kisses, as if he made no sense.

Conscience insisted he offer one more warning. "You can tell me who you are, Helen. Whoever you are, we both know that woman would never lie in Will Jones's bed. You could let me take you back to your people. You could trust me to recover whatever it is you want from that brothel."

"No."

He was gone. Helen lay where he'd dropped her. Cold air rushed over her breasts, and she shuddered. She heard another door open and close. By now she understood that his apartments spread across a row of buildings riddled with mysterious entrances and exits. She closed her eyes to consider the paradox. Will Jones didn't want her in his bed because he did want her there. He wanted to do with her the things Lord Thrustmore did with Miss Yeeld, the things Helen herself claimed to do with Paris. He wanted to make love to her breasts.

He admitted a frank carnal interest in her. Well, that was something new. None of her suitors had expressed, as Will Jones's burning gaze so freely did, an interest in her flesh. She laughed at the idea. How could they? She had once received a sonnet dedicated to her brow. The lines had not moved her to wish to see its author remove one article of his dress.

She wanted to see Will Jones's ribs, to put her hand to his flesh, as if she could heal him with her touch. She closed her hand around a fold of the silk coverlet. It was a stupid thought, not a Helen-like thought at all. His neighbors flirted and called him a devil. It was just a saying, but there was truth in it. No one healed the devil.

But her devil saw her. He really looked at her as none of her polite, virtuous suitors ever had. They courted her to catch her father's eye and win his approval. Maybe she should let Will Jones take her home right to her father's door. Maybe he could meet her father. She imagined the two of them standing face-to-face, her father robed and stern and trying to cow Jones, and Jones defiant. He would simply say, "Good to meet you, Your Grace, I've kissed your daughter and made love to her breasts and enjoyed it very much." At the idea of Will Jones confronting her father, a short, sharp tremor shook her, half laugh, half sob.

She stared up at the lush damask hangings of his great bed, vivid against the dark paneling. The cool air raised the gooseflesh on her arms. While she lay on his bed, her mother lay awake and helpless. With no daughter to comfort or distract her, her mother would be consumed with worry. With no daughter there, her father might question his wife's low spirits. Might badger a confession out of her. If she failed her mother . . . She shuddered.

She had been lucky tonight. Will Jones had walked away. She understood why. Even more than he wanted to do the things he said, he wanted to defeat March and find his brother. Their partnership was a flimsy thing. She needed a plan of her own. The idea of imitating Wilde that had seemed so promising in the afternoon had crumbled under Will Jones's tough pragmatism. But if the police investigated the house before Helen got there, her mother's letters would end up in their hands.

She roused herself to look again at Harding's plans of the brothel. There had to be a way to get those letters.

Will Jones did not return to the room until long after she had crawled under the coverlet in the great bed. She had no doubt where he'd gone. The pleasures of his neighborhood beckoned. He no longer cared where she ended up. That was a painful thought. All the time she had been insisting on her return to the brothel, his resistance had meant he didn't want to see her caught by Leary again. Now he seemed to have given up on her. She was not worth the trouble he was taking. Even her knowledge of Wenlocke's identity could not bind him to their partnership.

In the night she woke from a dream of her mother on the deck of a ship tossing on violent dark swells. She found Will Jones asleep beside her as if she didn't exist.

Chapter Twelve

❧

HELEN opened her eyes when something hit the bed. *Thwap*. Harding stood next to Will Jones's tousled head, a folded copy of the *Morning Chronicle* in his hand.

"Sir." Harding stared into space, seeming not to see them lying in the bed. "We have trouble."

Will Jones woke instantly, pushing himself up on his elbows and taking hold of the paper. He shoved himself up against the headboard, his eyes scanning the page. Helen could not look away from his powerful shoulders. His beard made dark shadows under his lip and along his jaw. His wild black hair fell across his brow.

"Bleeding hell." He threw back the covers and hurled himself out of bed with a backward glance at her. "Do what you need to do. We leave within the half hour."

Helen picked up the discarded paper. Under the heading "A Mother's Letter to Her Son" she read:

My dear son,

News that you are alive brings me back to London. These years without you have not been life. Wherever you are in London, I beg you to come home. You are meant to be with your brothers, with your own family. Daily we await your return and redouble our efforts to recover you.

Your loving mother,
Sophie Rhys-Jones

A separate notice immediately following the letter offered a reward to informants.

The Jones family of Hill Street seeks persons with knowledge leading to the recovery of Christopher Granville Jones, b. November 16, 1803 in St. Martin's parish. Please bring your information between the hours of nine and noon any day. All reports will be gratefully acknowledged.

T HE scene outside his mother's house on a foggy London morning was perfect for Kit's purpose. A score of people, darkly bundled against the cold, lined the pavement. Hawkers walked along the edge of the crowd trying to interest buyers in muffins, ginger nuts, and penny ballads. A restless movement twitched the line like a cat's tail as people shifted or blew on their hands or turned to talk with neighbors. Several clutched the newspaper in gloved hands.

It was the newspaper that had brought him back to his mother's neighborhood this time. He feared that her search for him would drive him away from Bread Street before he had a chance to rescue Robin. He didn't have Robin back yet, and an army of people on the lookout for Kit wouldn't help the rescue plan.

But as he walked the length of that line, no one took particular notice of him or his band. He had left off his usual coat and wore an old fisherman's cap over his hair. He sent the boys in pairs scurrying in and out of the line. Jay walked the length of the line on his hands to distract people while the other boys looked for anything that might have dropped.

Kit had written his answer to his mother's plea right on the paper itself. Now he needed someone to take his message inside. He decided the best candidate was a large man with a gaping jacket and crumpled hat about midway down the line. The fellow had an open face and talked readily with the people around him. Kit made toward the man as an elegant black carriage rattled around the corner at a fast clip. All heads turned toward the speeding carriage, and Kit took the moment to have little Finch press the message into the hand of the big man.

As the carriage careened closer, the driver seemed to lose control of his horses. The vehicle veered sharply, the wheels bouncing up over the pavement. The driver's whip lashed out, sending people scrambling out of the way. The muffin man lost his balance, and the tray of muffins on his head tipped, spilling his goods onto the pavement.

The coach sped away, and people righted themselves, cursing and shaking fists after the vanishing carriage, others scooping up the muffins. Kit whistled his band to him, and they slipped into the fog in the opposite direction around the corner where a wide frosted field led to Shepherd Market.

THE hack driver reined sharply to avoid an out-of-control black barouche as it rattled up Hill Street. Will noted the ducal coronet on the door as the vehicle flew past them. In its wake he and Helen descended alongside a broken line of people at his mother's door. The disturbed crowd was trying to reform a line. Will could guess what had happened. The situation was not a riot, but there was a restlessness about the crowd that threatened order. Tempers were getting short. At his mother's door, Amos struggled to keep order.

Will went to the beleaguered servant's aid at once to quell a disturbance around a man who had jumped the queue and was insisting he had an important message for the lady of the house.

Will took the man's measure, big, brawny, but genial-looking. "What's your hurry, mate?"

"A boy gave me this." He held up a torn folded piece of newspaper. "Brown 'air, so 'igh. Said the lady'd know 'oo it was from. Just now in the madness when that fellow lost control of 'is 'orses. I figure the boy can't 'ave got far if ye want to question 'im."

Will scanned the street. There were no mysterious boys in sight. "What did this boy say?"

" 'Please, sir, a letter for the sad lady. She'll know 'oo it's from.' I won't soon forget the boy's look. Barefoot, 'e was. And in this cold."

Will gave a nod to Amos and turned to face the crowd lined up along the iron railing. He gave a shrill whistle, and when he had their gaze, he made himself heard. "Will Jones here. It's my brother that we're searching for. You will all be heard, but this fellow comes with me now."

In Sophie's elegant blue-and-gold parlor, their visitor stared and hung back awkwardly, his self-possession momentarily gone when Sophie looked up at him. Sophie in her customary black silk sat on a tasseled blue velvet sofa. She clutched the framed linen sampler to her heart that had hung above her boys' beds. Major Montclare hovered behind her.

Xander sat at a desk, pen in hand, frowning over some pages. He shot Will a grateful look. Cleo Jones poured tea at a side table with admirable calm. Seeing her made Will realize why he'd brought Helen with him. He'd wanted an ally in this meeting with his family, but he had to treat her as Troy Tibbs, so he ordered her into the corner next to Cleo, where he would not be distracted by her in the midst of Sophie's drama.

He heard Cleo welcome her, and saw the two of them

exchange a look. Cleo plainly saw through Helen's disguise. He could imagine what Xander had said to his wife about the scene he had witnessed in Will's rooms. But his levelheaded sister-in-law simply invited Mr. Tibbs to have some bread and jam.

"Give her your message, man," Will prompted the stunned behemoth next to him.

The large fellow lurched forward, bowing, and holding out the folded paper in his hand. "Ma'am."

"What is it?" Sophie's tragic look seemed to paralyze the big man.

"A message handed to this fellow . . ."

He blinked. "John Neale, ma'am. A small boy gave me this for you just now outside your door."

"A boy?" The hope in Sophie's voice was unmistakable.

"No bigger than me belt, ma'am," said Neale.

Sophie's expression immediately sobered, and she took the note, unfolding it. She had it open and read in a flash. "Xander." She held out the note, giving Xander her helpless look. Will knew his mother was far from helpless.

Xander crossed to her side. He read the note and looked at Will. "It's the notice from the paper, crossed out and amended with charcoal."

He handed the paper to Will. Across the original notice someone had printed in large letters:

STOP YOUR SERCH. THAT BOY IS NO MORE.
YOUR ENEMY WON'T STOP.

Will studied the torn scrap in his hand. It could have been delivered by one of the boys from Bredsell's school, even Nate Wilde, or by some poor starveling. But the bearer of the note had mentioned the "sad lady" and thought she would know who sent it. Not likely one of March's messengers. Nor was the terse immediacy of the message in March's style.

"What do you think it means, *that boy is no more*? Kit's alive, and he knows we're looking for him."

Xander didn't answer. He and Cleo exchanged a steady look. Then Xander turned to their awkward informant. "Excuse us, Mr. Neale, we've heard contradictory reports this morning. You received this note while you waited outside?"

"Aye."

"What information did you come to offer before the child gave you the note?"

"I see a gang of boys regular as I make my deliveries. I drive a cart along to Smithfield Market. There's always boys after the carts you know, looking for what falls or making something fall. One gang's unusual, ye might say. The leader is a tall, fair fellow in a long black coat, looks like royalty, ragged royalty. And the boys, he calls 'em all by birds' names, Lark, Jay. And I've seen 'em on the rooftops, hopping along without a care, mind ye."

Sophie gave a rapturous sigh that momentarily cost John Neale his wits again. "Kit is alive, you see. Oh, thank you, sir."

Will watched Sophie. "Odd then, with your notice to

the papers, Mamma, that you get a message for the 'sad lady' to tell us to stop looking for 'that boy.'"

She turned on him with fury. "You think that message came from Kit, that he was here outside his home and did not come to us?"

Xander stepped between them, his wife at his side. "Cleo and I have a theory about why he doesn't come home, Will."

"Glad to hear it, Xan, but we also have a blunt message likely from Kit himself that says he is aware of a dangerous enemy and claiming that he himself is, what—changed? No longer who he was? And I think Mamma knows why she got that warning."

Sophie glanced at her major. "All I know is that Kit's alive, that it's been three years, and that I can endure this maddening delay no longer."

Xander thanked the gawking carter for his information. He gave the man fifteen shillings, a week's wage, and escorted him to the door.

Will turned to the major. "If you would excuse us, Major Montclare, this is a matter between mother and sons."

The major stiffened but took himself off to stand looking out of the window into the street.

Xander returned, and Will sat at the end of the couch from his mother. She regarded him uneasily. "Why does Wenlocke care about one of your bastards, Mamma?"

"Wenlocke?" Sophie ran her fingers over the edge of the sampler, now avoiding his gaze.

"You heard me, Mamma. His carriage just rattled up

the street, making all your waiting informants jump for their lives."

"He cannot possibly care. I never made any claim. Never." She shook her head firmly, clutching the sampler to her chest.

Will's gut gave a warning twinge. "He expected you to make a claim. Why?"

Sophie turned dark, pleading eyes to the major's back. Montclare didn't move.

"I married Daventry."

Chapter Thirteen

❧

XANDER had frozen. Will heard his own voice strangely hollow, asking, "When? Where?"

Sophie squared her shoulders. "Before he left for India. Here in London at St. Anne's, in April '03. There was a babe coming. It was a comfort to him to think of it. He wanted a son. He thought we would deal better with his family when he returned. He thought the duchess might forgive him the misalliance, even if the duke would not."

Will didn't trust himself to speak.

Married. All this time she had been a widow. Sixteen years earlier she had abandoned them, for a respectability they could never have. As Lady Daventry, her scandalous past would disappear, while her sons, her living sins, remained bastards, all but one. Kit was not base-born, but apparently he had been in danger from the time his ruthless grandfather, the Duke of Wenlocke, learned of his legitimacy.

"Mamma, you have proof of this marriage?" Xander asked quietly, in command of himself again, as far as Will could see. Xander would forgive her. Will could not.

Sophie nodded.

"I think we should examine this proof."

"I have letters." Sophie held out her hand, and Xander helped her to rise. The room was silent except for the swish of her skirts.

In her absence no one moved or spoke. Will glanced once at Helen and caught a look of love from Cleo Jones directed at Xander.

When Sophie returned with a leather box and held it in her lap, Will realized he had seen that particular box dozens of times, a simple box for a man's fripperies, his fobs, his cravat pins. The memory arrived unbidden, whole, his mother weeping over that box, her treasure, her comfort, a consoling possession to which she clung. He watched her open it now with a kind of reverence and remove a letter and read with a trembling smile. "*My darling wife*. He liked to call me *wife*, the novelty of it. He wrote letters for Kit, too."

Will heard Xander ask, "Are there any proofs besides the letters, Mamma?"

"He had a house. He drove me there after our wedding to spend the night. Hodge kept you, Will." She glanced at him then, with unseeing tear-brightened eyes.

"Daventry gave his old nurse our marriage lines to keep them safe until he returned."

Will could not believe she had spared a thought for him on that long-ago wedding day. Only habits of interrogation made him ask the questions they had to ask. "Who else knew of your marriage? Who stood up with Daventry?"

"Another soldier, a lieutenant of his regiment."

"Who?"

Sophie lifted her chin. "He's a colonel now, Ned Drummond."

"But you told no one else. The banns were not published?"

Sophie shook her head. "We were so careful. We married by special license. Ned procured it."

"Did you ever hear from Wenlocke?" Xander asked.

"Never. Daventry left for India within a week. We wanted the duke to believe the . . . affair had ended."

Will stood. He had to distance himself from her. "Hell, Mamma, Kit's the bleeding heir of the Duke of Wenlocke."

Sophie shook her head. "I never made a claim. Kit didn't need Wenlocke. He had us."

Xander spoke up. "But Norwood should pursue a claim in the courts. Kit should have his inheritance. I wonder if Daventry's nurse is still alive."

Will moved about the room trying to think not about Sophie and Daventry but about Kit, who believed he endangered them all because of the hatred of a powerful cold old man. He caught Helen's glance and knew she understood him. He turned back to his mother. "How did Wenlocke discover the truth? That's what this is about, Mamma. Wenlocke didn't want you to have a claim on him through Kit."

"I believe I know the answer to that, Will." Xander and Cleo exchanged a glance. "March."

Sophie turned to Xander. "I don't know Mr. March. I never had any dealings with him."

Xander spoke more gently than Will could have. "But March had a hold on Evershot's Bank, Mamma, your bank. Until last November he had access to all of Evershot's private dealings with clients. What did you have in that bank that would alert March to your marriage?"

Sophie looked uncomprehending. "Daventry had investments. He put them in my name when he left for India. He meant for me to have an income. But I didn't touch them for years, not after the news came of his death."

Will had to ask the next question. "When did you start drawing on them, Mamma?"

"I don't know, four years ago, maybe five for Kit's schooling."

Sophie collapsed against the sofa, realization stark in her eyes. She glanced again at her major's rigid back. His hands were clasped tightly behind him. Her voice fell to a whisper. "Was Kit taken because I used Daventry's money?"

Xander spoke. "No. Kit was taken because he is Daventry's legitimate son. March discovered the truth when you drew on those funds."

Will added, "And he used it to get to Wenlocke. He wanted Wenlocke in his debt. That's how March works."

"That evil old man. I am going to him. He took my son."

"Ah, Mamma, that's just what Wenlocke thinks of you. You took his son." Will took up the scrap of paper. "Mamma, you even put the duke's Granville name in the notice."

Sophie's look grew stubborn and aloof. She drew herself stiffly erect, her hands folded on the sampler in her lap. "My son, my husband's child, all I have left of him, is alive somewhere in this city. I will do everything in my power to bring him home. Do you think because you and your brother are so careful in what you say that I don't know what he's endured? What he has suffered?"

Major Montclare left his place by the window and came to stand behind Sophie and rest his hands on her shoulders. She acknowledged the support but did not bend to it. The major faced Will and Xander with his most martial bearing.

"Gentlemen, your mother has endured enough distress this morning."

Will accepted it. Sophie had another man to support her in her trials. He could not stay a minute more. Let Xander continue the interviews.

Will passed down the stairs with Helen beside him. In the street people still lined the walk, waiting to give information. He ignored them, walking rapidly toward the fog-shrouded square.

He didn't look at her as she scrambled to keep up with

him. "Go back to whoever helped you escape your parents, Helen."

"I can't."

He stopped abruptly and turned on her. "You see how it is with me. Be a smart girl, Helen. Leave me. Go back home."

"We have a plan."

"There *is* no we. Not any longer. You still want to take on March? Here, have some blunt. Bribe an errand boy and take his place. See if you can leave a window unlatched." He snatched her hand, opened it, and pressed a bill into her palm.

"Where are you going?"

"To find my brother. My legitimate brother, the Duke of Wenlocke's heir, if the old man doesn't murder him."

"I can help you."

"Help me? Is that what you think we've been about? Two good people helping one another, like blessed saints?"

"Like partners."

He smiled his sardonic smile. "We're not partners. You lie *to* me, and I want to lie *with* you. So now with a bit of luck, sweetheart, you've got a chance to escape me. Take it! From the moment I saw you I had undressed you in my head, enjoyed your lips, enjoyed your breasts, and speared myself so deep in you I didn't know my own name."

She punched him in the ribs, a swift, hard blow that made lights dance before his eyes.

"That's the first sensible thing you've done in a week." He smiled through clenched teeth.

"Listen to me. Your informant, that carter John Neale said something. And it explains a child I met in Bredsell's school."

"I'm listening."

"The boy was no bigger than five. He said his name was Robin, a bird's name, do you see? He was new to the school. He woke me when he tried to open a dormer window over the roof in the middle of the night. He said he had to open it because 'Boy' would come for him over the rooftops."

"Who are you?"

"Helen . . ."

He put a hand over her mouth, his eyes dark with anger. "Don't spin that story for me again. You know the ugly truth about me, but I know nothing about you, do I?"

She leaned into his touch, and he dropped his hand.

"I am your partner. We made a bargain. We both want to uncover the secrets of that . . . house."

He advanced on her, forcing her back through the mists of Hill Street. "Go home, Helen. Go back to whoever loosed you on London. Let me destroy March. If I succeed, March won't ruin any more of those good people you worry about."

Nate Wilde shoved his hands in his pockets and edged his way into Bredsell's library past an overturned cabinet. The place was a ruin. Nate liked a good mill, and always gave as good as he got when Bread Streeters took on a faction from another street. He had certainly seen a brawl wreck a taproom, but Bredsell's library gave him the shakes. Nothing had escaped the purposeful, methodical violence.

He'd heard it, too, like axes chopping. Since breakfast he had been locked with the other boys in the dining hall instead of being free to roam London. Just as the boys scraped the last porridge out of the bowls Bredsell had burst into the room and ordered Mr. Coates, one of the masters, to bolt the door behind him. With the assistance of the bigger boys, the men had barricaded the door with heavy dining tables. The boys huddled together, listening to shouting, pounding, and wood splintering across the hall.

Now Nate could see just what those sounds meant. Someone had overturned every piece of furniture in Bredsell's office. Drawers and shelves had been emptied. The floor was knee-deep in torn paper. Book spines gutted of their pages had been tossed in a tall pile like a midden of cockleshells. The walls had great gaping holes where the paneling had been pried off. The windows were smashed, and bits of china teapot crunched under Nate's boots.

"Don't just stand there, Wilde," Bredsell ordered. He righted a green velvet armchair. "Help me clean this up. Get a basket from the laundry."

When Nate returned, Bredsell was sunk in the green chair, his hand over his face, bits of the chair's stuffing clinging to his black coat. Bredsell lifted his head and gestured for Nate to pick up the drifts of paper. Nate began with a copy of the *Morning Chronicle*. He could see dozens of copies of the paper tossed about, one of them nailed to the wall.

Bredsell was a lump in that chair because someone terrible and powerful had reached into Bredsell's life and torn it apart. His golden hair stuck up in unruly spikes. He sat and stared into space while Nate worked his way through the drifts of paper to where he could read in quick glances the notice nailed to the wall. *My dear son*, a letter began.

Nate read on. A mother wanted her son back. The wanting in the notice was like a punch in the back you didn't see coming. Her name was Sophie Rhys-Jones, and she lived on Hill Street where Nate had spied on Xander Jones and his lady wife. He put it together in his head. Will Jones was the other brother, the copper. They were an odd family to have a starchy, top-lofty son like Xander Jones and a son like Will Jones. He was a copper, but he was tough and smart and mean as a Bread Street rat.

Nate knew the boy they looked for, too, the one Will Jones asked about when he took Nate's stash. The boy was a mystery, that one, always on the rooftops with his band. Nate had once seen him jump across a wide gap between buildings like it was nothing. Just watching that leap had made Nate's heart pound.

He went back to scooping paper into the basket. He thought about the boy in the notice, but he thought about his own situation, too. Other boys could answer the notice and get money for what they knew. Even a lie would probably get a boy some coin, but he, Nate Wilde, couldn't go into that house. They'd know him there from the times he'd spied on them and worse.

Nate considered the destruction around him. Leaving the newspaper behind was a way of saying that Bredsell had been punished because the boy was alive. The swift, brutal punishment unsettled Nate. Someone knew that Mr. March kept things in his books. Whoever it was had attacked the wrong library, but he would soon figure out where March's other books were. Nate didn't want to be doing an errand for Mr. March at the wrong time, in the wrong place. He needed to make a career change. He glanced out the broken windows.

Fog made it near dark as night outside, and it was cold as could be, not a good day for dipping a hand in anyone's pocket. People would be wrapped up to their eyes, and they would hurry along the streets, not stop to look in shop windows or gather to watch a street performer. Nate could see that he didn't have a lot of choices at the moment. If Will Jones hadn't taken his blunt, he could just walk away. He refused to think how long it had taken to collect that stash.

He'd come to just that stuck place in his thinking when March came into the room. His stride was abrupt and quick, not his usual toffy amble, and he was cloaked and wrapped in wool up to his eyes. The day was cold, but to Nate it looked as if March wanted to hide.

Bredsell immediately wailed, "What are we going to do now, March? Who's going to pay for all this?"

March crossed the room and pulled down the notice nailed to the wall and tossed it to the floor.

"Bredsell, I hope you're outraged at such an attack on a charitable institution." March looked about. "Did you make a speech? Did you send a message to the papers?"

"The papers?"

"To tell them how you did your best to protect the boys from the savages who attacked your work."

"I wonder that you're bold enough to come here, March. Wenlocke's obviously watching the school."

"You think Wenlocke was behind this, not Xander Jones? Now, I wouldn't say that to the papers."

"Look about you, March. Jones is looking for his brother, not for your—"

A look from March cut Bredsell off, but March halted at the ransacked desk and slowly took off his hat and gloves, looking about with a measuring glance. "Did they get yesterday's take?"

"Wilde must have it."

"Then get hold of yourself, Bredsell. Get those windows boarded up."

"Nate, lad, what do you have for me?" Mr. March's tone was hearty, but his face was cold, his look distracted now as his glance caught more of the room's destruction. He was noticing the books now, how each one had been emptied of its guts.

Nate pulled out the stash he'd received back from Will Jones and handed it over and watched as March counted and frowned.

"This is all Leary gave you?"

"Yes, sir, Mr. March."

"Nothing fell out of your pocket or got lost on the way?"

"No, sir, Mr. March. Oi'm not one ta 'old out on ye, sir." Nate held himself still under a sharp, searching look.

"Right then. Evidently, I must speak to Leary directly, but I don't want him to anticipate my visit."

"Forget Wilde and Leary, March. Take yourself off to the continent before Wenlocke finds you."

"I'll go when I receive the payments I'm owed."

Bredsell lifted his hand from his disarranged curls. "I'll thank you not to direct them here any longer."

"Where else would a generous donation to the school be sent? How are you to bring light to boys' souls without the kind support of your patrons?"

Bredsell groaned. "When are you expecting this payment to come?"

"Within a fortnight." March gestured to Nate to right another of the gutted chairs.

"How will I reach you?"

"I'll reach you. Just hold on to the blunt."

"What if Wenlocke's hired fists see you here?"

"They won't. They've done what they were sent to do."

"You can't fight Wenlocke, you know. Did you read this morning's *Chronicle*? Apparently Wenlocke did. His grandson is alive, and he knows it."

"A most inconvenient brat, isn't he? You'd think Wenlocke would see to the boy's demise himself."

"Why don't you simply send him a corpse, March? A

boy from the streets. They die with convenient regularity. Clean up the body, and how would Wenlocke know?"

"Bredsell, you surprise me! A little grave robbing? Or are you suggesting murder? Some poor lad, like Nate Wilde, here?"

"You want Wenlocke off your back, don't you?"

"I have a better way of handling Wenlocke. For a man of the cloth, you have so little faith." March smiled at Nate.

"Nate Wilde, here's your errand for today, lad. I've a book I'd like you to move for me from one library to another. That warehouse of mine, you know the one." He picked a scrap of paper from the basket Nate had filled and wrote a note on it.

He handed it to Nate. "Understand?"

Nate read it and nodded.

March reached in his pocket for a coin and tossed it Nate's way. "There'll be another when you've done the deed, lad. Not a word to Mr. Leary, mind."

Bredsell stood up. Under March's gaze he brushed the bits of chair stuffing from his coat and hair.

"Remember who keeps you in business. You'll continue to collect donations and hold them for me." He waited for Bredsell to nod. "And I think you might plan a journey to country to recover your spirits after this cruel blow to your life's work. I think you should arrange a post chaise for dawn tomorrow morning. Have the coach meet you here."

March took up his hat and gloves and muffled himself

to the eyes in a gray wrapper. "And Bredsell, let me know if you hear of any likely corpses of fifteen or sixteen years."

Nate waited for Mr. March to open the door and release him. He'd go one more time. He'd look about sharp and not let himself be trapped.

Chapter Fourteen

❧

H ELEN walked the neighborhood for an hour until
the seething rage Will Jones ignited had slowed to
a simmer. At least it kept her warm. She didn't need him.
She simply needed resolve and luck. She wound her way
through Shepherd Market. Her original plan still seemed
best—to pose as a delivery boy. She had Jones's money,
and this time she meant to spend it all and repay none.
At Kirby & Sons, Fruiters, she showed her money to the
proprietor, and asked for a sack of filberts and a tray of
Norfolk biffins, flat, swarthy baking apples. When he
pressed her for her master's name, she gave the number
next to March's establishment.

"Ah, for Mrs. Fairchild; why didn't you say so at the
first, lad?"

Helen made some demur and watched while he took pride in arranging the apples in a Kirby & Sons tray. The filberts he bagged in a paper sack.

Helen took the goods and tried her best to saunter off. In the lane at the back of March's establishment, she said a brief prayer that the brick-faced man would not be guarding the door and that she wouldn't see Nate Wilde about.

There was no guard, which meant something she was sure, but also that she had a chance. A thin fellow wiping greasy hands on a stained apron answered her knock.

"Filberts and Norfolk biffins for Mrs. Fairchild," Helen announced.

"Wrong 'ouse, boy." He leaned against the doorjamb of the open door.

"Can't be," said Helen. She named March's number.

The number made the fellow scratch his head and stare at the tray. Helen lifted the cloth cover, and the sweet scent of sugared apples filled the air.

"Nice goods, lad, but no Mrs. Fairchild 'ere."

"Oi got 'er number, in me pocket. Wouldjer let me look?"

"Yer a slowtop, aren't ye?" The man shrugged, and Helen lifted her tray his way. He came out of his slouch to take the tray from her.

Helen dug in her pocket while she squeezed the bottom of the bag of filberts. Filberts spewed out and rolled with a clatter all over the kitchen floor.

"Look what ye've done, ye clumsy oaf." The man backed into his kitchen and set the apple tray down on a tin wash sink.

Helen followed him and dropped to her knees, crawling after the rolling nuts. "Oi'll get 'em. Jest give me a minute."

"Be quick about it, lad, or I'll box yer ears for ye."

A kettle whistled, and the man turned away. Helen did a quick scan of the room for a window latch. Instead her glance caught a ring of keys hanging on a knob beside the door itself.

She jumped up, pulled the ring down, and dropped it in her bag. On her knees again, she kept the bag under her, reaching inside to loosen a key from the ring. She crawled after filberts with a wide sweeping motion of her free arm, keeping up a rattle of the nuts as she raked them in. As soon as she freed a key from the ring, she slipped it into her pocket and stood. The cook was still at his fire. She hung the key ring on its knob and took up the tray of apples.

"Got 'em," she called.

"Then best be about yer business, boy." He did not look at her.

"Done, sir." She backed out the open door with a quick glance at the lock and forced herself to turn and walk slowly through the bare garden into the lane.

She avoided the market and made her way back to Piccadilly. She should feel invisible, a smudge of gray and brown in the fog and bustle of midafternoon London. But she felt as if she were blazing across the soot-blackened stones like a comet, as if people would turn and stare. She tried to contain her exhilaration, shortening her stride and sticking her hand in her pocket to feel the key. It filled her palm, a flat head and a solid round shaft that ended in a row of three square, sharp-edged teeth.

She had an inexplicable desire to slap it on the table in Will Jones's inner room. *A mad thought.* He had made it plain what he wanted with her. But to show him how fearless she'd been, to share her triumph was tempting. To show him that she had truly become Helen.

You see how it is with me.

He had said the words, and she had not understood him in that moment, but she did now. He had his mother's eyes and her capacity for extremes. He was the lion in the old tale with a thorn in its paw. Wounded, trapped in anger at the world's evils, he would not find his lost brother. He could search all of London and find only injustice and pain.

She was the mouse, the partner, who could free him as he had freed her. She laughed at the key in her hand. It was the least of her powers. He had allowed her to become Helen. Who could she allow him to become? He was neither Paris nor the devil. Who was he really?

She would not know unless she went back to him and lay with him in his grand sultan's bed.

WHEN Will reached Bread Street, he found Xander's office a smoking ruin. A quiet defeated crowd had gathered beyond the fire wagons. People passed pots of ale to one another, but there was little talk and no humor. Will felt their hopelessness. Ordinary people could hardly believe in Xander's vision of London rising up and making itself great when bad luck seemed Bread Street's perpetual lot.

The captain of the fire wagon crew explained that his crews had been delayed by the long trench down the street. They'd not been able to save any of the tools, equipment, or plans that Xander had stored inside. There would be a delay of weeks in bringing light to this particular corner of London. Will soon heard talk that the school had suffered an attack, as well. That meant Wenlocke, not March was likely behind the destruction. The people suffered today not because Xander or Bread Street had failed in any way but because a powerful old man hated his own flesh and blood. The thought brought a grim smile with it. Maybe, he, Will, was the lucky one after all. His father, the debauched Earl of Oxley, was merely indifferent to his bastard son, not intent on his destruction.

Will took his time moving among the crowd, talking to people. He found himself invoking Xander's name, like a good-luck charm, planting the idea of Xander's determination and his inevitable rebuilding. He had no doubt that *Saint* Xander would be back with a plan and new equipment inside of a week.

He asked about Kit. Some claimed to have seen sweeps on the rooftops, but as one wit told him, everyone in the neighborhood had been looking at the ground for weeks, at the blooming ditch that now measured the length of Bread Street, soon to be filled with Xander's great gas pipe.

He left the crowd in the court and entered the tap. The place gleamed with new handles on the pumps, a grand mirror, and polished wood on the bar. Will could see Xander's hand again, or at least his pocketbook, had been involved in funding a rebuilding of the place after the flood. A conversation with the proprietor gained Will access to a stair to the attic. Together they pried open a sooty door to the roof. The steep pitch of it ended in the wall of the neighboring tenement. Will slid down that slope, and stepped up onto a flat roof and into Kit's world.

London stretched out in every direction, above a wide lazy river of fog in which shadowy gables, chimneys, and spires stuck up like boats mired in the muck of the Thames at low tide. The brewery's new vats dominated the skyline to the west across the street from the stark brick of Bredsell's school.

As Will scanned the expanse, he saw it for the first time as a kind of terrain to be navigated. From the street, the rooftops had looked like an unreachable other world, but now Will could see that once reached, links and paths could take a daring boy on countless journeys across London.

He set out above Bread Street to see where he could get. A gray pall of wet ash from the fire hung over the street. Here and there a group of huddled shapes suggested a band of boys in black but turned out to be a row of crooked chimney pots rising from their common stack.

He leaned at last on a gable looking down into the yard of Bredsell's school. Alone of all the structures on

Bread Street, the school did not touch its neighbors. Will was as close as one could come to it from above. A wide, high-walled yard separated the building from its neighbors. To go from the roof to the school, one would have to descend a vertical wall and pass along the top of the high wall surrounding the yard.

Helen believed one of his brother's band was trapped in the school, expecting a rescue from Kit. Thoughts of her had never been out of his mind since he'd first seen her on the makeshift stage of the brothel. No wonder Xander accused him of being derelict in his duty.

He was used to puzzles and danger, used to outsmarting the enemy on his own. Distrust, which they plainly shared, did not make a good partnership. Secrets withheld meant that in a tight spot, the other fellow could act in some wholly unpredictable way. No one in his experience acted with less predictability than his Helen of Troy. He was well quit of her.

But he had to admit that she had led him here. If Kit planned a rescue, he had likely studied the school from the very spot where Will now breathed the old city's dank, sooty air.

Will rolled on his back and laughed at himself. He was probably closer to his missing brother than he'd ever been in their long search, not because of all his expert police work, but because he had more of Sophie in him than either of his brothers, her disastrous emotions at least. Sophie and Helen, his lying mother and his lying sweetheart, they'd set him off. Of course, he'd come up short in his search.

He picked himself up. He was who he was. Sophie's one true bastard. He lacked Xander's saintly restraint or his belief in London's great future. The miracle of finding their lost brother was not for him. His role was the grim one of facing the worst men the wicked old city had to offer—March, if he could find him, and Wenlocke, if he could get close to such a powerful personage. He'd play the part fate had assigned him.

Chapter Fifteen

❧

"D ID you find him?"

She sat hunched by a bright fire in his outer room, wearing a chocolate silk wrapper of his, a towel over her knees.

"How did you find your way back here?"

"I followed Blind Zebediah from Oxford Street. Harding let me in."

She wasn't supposed to come back. He had resigned himself to the loss of her. She was not for him. Freeing her outside his mother's house was possibly his most noble act. "Not smart, making free with my wardrobe again, Helen." He shed his hat, gloves, and greatcoat, keeping to the shadows away from her.

"There's water by the fire for a bath. I've had one."

She leaned forward, silk sliding over her, and rubbed the ends of her shorn hair between the folds of the towel. Her breasts, freed from their binding, shimmied under the silk, a sweet vibration that held him motionless for a moment.

He glanced at the bed. Wild possibilities tumbled through his mind. The copper bath waited with a thick towel on the bench. A brace of candles glowed double in the mirror above the cabinet. It was the scene he'd left behind the night he'd gone to March's brothel to rescue her. "What have you been up to?"

She glanced up and rested her hands on the towel in her lap. A triangle of creamy flesh glowed against the dark silk of the dressing gown, and a line of twine or cord crossed her chest. "I read Lord Thrustmore."

He swallowed. "Tame stuff after Paris, I suppose."

"Instructive, I thought. I doubt Miss Yeeld could have had a better teacher than Lord Thrustmore."

Her lightness roused a spurt of anger. "Did you pay attention this morning at my mother's house? My brothers might be saintly Sir Alexander and lofty Lord Daventry, but I remain a bastard." He shrugged out of his jacket and looked for brandy.

"You always make yourself perfectly clear."

He poured a drink and sat opposite her. "The part of you I want is not your bleeding hand in marriage. I'm not a man who will make you an honorable offer tomorrow if I take your virtue tonight."

She didn't even blink. "The only promise I'm looking for from you is our bargain. Tomorrow you get me back into March's brothel."

"Don't be dim, woman. If I tumble Helen of Troy tonight, that other girl, the one behind that clever, wanton mask of yours, the girl you think you hide so well, loses her virtue too."

"You don't know that other girl at all, and you wouldn't like her." She smiled sadly. He knew that smile of hers. It appeared whenever she spoke of her other life, the life she was unfailingly willing to risk.

"So tonight is Helen's night." He raised his glass to her.

"Tonight is about healing those ribs. Just as you planned." With a sweep of a silk-draped arm she gestured toward the bed.

"You take quite an interest in my ribs."

"They are the only part of you not made of iron apparently. Do you want that bath?"

He drank his brandy and studied her. She was suddenly so sure of herself that it puzzled him. He tried to work it out, and his gaze came back to the incongruous bit of twine hanging around her neck. "You went back there, didn't you?"

"I did."

"Hell." *Why did she insist on risking herself?*

"You can see I made it out again."

"How far inside the house did you get?"

"The kitchen."

"Did you snatch a ball of twine from the cat?"

She grinned at him.

"What?"

From the open neck of her robe she drew a cord from which an iron key dangled.

She leaned forward, and he took it. His hand closed around iron warmed by her body, her breasts inches beyond his fingertips.

"Nice work; fits a rim lock by the look of it, likely an outer door." He thought his voice sounded ordinary, but she straightened abruptly so the key slid from his palm.

She stood. "You should have that bath now." Her voice had a quiver in it that shot a bolt of lust straight to his yard.

He didn't move. "Helen, I won't endure another night in that bed beside you and not make love to you."

She looked down at him as if he were a dolt of particularly weak understanding. "You'd best help me with the water. The buckets are heavy."

He put down his drink then and helped her tote the buckets to the tub. He could not read her thoughts. Did she understand him? That he could give pleasure and passion and nothing more? Was she so lost in her imagined life as Helen that she did not recognize the real consequences of their lovemaking?

"All Greece hated Helen, you know," he said.

She had her head down, concentrating on a steaming kettle of water for the bath. "Every woman for all time should thank her for daring to be herself and refusing to accept punishment for it."

They emptied the brimming buckets, and the heavy spill of water made the copper tub ring. He had cundums, didn't he? He glanced at the cabinet next to the cheval glass. In another life he had stocked it for an evening with a professional, the sort of pleasure he had allowed himself on occasion since his return to London.

He put aside the water pail and made short work of his clothes. When she saw the state he was in, she would call a halt to the proceedings. He could lock her in his inner room for the night.

But when he stood naked, it was not fear he saw in her gaze, it was a welcome, as if his deuced cock straining for her was an old and dear friend she was glad to see. *Hell.*

He stepped into the tub.

Helen liked looking at him naked. It made sense of him, the compressed energy that could be unleashed in sudden moves, the scars, the undaunted pride and glory of him. The room's mirrors gave him to her from all angles. His skin seemed molded to his frame, revealing the bulge of muscle and the lines of sinew and bone. He was a study in dark and light, the white of his shoulders and hips, a sharp contrast to the dark hair of his chest and groin. She had been right that he would still command a room naked.

She understood him better now. She had been wrong that her deception would be less wounding than the world's blows or his family's slights. He needed to believe in goodness, this man who thought himself Satan's own. It was his ability to believe in goodness that she must not wound.

Will sank into the heat and let it enfold him. It had taken a great deal of resolve not to push her back on that luxurious bed and pull the sash from her wrapper. He congratulated himself on his restraint.

She pulled up a stool and slipped her fingers into his hair and began to knead his head around his ears, his temples, his nape and knotted shoulders.

"How do you know how to do that?"

"An old woman taught me the trick . . . in Troy, a useful accomplishment for those times when Paris was in a foul mood."

"I thought he was your perpetually charming lover."

"You see, you think you know the story."

"So tell me about the *uncharming* side of Paris." He needed a distraction from the part of him that already beat with a steady pulse of desire. He had no plan for what to do when the water inevitably cooled. Sit until his privates shrank?

"All that armor polishing? That was Paris pouting. He would sulk and hold himself aloof whenever others questioned his soldiering. He had fifty brothers who seldom respected his work in war."

"How could they?"

"You wrong him like everyone else. He was swift and accurate with a lance, a bit showy in his gear, but all those Trojans liked their gold, you know. They had buckets of it."

"You learned a great deal in Troy." The lazy circling hands on his head seemed to tug invisible strings attached to his groin.

"One could go mad behind the walls without some study—people, that was my subject."

"Their virtues or their faults?"

"Their voices, who they truly were."

Will laughed inside at what a mad pair they were, Helen, happily prattling about Troy, while he was thinking of Lord Thrustmore's next move.

When he could endure no more, he simply rose and stepped from the tub, pulled her up off her stool, and walked with her to the great bed. He dropped her in a heap and pulled away the sash holding the silk wrapper closed.

She rolled away from him with a laugh, slipping free of the loose garment to lie gloriously naked on the deep blue coverlet. She was everything he remembered from that first night, everything that had driven him mad for days.

He toweled himself dry and flung back the covers, settling in the bed beside her. She removed the cord around her neck and handed it to him, a solemn ceremony of trust. He put it on the cabinet.

They lay on their sides facing each other. He looked into deep brown eyes, darkened with desire. The ends of her butchered hair curled softly around her face from the steamy warmth of the bath. The breasts he had done his best to forget rose round and free with only a faint pink line where the linen binding had cut her flesh.

He reached out a hand that he feared had a slight tremor and cupped one smooth, round breast. Its softness made him dizzy. He spread his fingers and ran his palm down her side to the valley of her waist and up again over the curve of her hip to trail down her thigh behind her knee.

He could hear her breath flutter unevenly though she held herself still under his touch. He turned his palm up and trailed his fingers back along the inside of her thigh to the valley of her sex and up her belly. He pressed his palm against her womb, his fingers splayed above her curls, dark gold against her pale skin.

"It's Lord Thrustmore you've got, Helen, no Paris, willing to die for love. I'll give pleasure and passion, not love."

Helen knew she should feel shamed, exposed, frightened, but she felt none of those things. She felt as powerful as Aphrodite herself. He needed her. In this moment he needed her like he needed air itself. Every limb rejoiced in its power.

She knew that power would shift from her, that in the end the goddess demanded helplessness before desire. But as Helen had borne it, she would, too. She smiled at him.

Will watched her smile a smile he never expected from a virgin as if she knew something he didn't.

He would show her that reading Lord Thrustmore meant nothing. He reached out and snagged her waist and dragged her body up against his, molding her to him, her breasts crushed against his chest, pulling her leg over his hip so that his cock nudged the folds of her sex. He brought his mouth down on hers.

She opened her lips to receive the fuller joining he demanded and twined her limbs with his.

It took several minutes for him to realize that his strategy wasn't working. Instead of a blushing maiden, offended by the taste and smell and heat of carnal embraces, he was in bed with a willing and attentive partner. He lifted his mouth from hers.

"We can stop now. Technically you remain a virgin, and I don't recommend testing the boundary between maidenhood and experience any further."

He fell on his back next to her, his blood pumping like a steam engine.

Her breathing, like his, was ragged. Her breasts rose and fell with each warm exhalation. Her golden skin was flushed, and her nipples, glistening from his attention, stood up in sweet peaks.

"You've a good bit of knowledge to take back to your other life after tomorrow. Maybe you'll want to add Lord Thrustmore to your storytelling." It was a cold thing to say. It made a romp of their lovemaking, a lesson.

His coldness drew that smile of hers, but she sat up, her legs folded under her. He couldn't help himself; he reached up to cup one breast, to hold that trembling fullness in his palm.

She knelt above him then and ran her hands over his chest and belly and down his thighs. He saw her glance at his pulsing cock, tempted to touch that, too. And he would have laughed at that one maidenly hesitation, but she bent down and kissed his ribs. Her breasts brushed his chest and his groin.

Don't. Don't know me. Don't see my need. Don't give so generously of yourself.

Her kisses changed, and he knew that the real woman, the person behind the mask was kissing him. He understood what the girl behind the mask was about—she was giving up her respectability for him.

He rose up and let Lord Thrustmore take over, pushing her down on her back again, kissing her lips, her breasts, her belly, hooking the little lip of her navel with his finger, and dipping down to take possession of her cleft with his hand, until she arched up into his touch. He stopped, rolled away, and stood on shaking legs beside the bed to open a cabinet drawer and pull out a cundum.

"That's not how it ends, is it?" she asked his back.

"Not at all. I'm just making a preparation for what comes next."

He turned and held up the device and watched the open joyfulness fade in her eyes. And felt how unreasonable he was to regret the passing of that look.

"Just doing my part to support neighborhood industry—there's a cundum warehouse across the street."

Helen lay back against the sheets, her body pulsing with life, her soaring spirit momentarily checked.

On her fifteenth birthday she had stood invincible on a bluff, leaning against a stiff October wind, letting it billow her skirts and cape and hold her up. But the fickle wind had died, and she'd just caught herself back from the lip of the bluff in time.

She covered her eyes with the back of her arm. Helen never weeps, she reminded herself.

"Finally too much reality for you, Helen?" Will turned away from her, securing the damned thing to his cock, tying the frivolous ribbon with ruthless efficiency. He glanced over his shoulder at her face, hidden for the moment. "I bring no bastards into the world."

He rolled back on top of her, stretching her hands above her head with one of his, kissing her breasts, and reaching with his other hand to tease again the place he had made ready for their joining. "There will still be pleasure, that I promise."

Helen opened to him. This was the helplessness the goddess demanded. He could reason and draw back and think of the world beyond the bed they shared, while she could not, her body clamoring for a completion he must give. She gave into it. Miss Yeeld, indeed.

He slipped his hand under her, lifting her body up to his, and plunged himself deep inside her. He caught her gasp at the pain of it and stilled. Then he began a slow slide inside her, and as it built, Helen discovered the final secret the goddess had to give, the secret of the mysterious power of love itself—in helplessness, one came fully alive.

Pleasure came and filled her body.

He turned away again, to remove the little sheath, the barrier that had kept him from yielding as she had.

"Sleep. I'll wake you when it's time. My word on it." He picked up the cord with the iron key. The key felt cold in his hand, and he saw her shiver when he looped it over her head and let the iron fall against her breast.

Helen curled her fist around the cold iron. Her heart felt bruised, but it was only from beating so hard. The feeling was bound to pass.

He pulled the covers up around her and slipped away to the inner room. If he meant to get her in and out of March's place safely, he would be wise to study Harding's sketches again.

Chapter Sixteen

❧

H E lit the lamps again after two. Though the ancient paneling of his rooms muffled the bells of the neighborhood churches, this night he had heard the tolling of each passing hour.

She did not wake at once, his sleeping queen, and he allowed himself the pleasure of watching her as he dressed. He had plucked her from the midst of dishonorable men with no idea of her truth worth. Even he, who had offered a reckless sum to retrieve her from their hands, had underestimated her value.

She had more courage than he, for she had taken on March with only her wits and her queenly disguise. Setbacks had not stopped her, and he had not stopped her with his mockery or his desire. Tonight he would use every skill and instinct he had honed as a spy and a Runner to help her succeed in her mission.

He touched her shoulder, so warm and silky he almost groaned, and her eyes opened, those deep brown eyes with their queenly bits of gold and violet that seemed to know him better than he knew himself.

"It's time?"

He nodded.

She rose without coyness or concealment and began to dress.

"You're not expecting any sudden display of gallantry, I hope."

"Just our plan." She took up the strip of linen from her pile of garments and bound her breasts.

At the door to the street, the mastiff growled low in his throat, and she hushed the beast with a word.

Will caught her by the arm. "A kiss for luck, sweetheart?"

She came up on her toes and met his mouth with hers, a full and open joining. She broke it off, and they stepped out into the dark street.

IN the lane behind March's brothel, Will Jones reminded her, "My rules, sweetheart."

Helen's stolen key unlocked a lower door to the kitchen. Will Jones entered ahead of her, moving swiftly and surely, while she halted to adjust to the shadowy gloom. A banked fire on the hearth outlined tables, chairs, and cupboards. For a moment her trembling nerves held her frozen. If she moved, she would knock into something. Her whole reason for being in London came down to this chance to save her mother. She had to keep her mind on that and not on fear. They might meet some of March's men, but Will Jones was armed, and if he had showed her the dagger in his sleeve, that meant he had other weapons on his person elsewhere.

From the kitchen a hall forked left into a long, dark path under the house itself and right into a short passage to the base of some stairs. Will Jones opened a tin device that released a single candle beam. Its light revealed a row of closed and bolted doors along the long inner wall. On one door a pair of padlocks hung from the bolts. Though Will Jones had rejected the basement as the location of March's secret files, he took a long look down that passage before they climbed the stairs to the main house.

On the ground floor they edged in darkness past a back bedroom. Helen knew he counted every step, relying on his knowledge of Harding's drawings. He stopped, and Helen felt the change in the space around them. He caught her by the arm in the same instant that she recognized the place as the dark well of her drugged memory.

They stood in the shadows between a pair of pale marble columns. Faint light fell from sconces far above them where the open balustrade marked the upper story. Helen's memory threw up a flash of leaning over that balustrade. As her eyes grew accustomed, she saw that the room was a library, not a well, its double height

supported by eight magnificent columns, the curved seg-
ments between the columns lined with books from the
ground floor to the story above. The sight made sense of
Nate Wilde's cheeky comment that he spent his time in
the brothel reading books in a library.

"Damn! March bought the place for this room." Will
Jones reached in the dark for a book. He found them
wedged tightly together and pried one loose from its
row. He gave her the tin light-box and turned over the
book in his hand, opening it and fanning the leaves.
The pages were cut. The book was real. He took it by its
spine and gently shook. Nothing. He took another, and
another, and slowly, carefully, noiselessly repeated the
procedure.

At the end of the first row, a letter slipped from the
leaves of the book. He stepped back into the hall and held
the letter to his light, reading quickly. He looked from the
letter to the spine of the book in his hand. "It's an infer-
nal filing system. Alphabetical, no less. March must have
hundreds of documents stored here." He showed her how
the first letter of the signature matched the first letter of
the author's name on the spine of the book. "You know
where to find what you're looking for."

He held up his hand with the fingers spread. It was
their sign. *Five minutes.* He had promised her five minutes alone. The candle would last no longer. When it
went out, with or without him, with or without what she
came for, she was to find Harding at the appointed meeting place. He had made her swear to it. In that dark hour
before dawn there had been no kisses, no touching.

Now he gave her his beam device. It was a reminder, that candle, of how small a chance she had to save her mother. He stepped back in the darkness and was gone. She did not hear a sound.

Helen turned to the walls of the library, moving carefully, reading the spines. Halfway in her circuit of the room, she realized that *R*, the letter she needed, was in the space above one of the wide openings between the columns. She looked around for a book ladder and found none, though she could see the high iron rail over which such a ladder usually hooked. No ladder. It made her doubt their theory. Maybe there was a different system, not names, but numbers. She reached for a volume by Pope, tugged it free from the tight grip of its neighbors, and gently shook its leaves. A letter fluttered out and dropped to her feet. Helen bent to scoop it up and read the signature. *Palgrave*.

She spun back to the room then, studying the furniture—a heavy desk, a pair of wing chairs, an ottoman, and a tall candle stand. Even mounted on a chair seat she could not reach the height she needed. She made herself look again. Nothing. She took a slow breath. She could not come so close and fail. She turned to the shelves, stuck her foot on a shelf about two feet off the ground, grabbed a shelf above her with both hands, and pulled herself up. The shelves held.

She could not climb and carry the light. She descended, positioned the wing chair near her target shelf, and stood the candle stand on it, hooking her little beam to the top of its branches. Then she began her climb again. When she had her foot on the fifth shelf, she felt dizzy with the height. Her arms trembled with effort, and below her her little light flickered.

Her pulse pounded in her ears. Voices filled her head. She seemed to hear her father saying, *frailty thy name is woman*, her mother murmuring a plea, and Will Jones's dry *sweetheart*. She leaned her forehead against the shelves and cleared the male mockery from her thoughts. Only her mother mattered now. She opened her eyes and read the spines of the books across the top of the opening. *Reeve, Reynolds, Richardson, Robertson, Rousseau, Rymer.*

Her light sputtered again. If March had her mother's letters, they were likely tucked in one of those books, and she had one chance to choose. *Rousseau.* It was nearly the farthest from her reach. She edged as close to the top of the opening as she could and stretched until the fingers holding her in place cramped and her left shoulder made a faint pop. The middle finger of her right hand touched *Rousseau's* spine.

She stretched further against the strain through her shoulder. With her nail she hooked *Rousseau* by the top of its spine and tugged and coaxed until it budged. She picked at it again until she could grip the spine between her fingers to pull it free. When her trembling left arm threatened to give, she rested *Rousseau* on the lip of the opening while she held on with both hands.

WILL moved fast. It divided his mind to leave her alone for the five promised minutes. Thoughts of Leary and Brick Face and March distracted him. He did not believe March had left London. Helen's desperation was a sign that March was near and getting reckless in his efforts to squeeze money out of those in his power. Whoever Helen meant to save from March was not one of the man's usual pigeons. And Castle's snooping in the neighborhood suggested that Bow Street thought March was guarding something nasty. Will did not like the way the details added up.

He was down the back stairs, through the kitchen, and into the long passageway in under a minute by his count. He would not leave her alone a second longer than his promise required.

All the doors along the passageway had simple sliding bolts at the top and bottom, except the one he'd noted earlier, where the bolts had been secured with a pair of padlocks. He grinned in the dark. Trust an amateur to signal his hiding spot. He slid his skeleton key into first one padlock and then the other and stepped into the deeper darkness of a small storage room. His outstretched hand instantly met a stack of rough crates.

He quieted his mind, concentrating all his senses, while his hands worked to count the crates. The room must have once held small beer and spirits. Stale liquor was the dominant smell and damp and must. Then there was the scent of new-cut wood from the crates themselves and the odor of packing straw. There was more. He waited for his brain to sort the remaining threads of scent under the stronger odors. Beneath the smell of packing straw was another smell he knew well, rifle grease.

He counted a score of crates at least, in rows of four, piled five tall. They filled the room so that he could not get around them. He took the knife from his sleeve and jabbed the point through the end of one slat where it met the corner of the box. He pried the slat loose and reached through straw to find a cold steel rod, the British soldier's best friend. He ran his hand down to the stock, measuring, verifying his suspicion as to the gun's make. Thirty inches, more or less. There could be no doubt. The length, the distinctive groove in the butt marked the weapon as a Baker rifle.

March was selling arms. To whom was the question.

Will's hand shook a little as he pushed the slat back in place. He had been alone with dangerous intelligence before, in Spain, in France, but not in the center of London. Before he'd always known exactly where to take such information. Here, he wondered. What did Castle know? Who planned to use such weapons against whom in the heart of London? Had Castle traced the buyers to March? Questions multiplied in his head even as he covered his trail. He slipped into the passage, closed the door behind him, and fixed the padlocks in place, his movements quick and steady. He had to get Helen out of the place before he could bring in the authorities.

As he reached the top of the stairs, he heard the loud smack of a book hitting the marble floor. *Helen.* Faster than he thought he could move he reached the entrance to the library.

Too late. She clung halfway down the shelves on trembling arms. The sputtering candle from his device cast her shadow on the spines of the books. He glanced at them and saw one book missing from the shelf over the opening to her right. She had taken just the one. Hell, she, too, was an amateur.

"What an ambitious thief," a male voice drawled. March lit the lamp on the desk and stepped into the center of the library, his smooth face plainly illuminated. Will faded back into the darkness of the passage. The inescapable architecture gave him no way around the library to come in behind Helen or March.

"There's nowhere to go, so you'd best come down, boy." March was dressed for the road in a caped greatcoat, hat, and boots. It fit Will's theory that the man was collecting as much blunt as he could before fleeing London.

At least March thought her a boy. For the moment.

When her feet touched the floor, she staggered against the shelves, caught herself, and turned to face March. She stayed out of the beam's direct path, but Will could see the fine tremor running through her. He scanned the floor for the missing book. A slim red volume, it lay openly on the marble tiles under the shelf from which it had fallen. *Had she retrieved her letters?*

She opened her mouth and Nate Wilde's accent came out. "No thief, sir. Jest readin'. Ye've a great library 'ere, sir."

"Ah, but so late to be reading, and so particular about your reading matter, aren't you?" March closed in on her, and his glance slid up the oddly positioned chair and candle stand to Will's dangling beam device. The instant March's glance shifted, Helen moved toward the fallen book. Will's heart lurched madly. *Hell*. She was going to give herself away over those damned papers. The only hope of March letting her go was to pretend the papers didn't matter, and her face plainly said they mattered the world to her.

It was then that March found the gap in his perfect lineup. There was no doubt he knew exactly which volume was missing. Will could read the calculation in his eyes. Another moment and he would solve the puzzle of the thief's identity.

At that moment the candle in Will's device fizzed and guttered and went dark. Helen reacted with a sideways lunge and a kick sending the book hurtling across the slick marble in a whispering glide.

Instinct had Will bending down as soon as her foot connected with the book, arresting its slide in the dark, and scooping it up. He shook it, and a pair of letters on crisp lilac-scented paper fell into his hand. He had palmed them up his sleeve before March reached her and backhanded her across the face, sending her to the floor, leaving Will no good options.

He stepped into the room, as she crumbled under the blow. He held the volume in his outstretched hand, controlling a rage that threatened to blind him. "Evening, March, I see you've met my clumsy apprentice. Were you looking for something to read?" Will placed the book on the edge of the desk, and rested his hand on it. He had March's attention for the moment. Helen picked herself up, her desperate gaze fixed on the slim volume. Her shocked look could not comprehend his betrayal.

The fall had knocked her cap off, but Will had March's attention and meant to keep it.

"Jones. Once again you intrude into a gentleman's private space." March looked him over. "You're no longer on the force, are you? You've no authority, no stick with a golden crown on it. You're just a thief I can have arrested. And transported. Or hung. You and your . . . accomplice."

Will pressed his palm flat on the book. "You might find it inconvenient to bring the police here tonight, March. Bow Street's onto you. They think you're hiding something of interest to the government."

"Jones, you and your brother underestimate my influence on our government."

"I think not, March. We're just curious about the nature of that influence." It was the sort of conversation with a bully that Will had had too often in his life. He was weary of it. If he didn't have to distract March from Helen, he'd end it.

He needed to goad March into moving just enough toward Will that the girl could make a break. But she hadn't moved again. Her whole gaze was on the book under Will's hand. He had deliberately repeated March's name. She knew who they were facing.

"Jones, your sort can't appreciate the charitable works of men like Bredsell and myself."

"March, if you'd stick with philanthropy, I'd gladly

leave you to it. It's murder, blackmail, larceny, and . . . treason . . . that I find so unacceptable."

Treason got March's full attention. Will lifted his palm and shifted the book under his fingers, like a mountebank moving his thimble over the hidden pea, duping the spectators into following the hand motion.

"Jones, you have the most tedious way of interrupting my business and interfering with my plans. Really, it wearies me." March pulled his gaze from the book and crossed to the bell rope.

Will shot Helen a quick glance. *Run*. All he got in return was that outraged look of betrayal.

Somewhere the bell sounded and brought a quick shuffle of feet in the passageway. *Hell*. Leary and Brick Face entered the room, the one all freckled meanness and the other a bloated tub of lard on legs. The lard, however, possessed a lean, mean pistol. He pointed it at Will.

"Time to take my bow, Jones, and make my exit. The London scene no longer suits me. I'll trouble you for that book and be on my way."

The girl stiffened, drawing a look from Leary. Will felt his gut twist. He tapped his fingers on the book. As long as March believed the letters were still in place, she would be safe from him. Will could worry about Leary and Brick Face next. "A rare first edition, is it?"

"Merely a bit of reading for the journey." March nodded to Leary who stepped behind Will and gripped his arms in savage hold.

"I leave it to my household staff to deal with intruders. Whatever his faults, Mr. Leary is an efficient apothecary.

I'm sure that under his care, you need not feel another moment's pain in life."

"Is that how your brother died, March? Doped up and shoved down a flight of stairs?"

"Jones, your years in the gutter are showing. You really have no idea of how to speak to your betters." March picked up the book and dropped it in his greatcoat pocket.

Helen's whole gaze was on that book, and the situation deteriorated when March turned and caught that look.

"On second thought, I'll take your assistant with me as well." In two strides he reached her and seized her by the arm, his expression changing, as he felt the female flesh in his hold.

Will made himself speak lightly. "He's a small fish, March. Just toss him back in the sea and be done with him."

"Insurance, Jones." March looked at her sharply, and Will felt his heart stop.

"Mr. March, ye'll not give me ta the police for tryin' ta read a book, wouldja?" The mimicry was perfect, enough to confuse March.

"Say another word," he told her. "And you'll lose your lying tongue."

"Don't listen to him, Troy. Holler for all you're worth. Trust me." He hoped she understood him.

Chapter Seventeen

❧

I T was the last she heard from him as March hurried
her along through the house. Will Jones wanted her
to cry out, to alert Harding, but if Harding interfered,
March would get away with the book and her mother's
letters. She let him drag her through the garden to a
waiting hack. He yanked the door open and shoved her
up the little step. Just for an instant she braced her arms
on the hood, resisting March's push, looking to signal
Harding to follow.

"Spring 'em," March called to the driver. "Bread
Street."

She saw Harding rise from concealment and start
toward them. March spun and fired a pistol. Her ears
rang as Harding crumpled to the ground. She almost

cried out then, but March grabbed her arm and twisted, forcing her in the hack. It lurched forward, and she collapsed into the narrow seat. March landed beside her. The hack tilted as the driver took a curve.

March seized her chin and twisted her face to his. "Well, miss, let's drop the masquerade, shall we? Of all the young women to land in the bed of one of the Jones bastards, a maiden of your impeccable breeding. But perhaps your blood is not so unblemished after all. Perhaps it is a case of a daughter following in her mother's footsteps."

She spat in his face.

He wiped the spittle from his cheek and drew back his fist.

Helen flung herself back against the side of the cab. March's blow stunned her shoulder while her left cheek collided with the cab frame and split open. She tasted blood.

He yanked her upright. "How very unwise of you. I'm your savior, my dear. Without me, you'd merely be Will Jones' discarded doxie. The scandal would kill your frail mother, I think, and ruin your father. Who would listen to him preach on the moral training of women after his own daughter fell so far from grace?"

Helen said nothing. Under the blood and the sting of her split cheek was a deeper burn, like nettles on the inside of her skin. No doomed, god-tricked Trojan in the walled city had been more deceived by the fates than she had been by Will Jones. Her first mistake in presenting herself at the brothel had been a mere miscalculation of her mind, but trusting Jones had been a colossal blunder of her heart.

She struggled to breathe through a terrible tightness of her chest. March had the book with her mother's letters in his coat pocket. That must be her one thought. She could spare none for her betrayer.

I know you. Vicomte." Leary hissed in Will's ear while Brick Face held the pistol. Brick Face with a pistol was bad. Leary meant to kill Will in time, but Brick Face might do it because his thick finger was too large for the trigger.

"Bien sûr."

"'E's the toff wot stole the girl?" Brick Face's slower brain caught on.

"He is, Noakes."

"Be 'appy to 'urt 'im for ye, Mr. Leary."

Will made no resistance to Leary's wiry hold. He kept his gaze on Brick Face, Noakes, with the gun. At last the idiot put it down on the desk.

"'Old 'im steady now, Mr. Leary."

"Smash his ribs for me, Noakes."

"'Is ribs it is." The big man planted himself in front of Will and grinned. He was still grinning as his big right fist connected with Will's ribs. Wheels of light exploded in his brain. He let his weight go dead in Leary's hold, and against the pain he swung his booted feet up, catching Noakes as he drew his fist back for another go—in the stones.

Noakes folded in half, cupping his testicles, a high keening sound wheezing from him. He staggered, weaving backward, and collapsed. Leary yelled abuse at him, but Noakes didn't rise.

Will knocked his head back against Leary's nose and heard the crack of cartilage. Leary dropped him. Will rolled away from Leary's feet, reaching for the knife in his boot. He pushed to his feet.

Leary leaned against the bookshelves, pressing his sleeve to the flow of blood from his smashed nose, his hands bloodied, madness in his eyes.

The next instant he charged Will, lunging for the knife. His slick hands couldn't grip it, and Will drove him back with a shoulder in his gut to sprawl over the desk, his head hanging over the edge. Will jabbed his blade through the armpit of Leary's waistcoat and shirt and tied Leary's free, blood slick hand to a drawer pull with his neckerchief, pinning him helpless against the desk.

He left Leary roaring for Noakes as he ran through the house, each breath a stab of pain.

He found Harding lying in the lane and dropped to his knees beside the fallen man. At Will's touch Harding opened his eyes and raised his head. "Just a scratch, sir. March took her."

Where? The word stuck in his throat.

"Bread Street."

The school. Will found he could speak again.

"Harding, can you get to Castle? There are more than twenty cases of Baker rifles in March's basement, two angry employees, and no guards."

Harding nodded, and Will was off. He thought he heard Harding call something as he rounded the corner.

KIT looked out across the roof edge to find his lookouts in their places. It was the hour of stillness, the last hour of the night before the carts started rumbling through London streets to the markets. The chill was deep. He gave a birdcall and heard it answered from spot to spot around the school. His band was ready, armed with a plan, their pockets full of rocks. Lark had found a knife of sorts, a rusty item he had pulled from the river mud at low tide in September and not yet used.

Their plan to save Robin had been delayed by the attack on the school. Kit had considered the meaning of that attack carefully. Since it happened there had been laborers about repairing the windows and walls. The rough talk of those men had been of Bredsell's fear and of the thorough destruction of his library. No one believed Bredsell's explanation that a rival street was to blame.

Kit gave the signal. His boots hung around his neck and his tools were in one of the deep pockets of his long velvet coat. He crossed the roof and slid down to the high wall around the school and walked its icy length barefoot to the building's edge, then caught an iron pipe to climb to the roof of the school itself. He ran lightly across to the first of the dormers and tried the window. Locked as he expected. He rapped the glass sharply above the latch, making a crack and reaching through, and turned the latch, to swing the window wide. He dropped down inside and swiftly drew the window closed. His heart pounded briefly, feeling at once the confinement of walls around him and a roof over his head. But he held himself still to listen for any sleeper roused by the breaking glass. Rustles and snufflings and the quiet exhalations of deep sleepers filled the silence.

He knew the layout of the sleeping quarters from Lark's account. The boys slept oldest to youngest, usually two to a bed. Little Robin would be at the end nearest the inner door. Kit made his way by stealth, counting the ends of the beds with a light touch, but the smallest boy he found was a good bit bigger than Robin.

He made his way back to the dormer, stepped on the edge of the nearest bed, and hoisted himself up and out. On the roof again, he gave a signal to the lookouts, heard their calls, and crossed to the second gable.

N ate could not sleep. It must be near day, and his head felt like it held a spinning wire cage with a firedog running and running to turn a spit. Coming back to the school from the brothel had been a mistake. Everything was unsettled. Leary had given Nate no letters and no money to bring back. March and Bredsell were at odds, and it was plain they feared the powerful person who had wrecked the school. Nate realized that March was a hunted man now. He would have to leave London to escape his enemies.

March was the first toff Nate had ever seen close up. His first thought had been—what a fortune a fellow could earn by selling such a rig. A Bread Street family could live high for a year on the clothes off March's back. Yards of white linen, a bottle green silken waistcoat, a fine wool jacket and trousers, a pair of fobs with two glorious watches big as cockles, boots soft as butter, and a signet ring with gold enough to fill all the teeth in a grown man's head. His second thought had been wiser. To wear such riches as Mr. March did so regular and careless proved his boundless wealth. It had seemed to Nate that with March's favor he would soon make his own pockets jingle with coins.

Tonight that memory tasted sour. He could hear instead copper Will Jones warning him not to trust March, not to go back to Bredsell's school.

Tonight he hadn't liked seeing Mr. Coates lock the sleeping room doors. He had an uneasy feeling he would not get out again. Something bad was brewing, and someone, maybe the police, would come and take over the school. Boys who were trapped inside could be sent to the workhouse or worse. He, Nate, would get no birching from the magistrate but a lagging. Transportation. That thought made him shudder so that his bed shook.

Will Jones laughed at transportation like it was a lark, but Nate's stomach lurched at the idea. He could see a big wave rising and behind it another and another. To cross thousands of miles of ocean, to see no land for days, to toss and heave on those great rolling waves, he who didn't swim could think of nothing worse. It made his heart pound so hard he almost missed the crack of the glass.

He froze, listening, and felt a stir of icy air, and the click of the window closing. He opened one eye a slit, but saw nothing. Then he heard a slight stir at the end of the room for the smaller boys. He shifted to his side so he could get a better look. A tall shadow stood over one of the beds.

"Boy!" Nate heard pure joy in the quiet exclamation. The little one leapt for the tall, slim figure in the black cloak.

The figure held still, enduring a fierce hug. "Come, Robin, we've got to get you out of here."

Out of here. The words crystallized in Nate's mind. If they were leaving, so was he. He kept his eyes half closed to view their movements.

The tall boy stood by while Robin pulled on his breeches, jacket, and cap. The younger boy's shoes disappeared into the pockets of the long flowing coat of the stranger.

The tall figure strode to the door, sprung its lock, listened, then stepped out onto the landing at the top of the great stairs. Dim light from a lamp left burning there revealed him to Nate, and he knew for sure that this was the lost boy for whom they all searched, the boy March wanted dead. He was going to walk right down the stairs and . . .

Nate was up and in his clothes in a flash. If anyone was getting out of Bredsell's school, Nate Wilde was.

KIT led Robin down the wide, dark wooden stair that circled the center of the sleeping school. Only an occasional sconce lit the way. They went cautiously, alert for early risers. The plan depended on timing. Once carts started rumbling by on the street outside, any sound of their breaking out could be covered.

At the top of the last flight of stairs Kit halted to scout the situation. A landing with a balustrade ran around three sides of the entry below, and on the fourth side a pair of half flights descended to meet at a landing and join in a wide stair to the tiled entry below. Directly opposite the foot of the wide stair was the door to the outside.

But light poured from the open doors of a room off the entry, and from inside came the sound of someone in hasty motion. Kit could hear drawers opening and closing, a man muttering and rustling papers. Kit and Robin would have to pass directly in front of that open door to reach the main entrance. The only other ground-floor door led into the walled yard.

Kit would like to know whether that main door was locked. An unlocked door would give them the time they needed to escape. They could count on the preoccupation of the busy person in the lighted room, but if the door was locked and they were spotted, a shout would bring the masters down on them trapped there.

He sat Robin down in the shadows of the rail to put on the boy's shoes and his own boots while he considered how best to handle the problem of the door. He might send Robin alone. If the boy were discovered, he would rouse no alarm of an intruder, but if Robin were caught and they did not escape, the boy would be harshly punished. As he weighed his strategy, the great door rattled from the outside and burst open.

A tall lad staggered in followed by a gentleman in traveling attire, holding a gun. Kit instinctively drew back. The tall boy stumbled and fell and rose slowly. His cheek bled from an open gash. When he lifted his head, Kit could see that the lad wasn't a boy at all. At his side Robin started.

"Troy!" The cry came from Robin before Kit could stop it. "Boy came. Boy's 'ere." The little boy waved at the wounded girl.

She and the gentleman with the pistol both looked up, and the gentleman leveled his gun at Kit. He bellowed, "Bredsell!"

"Go back, Robin," the girl shouted.

The man in the greatcoat shoved her to her knees. Robin was in motion as Kit's hand shot out, too late to catch the boy.

"Robin, stay back," the girl cried again.

The gentleman kicked her violently.

A man in clerical dress came rushing from the lighted room. "March, what is this?" He glanced down at the girl. "Who have you got?" The clerical man stopped when he saw the gun and took a step back. "Are you mad? You're on your way to the continent."

The gentleman held the girl down with his boot. "Calm yourself, Bredsell. Look what I've found." He gestured with the pistol at Kit and Robin on the stairs.

As he spoke, a long-closed door in Kit's memory opened. *March*, he knew the name, and he knew the voice. He had heard that voice speaking to his abductor, Harris. *The boy disappears—you understand, Harris? Aye, Mr. March.* Those were the words. How many nights had he puzzled over the mystery in those words? Why had he been chosen to disappear? Who was the man who ordered it so? Now he was face-to-face with the man who had stolen his life, a man he didn't know. Hatred and puzzlement trapped him equally in the moment.

Caution held him, too, caution he had learned in a hard school. They could flee. They could be up the stairs and out the dormer before either March or the one called Bredsell could catch them. Kit could escape over the roof, but not with Robin. Robin couldn't walk that wall. Robin clung to the railing, his small body inclined full tilt toward the girl.

"Good lord," Bredsell said, looking at Kit. "Is that him? Wenlocke's grandson?"

Chapter Eighteen

❧

H ELEN knelt, praying with her whole being for the two
boys to vanish up the wide stair, but neither moved.

"One shot, Bredsell, and I earn His Grace's undying
gratitude."

Bredsell looked from the boy to March. "Are you
mad? You can't shoot Wenlocke's grandson here."

"Ring for Coates and Syme. I want them outside with
weapons." March smiled. He reeked of satisfaction. It
came off him in hot waves. "I have such evidence of His
Grace's gratitude for my work on his behalf that he can
never act against me. Move, Bredsell."

As Bredsell grabbed the bell rope, the boy in the
ragged velvet coat whistled to Robin, but Robin only
cast a helpless glance at Helen and slipped further down

along the banister to the landing where the two wings of stairs joined. The little boy stood with his hand on the newel post, his red cheeks bright.

The distant bell jingled. The older boy—he must be Kit Jones—could easily escape, but she saw that he wouldn't. His face, in torment at the trap, said he wouldn't leave Robin. He remained fixed at the top of the stairs, his gaze on March and the gun.

The little boy took another step down. A whisper of the velvet coat made him check and turn. Then from above the boys two large men closed in from either side.

Kit Jones vaulted with light grace over the railing and dropped to the floor below. It was a move so like his brother's that Helen felt her heart lurch.

Bredsell squeaked. March took an involuntary step back.

One of the two brutes scooped up Robin and carried the boy down the stairs to drop him at Helen's feet. She pushed herself up and gathered the little one to her.

Two vehicles parked at the top of Bread Street gave Will a moment of relief so profound he leaned his hand against the foul bricks of the wall beside him. A hack driver wiped down his heated horse, and a large traveling coach stood in the road in front of the school. March had not left London with Helen. Will could get her back.

The coachman and a guard warmed themselves, exchanging swigs from a flask. Two brutes wearing coats over their nightshirts barred the main door of the school.

Each man carried a pistol, not a fine dueling pistol, just a blunt instrument for blowing a hole in a man. March did know how to find muscle, Will would give him that.

He kept to the shadows and moved closer. Slipping into a narrow court, he collided with a small body that produced a snarl and the quick slash of a blade across Will's forearm. Will subdued the writhing boy in a ruthless hold. His prisoner gave a bird's cry, and a chorus of answering calls came from dark corners nearby.

He let the boy feel the strength of his grip. "You're one of Kit's boys. Where is he?"

There was no answer, just the shallow, panicked breathing of a trapped creature. But Will could piece it together.

"He's in the bleeding school, isn't he? He went to get one of your mates. He went to get Robin. Who else is in there?"

Will waited until the boy's breathing calmed. He knew better than to relax his hold, until the boy was thinking again. He cracked as Will's patience reached the breaking point.

"'Oo're yew?"

"His brother. Can you and your mates get me inside?"

HELEN tried to think. She was standing with Robin clinging to her legs. Bredsell had a pistol, but he shook so that she feared the weapon would fire any moment. She and the quaking Bredsell probably wanted the same thing—for March to leave without killing anyone, but Bredsell seemed incapable of stopping March.

March's gaze focused on the boy who had dropped from above. "Another Jones. You should be dead, you know."

The boy's stark lean face showed no fear. "Let Robin and the girl go."

"You absurd whelp." March gestured with his gun. "You have no say here."

"Take me with you, not them."

"March, you can't kill children here." Bredsell's voice was a dry croak.

"Bredsell, calm yourself. The girl goes with me. She offers a neat solution to some pressing difficulties. Once you marry us, her family will come down handsomely, and her company will draw less attention to my journey. I will merely be a gentleman taking his young bride abroad."

Bredsell stared at March as if he were mad. "March, you're not making sense. A forced marriage?"

"Oh, she's quite willing to marry me, Bredsell. In exchange for my silence about someone near and dear to her."

"But you've no license."

"Bredsell, I begin to think you are impatient for my departure. Are my trunks ready? Did you pack everything as I asked?"

"Your trunks are in the library. I was just finishing when you arrived. Let me take care of it."

"No, I will. Keep your gun steady, Bredsell."

As soon as March left the room, Kit Jones began

to move. He circled to his right toward the foot of the stairs. Bredsell swung his gun arm to follow the boy. "Stop now."

Helen could see that the boy's movement made it impossible for Bredsell to cover them both. She took Robin's hand and tugged the little one toward the front door. Bredsell's gaze shifted uneasily between the moving boy and Helen and the child.

WILL came through one of the attic sleeping rooms and sent the boy Lark through the other. He roused all the sleepers in his path. It was time to declare a school holiday. He told them to follow him and they'd be free. He and Lark led their ragged troops down the stairs. The waking boys shuffled along, murmuring through chattering teeth as they came, a distraction Will hoped would soon be heard below.

He reached the level above the entry hall when the sound of a door opening made him spin, his knife in hand, but he checked himself as Nate Wilde emerged from a closet with a grin on his lips. He came to stand beside Will.

Will studied the scene below, not liking what he saw. Bredsell's unsteady hands held a gun loosely. The barrel wavered like a fish squirming up current. One minute it threatened Helen and a small red-cheeked boy who clung together near the door, the next, it pointed at Kit. He didn't see March.

Will spoke quietly to Wilde, outlining the plan forming in his head. Wilde nodded.

With a boy from Kit's gang stationed at each pillar, Will signaled Nate Wilde to let the shivering urchins go. Bredsell certainly didn't waste his donors' money on heating the place. Boys surged down the stairs until they filled the two wings leading to the last landing, the babble of their voices and the pounding of their feet on the stairs rumbled down the open stairway.

Bredsell looked up and shouted, "You boys, go back to bed, all of you. Master Coates will whip you soundly. Go."

Still the boys pushed forward, waifs in dingy night-shirts and worn jackets, carried along like a dirty froth on the Thames. Below Will, Kit shifted nearer to Bredsell's side. Bredsell backed away, his gun swinging wildly. "March," he yelled.

March strode out into the entry, with a pistol and a black book in hand.

"Run, boys," Will hollered. The dash began, the boys fanning out in a mob intent on the door, Nate Wilde swept along in the rush.

Bredsell backed against the wall. Helen whirled the little one to the side as the flow of boys filled the entry, jostling each other for the door. March angled toward Helen, yelling for Coates and Syme.

The door swung open as the first boys reached it. They swarmed out. The two masters, caught in the rush, grabbed at collars and swung pistols at small heads. Shrieks and howls erupted. Kit's band answered from above with a volley of rocks, driving Coates and Syme back. The two masters struggled to close the door.

"Let them go," March yelled. "Mind the girl. Don't let the girl escape."

"Morning, March," Will called from the wide stair.

March spun. "Jones!"

Everyone froze except the last of the fleeing boys. Four guns were now aimed mainly at Will. And to think he'd objected to Noakes with one pistol.

"Unexpected of me to call, I know." Will caught the girl's grateful gaze. At least he thought for a moment gratefulness had flashed in those dark eyes. He would have to explain about her letters once pistols weren't pointing at him.

"Morning, sweetheart." He kept moving down the stairs.

March signaled to one of his brutes to grab Helen. The fellow tried to dislodge the small child clinging to her and couldn't. Will knew how the boy felt. He didn't mean to let her go, either, once he got her back.

"Jones, come closer, and your brother dies."

Will stopped and turned to Kit and grinned. "Hello, Brother. Good to see you. You must be wondering why this maw worm keeps trying to kill you."

"Jones, we're about to have a wedding here. I'm going to make an honest woman of this poor girl you've deflowered."

"Are you?" He met Helen's shocked gaze. It was foolish, but he grinned. He was that glad to see her. "He's won your love with those letters, has he, sweetheart?" Will shook his head. "I'd ask to see the letters first before you repeat any vows."

March jerked as if stung. He dropped the black book in his hand, fished in his greatcoat pocket, and brought up the red volume from Half Moon Street. He held it by the spine and shook its leaves. Nothing fluttered loose.

The instant his disbelieving glance shifted, Will threw his knife. It caught Coates in the pistol arm. The big man screamed and released Helen. Will lunged for the banister, rolling over it and dropping as Syme fired. The bullet caught him high on the right side, and he landed awkwardly.

When he turned, March had his pistol aimed at Helen and the child.

The first hint of dizziness fluttered behind his eyes. He fought it. He just needed another moment of consciousness to finish March. He took a careful, deliberate step forward.

In that moment Kit seized Bredsell's wavering hand in both of his. He swung the gun toward March, and squeezed Bredsell's fingers closed over the trigger. The shot hit March full in the chest, and the kick sent Kit and a squealing Bredsell sprawling.

"Well done, Brother," Will managed as the floor came up to meet him.

Helen watched the blooming look of surprise on March's face, and then his hand fell, and his body crumpled. His head hit the floor with a heavy thud.

Bredsell flung the gun away from him and it clanged against the tiles.

Helen rushed to Will and skidded to a stop on her knees. He lay stretched on his side, his hand extended toward his brother. She rolled him gently to his back and leaned over him, kissing him frantically on the mouth, the cheek, the eyes. His eyelids fluttered open.

"Sweetheart, got your letters."

"Where are you hurt?"

"Ribs. Tell my brother he's not a bastard. Tell him, he's the bleeding Marquess of Daventry." His eyes drifted closed again, and Helen tore at his waistcoat, popping its buttons. The shirt under his right arm was soaked with blood. She pulled it free of his trousers. His ribs were a livid purplish blue, and a hole high on the side of his chest oozed blood.

She took his hand in hers. His was bloody. She tried to tear his sleeve open and couldn't. And then Kit was kneeling beside her with a rusty knife, slitting open the sleeve of coat and shirt.

Helen peeled back the edges of the fabric and found a gash on his forearm and a bloody furrow along the white flesh of his underarm. She tore off the tail of her shirt to bind his wound. When she lifted the arm gently to wrap the cloth around the wound, she found, caught in the cuff of the shredded sleeve, two bloodstained letters on lilac-scented pressed paper.

Her mother's letters. She lifted them gently.

Oh, my love, if I've killed you for those letters.

She bent her head and pressed her lips to his open palm. She loved him. Oh, dear lord, she loved the devil, the surly madman who leapt into danger. It hurt with an ache that momentarily stopped her breath.

No tears. "Helen never weeps," she heard herself telling him. She kissed his still lips, and he breathed.

The closing of a door made her look up. Coates and Syme were gone, and Bredsell had risen to his feet and was edging his way toward the door. "Stop him," she yelled. "Don't let him take that coach. We need it."

At her cry, the boys in Kit's band hurled more stones and drove Bredsell back into his library. She heard him bolt the door.

Ragged and panting, the boys came pounding down the stairs. They looked ready to bolt.

"Troy?" came a voice. "Oi can 'elp yew."

"Nate Wilde." He was standing inside the door. She smiled idiotically at him. "Of course. Get that coach ready to take Will. We must get him to his place."

He grinned back at her, all his strong white teeth gleaming. "Done, Troy."

She turned to the boy kneeling beside her. His stark face was unreadable. "He needs Xander."

"I'll get him," he said.

He rose from the floor and crossed the room, bending over March's body. He coolly turned the dead man over and reached into his coat, searching until he found a leather purse. He opened it, and took a handful of notes.

He turned then and tossed the purse to the boy who seemed to be his second in command. The boy's hand shot out, and he caught the purse. Kit looked at his band until he had them all looking back. "Stay with my brother," he told them. "Don't leave him." He turned to the tallest. "Lark, keep them together, mind. And do whatever she says."

Lark nodded.

Chapter Nineteen

ॐ

O UTSIDE the school Kit found Nate Wilde convinc-
ing the coachman to make room for Will. Carts
had begun to fill the street. Kit trotted along the thor-
oughfare until he found a hack. He showed the driver his
wad of bills and told him, "Half now, half when you get
me to Hill Street mews."

He could not judge how long the journey took, an hour
or a few minutes. He had not ridden inside a vehicle in
four years, odd to be rocking along closed in, the noise
of horse and wheels cutting him off from the sounds of
the city itself.

In the mews the driver accepted the rest of the money
and drove off. Kit scaled the garden wall and dropped
down outside the kitchen. He had come to this garden

dozens of times, but had always stayed on the outside looking in.

Mrs. Wardlow turned at the sound of the kitchen door, saw him, and dropped the pot of oatmeal in her bony hand. It smashed against the slate and splattered hot, steaming oats everywhere.

"Master Kit, lad, we've wanted ye home so." She wiped her hands on her splattered apron, tears streaming down her face.

"Mrs. Wardlow," he said, "I've come because Will needs Xan. Will needs a doctor. Straight away, ma'am."

She looked uncomprehending, but she said, "I'll get Amos." She started off in a swish of skirts but huffed right back. "Now, see here, young man, don't you leave this room. We'll get a doctor, but . . ."

Kit sat.

". . . Your mother, dear lord, your mother must know."

He nodded.

He heard Mrs. Wardlow shouting for Amos. He rested his elbows on the table then and tried to hold back the tide of memory washing over him, like the Thames at ebb, sweeping everything in its rush. In this, his mother's house, the sleeves of his worn coat, which smelled of London itself, of soot and stone, and river and tide, reeked. He felt the self he'd become, the tough self he had forged to survive, in danger of being shaken loose like a bit of drift on the shore and washed away. He fought to hold on.

He had only the warning of a light swift footfall on the stairs, and she was there. He stood to meet her, his beautiful mother, a swirl of silk and spice, her black hair, her great dark eyes. A sob caught her and stopped her.

He remembered. She had been teaching him to dance, but he had wanted to learn to box. They'd quarreled, and Xander had taken him to see the champion box in that exhibition match.

"I'm sorry, Mamma," he said.

She did not move, did not take him in her arms yet, just stood and wept and wept, smiling absurdly through the tears.

One thing he had forgotten was how a houseful of servants could make things happen. Isaiah showed up to say the carriage was ready. Amos came next to say that Xander had been alerted and was headed for Will's rooms with a doctor.

Kit offered his mother his hand. Where had he remembered how it was done? No matter. He had and she accepted. Mrs. Wardlow threw her own cloak over Sophie, and Isaiah led them to the waiting carriage.

S OPHIE Rhys-Jones knelt at the side of Will's bed with her forehead pressed to his slack hand. Helen stood behind his brothers and the physician, his sleeves rolled up, his instruments and basin now bloodied. The crisp edge of her mother's letters, where she had tucked them into the linen around her chest, made a sharp point against her breast.

The doctor finished his work. The bustle hushed around the great sultan's bed. Will Jones's family, whose love he had doubted, had come to him. He would wake, in time, surrounded by the goodness in which he needed to believe. Maybe she had betrayed him by bringing them all into his hidden rooms, but it seemed that now his long exile would end. All the lost boys had been recovered. Even Nate Wilde had watched anxiously as the doctor worked on his patient.

Only Cleo Jones was missing, and her absence at Will's bedside gave Helen an idea. She slipped away under the guise of speaking to a footman waiting outside to take the news of Will's condition to Cleo. It was time to stick to her mission, and return with the letters to her own mother. If Sophie Rhys-Jones, with the support of her sons and would-be lover, felt such solicitude over a son, how much more troubled must Helen's own mother be, helpless to save herself, and enduring weeks of uncertainty without the least word of her only daughter's well being. Helen could return now to her father's house and embrace her mother and laugh to hear her father say, *Frailty thy name is woman*. What did he know of women? Nothing.

In a minute she was down the stairs and past Blind Zebediah's sleeping mastiff. A few twisting blocks away in the Strand, she found a hack driver looking for an early morning fare. She did not look back to see the youth following her and never caught the flash of his toothy grin as he mounted a cart heading west behind the hack.

Chapter Twenty

WILL woke alone in his grand bed from a vivid dream of Helen arching under him, her lips parted in passion. His body came back to him on a tide of pain. He groaned.

"Yer awyke, are ye?"

The voice didn't belong in his room, and he thought he had imagined it. "Wilde?"

"Aye."

Will lifted his head. The boy sat by the fire in one of the room's ancient nail-studded armchairs, his feet on the fender. He grinned at Will. "Oi'm going to let ye reform me, copper."

"Since when?" Will pushed himself upright cautiously, testing for specific injuries. One by one they made themselves known—his arm, his chest, his ribs. His whole body felt disappointed, empty, beyond the specific sources of pain. He ran a hand over his face, rough with beard. Three days maybe. His mouth tasted dry and medicinal. Someone had given him a foul potion to drink.

Wilde swung his feet to the floor and crossed the room to peer at Will. "Since March croaked."

A chaotic jumble of scenes tumbled through Will's mind at the words. March pointing a gun at Helen. Bredsell pointing a gun at Kit. Boys running and tumbling down a wide stair. Himself . . . He could only go so far in reconstructing the scene before he encountered blankness and blackness. A single question consumed him, but he wouldn't utter it before the boy.

"Ye want cawfy?" At Will's nod Wilde turned away.

"Trying to take Harding's place, Wilde?" It was unlike Harding not to hover when Will had an injury, so where was the man? He had been shot by March, but surely a tough old soldier like Harding had survived.

Wilde came back with a tray and a cup of dark brew. "Oi like yer place. It's a good setup. Ye can get in and out a dozen ways."

Will accepted the tray and put it on the bed beside him. He took up the cup. "You've made yourself at home, apparently, you limb of Satan."

"Try the cawfy."

Will took a swallow. It was more than drinkable. "You made this?"

"'Arding is teachin' me. Ye want yer shavin' gear?"

Wilde crossed to the cabinet beside Will's great copper tub.

"What! Are you my valet now?"

Wilde shrugged. "More like a 'prentice."

"The devil's apprentice then." Will fell back against the pillows. "What do you want to learn from me?"

"Policin'."

That stopped him. He swallowed more coffee. At least the boy hadn't robbed him and taken off. That was remarkable in itself. "Where is Harding?"

"'E's 'elping at your mother's 'ouse."

"You've made yourself very familiar with the details of my life."

"It's them boys. They all went with yer brother to yer mother's 'ouse. Needed someone to 'elp 'em stay in line."

More fragments of the lost episode came back to him.

"Kit decided to come home?"

Wilde nodded.

Sophie must be happy. He could imagine her joy. Imagining it made him shake all over. He had to put the coffee cup down and concentrate on subduing the tremors that shook him.

"That's likely the fever. It'll pass. Yer brothers'll come soon. They come every day, waitin' for ye to wyke up."

"They both come?"

Wilde nodded again.

"And Troy? Helen?"

"Gone." The boy didn't hesitate, but his face concealed

some part of the truth. "There was a crowd 'ere when we brought ye back from the school."

"A crowd?"

"Yer brothers, Troy, 'Arding, me and yer brother's gang, the sawbones, yer mother."

"You exaggerate, Wilde."

"'Onest truth."

"My mother, here?"

"Oi swear."

Two days passed before Will felt strong enough to feel both restless and surly. He woke each morning to Helen's absence. She had disappeared without a trace into her other life. It was as if he had dreamed her. It was as it should be. He was sure they had made no babe. She might have to explain herself to a husband eventually, but there would be a husband to free her from whatever constraint she lived under. At least he hoped there would be. He hoped she would find . . . what? What was that elusive thing she was supposed to find with someone who was not him?

He was growing used to Wilde's cheeky watchfulness. Not much escaped the boy's notice. They had spent hours in Will's inner office, while he was mostly confined to a chair, talking about each of the maps on the walls. The boy had a wealth of street-level information, some of which he shared readily. Will made him add names and places to his map of London's criminal underworld. And they laughed over those questions that made Wilde shake his head and say that he couldn't nark.

Wilde didn't appear to have a family of his own, like

Harding. He didn't explain, and Will didn't ask. He recognized the pattern of connection men made with their fellows when cut off from any family.

Will's brothers interrupted one afternoon. On this visit Kit said almost nothing. He had submitted to a haircut and some new clothes, but he still wore the long black velvet coat he'd come by from some masquerade warehouse. Will understood. Disguise became familiar, comfortable, safe. To go back to being who one truly was, to the inescapable realities of birth and family, it was a difficult waking. Kit would not find it easy to go from who he was in the streets to this other person he was supposed to be, the Marquess of Daventry. Still Kit and Xander seemed to understand each other, and on one point the brothers were united—Will should visit Sophie. Still he put off the visit.

Gradually, he rebuilt a picture in his mind of the confrontation with March. He could now recall the sequence of events leading to unconsciousness. Once he had that clear he found himself perplexed by questions. How had he gone from lying bleeding in the school to waking up days later in his own bed? One question dominated the others.

Wilde, sitting at the table, spread mustard on a beef pie.

"Wilde, tell me again why I'm keeping you here?"

The boy looked up from the crumbling pie in his hand, a quick answer on his lips. He caught Will's face and sobered. He put down the pie and wiped the mustard from his fingers on a napkin. They had been working on such niceties. "Because oi know things ye'll be wantin' ta know."

"Like?"

"Where she is."

It stunned him. The tremors threatened, and he ruthlessly subdued them.

"Ye don't want to see her now." Wilde shook his head solemnly.

"That was never the plan." He would not interfere in her life again. She had succeeded in her mission, as he had in his. And there an end.

Wilde shrugged and picked up his pie again. "Smart. Ye look like a rat the cat's killed and dropped on the kitchen doorstep."

"Cheeky whelp. I just want to know she's safe."

Wilde nodded, tight-lipped. "She's safe." He bit into the pie.

And Will discovered that was not what he wanted after all. *Safe*. It hardly seemed the right state of being for Helen of Troy. *Safe* was not free, not happy, not vibrantly alive. He had a feeling safe was dull, constrained, a half-life.

It made him impatient. He decided to visit his mother after all. "Wilde, I'm going out."

"Out?" The boy put the pie down again.

"To my mother's."

"Oh."

"Come, meet them."

"They don't like me there. Oi spied on your brother and his wife."

"You bleeding tried to get Cleo kidnapped."

Wilde shrugged. He seemed incapable of regretting his past life. "Let me 'elp ye ta get rigged out."

"Just heat my shaving water, whelp."

WILL did not recognize his mother's drawing room. Cleared of gilt and velvet in favor of oak and chintz, the room looked warm and welcoming. There wasn't a tassel anywhere. Chairs, sofas, and tables had a sturdy worn look, and boys were playing games everywhere—spillikins, chess, and a game of tossing beanbags. Harding and Major Montclare each led a group of boys in a game.

Harding crossed the room and shook Will's hand.

His mother was in the middle of it all, laughing. She wasn't wearing black or silk, but a vivid blue kerseymere. Sophie plain, Sophie laughing? When had he last seen that? Major Montclare seemed to be holding up in the face of it, but Will knew what heady stuff such laughter was. The woman a man loved, with laughter bubbling up inside her, was irresistible. Will wondered if Xander had asked the major his intentions regarding their mother, though those intentions looked fairly clear.

Sophie came to him at once and took him in her embrace. She clung as she always did, but her embrace, too, had changed. He decided she was giving, not taking. She stepped back to look up at him and nodded her approval. "You're mending, aren't you? I needed to see it for myself, as reliable as Xan and Kit are. Still a bit thin, I'd say."

"You've transformed the place."

She nodded. "I think they were afraid to move among the old things. They don't feel at home, quite yet, but the older furniture helps. And thank you for lending us Harding."

"Of course." *He had lent them Harding?* He wondered if he should step out into the street to check the house number. "Have you adopted them?"

"Temporarily. They loathe baths and shoes, but love Mrs. Wardlow. Kit will say what becomes of them I think. They have quite a way of working things out among themselves, but he is their leader."

"Is he happy?"

A quick rueful look passed over her face. "It is far too soon for that. He's content, I think. In time he may learn to be happy. And I have you to thank for his return."

"Me?" The sequence of events he now remembered did not seem to him to rest on his shoulders.

She looked at him then, and he tried to figure out what had changed. It was an honest look that didn't seek to persuade him. Sophie had just told him something she believed sincerely. He thought he needed to sit down.

"I'm so glad you've come. All my sons under my roof together." As she spoke, her eyes turned bright with tears. The boys noticed instantly and stopped their games, and Major Montclare crossed to her to offer his handkerchief. Will laughed. His mother's beauty still retained its astonishing power to stop all functioning of a male brain. At once she was back to laughing at herself and urging everyone to continue their games.

Over a dinner of beef pies and porter, an unexpected menu, Xander surprised him again with an offer. "Wellington wants you to meet someone."

"You move in exalted circles these days, don't you, Xan?"

"He came to me when he heard about your recent action."

Will pushed the food about on his plate. He wasn't hungry, and he was puzzled as to how old Hookey could have heard about anything Will had done.

"The government is very grateful to you for uncovering that cache of guns in March's basement. Castle did some explaining direct to Wellington, as I understand it."

Will didn't look at his brother. "Who is this person Wellington wants me to meet?"

"Peel. He's just returned from an administrative post in Ireland, and he's got an idea for a metropolitan police force."

"He wants to do away with the Runners?"

"I think rather that the Runners have sparked his thinking about an expanded force with more effective methods. It strikes me as a good sign that they want to talk to you about the idea."

"Trying to save the devil, Xan?"

"Just a Londoner doing my civic duty. With new lighting and an effective police force, London might be a great world city yet."

Will cast a glance at Kit. "You've seen the city at its darkest; what do you think about a new police force?"

Kit put down his fork in his serious way. He had a

look about him as if he were a visitor from Asia or the Indies puzzled by the strange customs of Londoners. But at the moment his look was dead earnest. "Change the law first. Stop sending children to prison for stealing bread. Then the police might be of real use."

"Get Xan to run for Parliament, then." Will offered the suggestion lightly. Kit was someone else, this brother of theirs, who had been lost and now was found. It would take time to get to know him. Will found he liked the idea. He could see that Xander and Kit had worked out an understanding between them.

"Will you meet Wellington then?"

"When?" He didn't know. He felt no hurry to take up his life again.

"You're joking. Wellington would find yesterday convenient."

"I work best alone."

THE Duke of Wenlocke's right leg was giving him trouble. It put him out of sorts and tested his nephew Aubrey's patience. Wenlocke preferred to stand, his towering height undiminished in spite of his eighty years. While the duke stood, men of lesser rank and stature could not sit in his presence. The fierce brow and hooded eyes retained the energy that had made Wenlocke a formidable opponent in any contest of will or power for over fifty years, but the uncompromising face was deeply lined.

And now the duke's leg had a give in it at unexpected

moments that had obliged Wenlocke to sit through a meeting between his solicitor and the solicitor of Sir Alexander Jones. Aubrey saw that the experience had goaded his uncle into an unreasoning state of fury.

Aubrey considered it his best interest to restore the duke's customary coolness and wiliness. It would not do to have Wenlocke commit an actual murder. To have his uncle tried in the Lords for murdering his grandson would hardly serve Aubrey, his rightful heir.

"The whelp lives on apparently, Uncle." Aubrey made light of it. He poured a glass of good Madeira and brought it to the duke. No refreshments had been offered to the lawyer for the bastards' side, and his uncle must be in need of a drink.

"They've produced a youth at any rate." Wenlocke propped the offending leg on a kilim-covered ottoman.

"Who's to say he's not some pretender? Have they any proofs of this gutter rat's origins?"

"I'm to believe there is an army of credible witnesses."

"Really?" An unalarmed tone was best, Aubrey thought. He took a chair and leaned back in it, so that the duke looked slightly down at him. Aubrey knew that in part he owed his uncle's favor to his own significant stature and his reputation as a bruising rider. The duke had only contempt for men of inferior bodily strength.

"Cooks, footmen, schoolmates, a tutor."

"Ah, the sort of witnesses one can buy, and cheaper by the dozen, I suspect."

"This lawyer, Norwood, claims they have the marriage lines and baptismal records, as well."

Aubrey frowned. It was unlike his uncle to let the other side have any hope of success. Maybe the old man's mind was giving out as well as his leg. "You've checked church records and arranged to have any inconvenient entries removed from the books, I trust, Uncle."

"Had all the churches in London searched four years ago."

"And?"

"Nothing turned up." Wenlocke stared glumly at his wineglass without drinking.

Aubrey took a drink of his own wine. "That rather helps your case, doesn't it? If the 'whore of Hill Street' has no record of her marriage to your son, what claim can she make?"

"Damn her, she dares to wear widow's weeds."

"Black bombazine is not an argument in a court, however, Uncle."

"Do we go to court, then, Aubrey?"

Aubrey lifted his glass again, regarding his uncle carefully. The question could be a ruse to lead him to tip his own hand. He did not think Wenlocke ever felt a doubt, or shared one. Or it could be an unexpected opening, a chance to influence his fortune for once. "Uncle, I doubt you can lose in court. Your influence there is boundless. You can tie this upstart down for years. I doubt he has the money to keep a case going for long."

"And if we need a resolution of the issue sooner than years from now?" The duke gave him a piercing look.

Aubrey shrugged. He found in the sharpness of that

gaze that perhaps his uncle's state of unreason had passed. "Buy a decision if you want it done quickly."

Wenlocke rose, the leg quite steady under him. "If she dares to call herself Lady Daventry, I'll have her killed."

I T was a week before Will returned to Sophie's house. He took Wilde shopping, transforming the boy into quite a young pink of fashion. Wilde's own natural flair influenced his choice of waistcoat and the style of his neckcloth. But no gentility of dress could hide the cockiness of the boy's stride or his grin. As soon as he opened his mouth, he was an East End tough. The trouble was Will could not hear that cheeky voice without also hearing another voice mimic the accent.

The shopping had been a reward for Wilde's being willing to put his substantial stash in Evershot's Bank. The boy had not been entirely convinced of the greater safety of a financial institution over a sack in the crypt at St. Clement Danes. They talked endlessly about the future of police work in London. Wilde liked the idea of method in the work. Will's system of mapping crime appealed to him, and together they were making a list of the principles of good policing. There were hours, too, of testimony, answering questions about March and Bredsell and preparing for Bredsell's trial.

When Will did return to Hill Street, he found his mother's household in disarray.

"Good you could come, sir." Amos's long face looked bleak.

Will showed himself up to the drawing room. The place appeared to have been sacked by an army of dwarves, who had wrecked havoc on everything below the wainscot. Abandoned beanbags and spillikins, chess pieces, and blocks lay strewn across the floor. Chairs were scattered and overturned. And a trail of discarded shoes and stockings led from the center of the room to the stairs.

Sophie lay collapsed on a sofa, wracked with sobs. Her major stood behind her couch, murmuring her name, his fists closing and opening helplessly, constrained by his absurd honor from touching her.

Xander sat at the desk, reading a bundle of papers.

"What's going on?" Will asked.

"Kit has decided to leave. He's called his band together to tell them." Xan was grim-faced.

"You're as bad as that honorable nodcock, Xan." Will nodded at the major. "It's not your fault."

"It is." Will knew that grim look of self-blame. "I explained Kit's inheritance to him this morning, and told him Norwood is bringing a motion in chancery to get his legitimacy confirmed. He didn't like the idea."

"You spooked him, I imagine."

"Here, read these." Xan shoved the papers Will's way.

"What are they?"

"Daventry's letters to Kit from India. I'm hoping that getting him to read them will change his mind."

"Hell." Will took the letters, righted a chair, and sank

into it. Just what he needed—the maudlin outpourings of the heroic young father-to-be, now dead, to the son he dreamed of meeting in some happier time.

Xan glanced back at Will from the door. "Will you talk to Kit?"

"Me? You think I can influence him?"

"Will you talk to him *with me*?"

Will nodded. Xander strode off.

Halfway through the first letter, Will looked up at the major. "Montclare, make yourself useful, man. Sit on the bleeding couch and put your arm around her."

Montclare's expression wavered briefly between stiff offense and grateful relief. Then he came around the sofa, scooped Sophie up in his arms and began stroking her back, murmuring endearments to her in soothing French.

Will turned to his reading. At least Daventry's style was less flowery than Montclare's. The man was fairly plainspoken and direct and not without a sense of humor. He would have been good for Sophie had he lived.

Abruptly Will came across a passage that shook him. He put the letter aside, surprised at his reaction. It was a full minute before he could take it up again.

My own father is not a fatherly man. And you, perhaps, will never know him. But he will not be my model for our relations. You can rather expect me to be your disinterested friend, to encourage your studies and your interests, and to recognize and respect your nature whatever sort of person you prove to be.

He folded up the last of the six letters as Xander came into the room.

"We're meeting in the breakfast room."

Kit stood at the window, looking out on the street, his black velvet coat loose on his thin shoulders. Will recognized the shabby garment's source, some costume warehouse off Holywell Street. He favored the area himself for fashions that let an officer of the law pass unnoticed among the disreputable denizens of London's hard districts.

He lay the bundle of letters on the table.

Kit spoke to the window, apparently in answer to some question Xander had asked. "This house is no place for us. We are unused to walls."

"You know Mamma will make adjustments if you ask her," Xander replied.

Kit turned. "The boys think I'm one of them, but I won't be if I stay."

"You're one of us, aren't you?" Xander asked.

"Am I?" Will could see that the boy was struggling with it.

Xander pushed on. "Mamma doesn't want to take your independence. She merely wants your safety."

"There is no safety, Xan."

"But in the face of danger you have brothers," Will offered. "And you know your enemy, and you can fight him in court, where you stand an equal chance of winning."

The stubborn, closed face remained unmoved.

"Let Xan take Wenlocke to court. You'll get a place

for yourself and your band and likely an income for life—all the independence a man could wish."

Xander spoke. "It's a decent house, Kit. It came to Daventry on his majority. It was his before he married our mother. The income from the estate alone will keep you and the boys for a lifetime."

"Does accepting the house mean I become Wenlocke's heir?" Kit asked.

"It does." Trust Xan to be honest.

"The heir of the man who tried to kill me?"

"And failed," Will pointed out. "You are a tough man to kill."

"And if I don't want to be the Duke of Wenlocke, now or ever?"

Will met Xan's gaze. Kit was one of them, a man who rejected the world's willingness to fix his worth in advance by the accident of his birth, a man who would define himself.

He slapped the pile of letters on the table in front of Kit. "Forget Wenlocke. We'll take on Wenlocke, and win. This good man"—Will rapped the letters sharply—"wanted you to be his heir. That's who you are—his son, the son of a man who knew how to love and how to die. He was willing to do both for you. What can you do for him?"

He found himself shaking. He was perhaps less recovered from his injuries than he thought. Hell, he sounded like a bleeding idealist, like bleeding Helen of Troy. He covered the tremors by pressing his palm flat against the table. "Read them. It's too late for him, but not for you."

Kit's head was bowed. Will did not dare move. He didn't know whether he'd reached the boy or blundered irretrievably.

Then the boy reached out and took the letters; just like that, they were in his hands. He held them loosely a moment before he looked up and leveled that too grave gaze at Will. "If I read these letters, will you meet with Wellington?"

Hell. He could see the bleeding trap about to close. "Read the letters today, I'll meet with Wellington tomorrow."

Suddenly, they were all grinning, Xander and Kit exchanging a glance.

"We had a wager going," Xan confessed.

Chapter Twenty-one

HELEN pushed her mother's chair into place in the high-ceilinged red silk drawing room of the Bishop of York's Grosvenor Square home. Guests continued to pass through the great double doors assembling for the bishop's dinner. Her father laughed heartily from the crowd of clerics around the bishop, willingly letting his wife and daughter retire to a less prominent spot in the room. Helen's mother seldom came to London. It taxed her strength to endure the maneuvering of her chair up and down stairs. And the awkwardness of being wheeled about a crowded room meant that her mother liked to remain settled whenever she found a spot that suited her. At the moment their position afforded them a view of the new arrivals but meant that they were out of the way.

From her girlhood Helen had been used to being her mother's legs. Almost from Helen's birth Jane had suffered from a crippling arthritis that had eventually withered her limbs and confined her to her chair.

Helen had slipped back into the pattern of that life more easily than she'd expected. With Cleo Jones's help that morning, she had been restored to the appearance of a young woman of respectability. Together they had devised a story to account for her absence. By noon she had returned to cousin Margaret. By teatime she had convinced her cousin to accept an account of her missing days. It had been her last foray into fiction.

Since her return with her mother's letters, Helen had been rethinking her life. She must marry. Will Jones had said she couldn't go back again, but she had. The real Tibbs had given Helen's hair the appearance of being bound up rather than cropped. Her mother's modiste had created a new wardrobe, and Helen had agreed to attend whatever gatherings were likely to include eligible men. She had not yet brought herself to smile encouragingly at any potential suitor, but that was a step she meant to take soon, perhaps even tonight. *If the bishop had invited any single men under the age of forty.*

A stir at the door meant some guest more prominent than the others had arrived. This time it was the Duke of Wellington with his famous profile and a following of younger men, all elegant in black evening dress. One of them laughed at a sally from his companions, and Helen froze, tightening her grip upon the handles of her mother's chair.

"What is it, dear?" her mother asked, instantly alert.

Helen murmured that it was nothing, keeping her head down. The room was large, the company numerous, and Will Jones was with the most prominent man in England at this moment while the prince lay ill upon his bed, as yet uncrowned. Will Jones would not see her because he did not expect to see her. She was visible and invisible at once, a neat trick that she thought even he, the master of disguises, would admire.

She forgot that Wellington never neglected the ladies, and that there were few young women in the crowd. Her role as her mother's aid was her only reason for being there. The old soldier began to move around the room, bowing over ladies' hands and exchanging raillery like the flirt the gossips claimed he was.

Instantly, she thought she might excuse herself for a moment, as her mother was settled and the dinner would not begin for an hour. She leaned down at the thought to speak to her mother. *Too late*. Wellington's party reached them. Helen straightened.

"Mrs. Rossdale, good evening. Always a pleasure to see you."

"My lord, have you met my daughter, Marianne?"

"Miss Rossdale, my pleasure. Let me introduce my companions, Sir Robert Peel, our man from Tamworth, and Captain Will Jones, formerly of my intelligence staff."

Helen curtsied, her hands tight on her mother's chair.

She felt Will Jones was equal to the moment as she was not. His look was on her mother, with only the briefest nod for Helen herself, only she was not his Helen any longer. Surely he could see that.

It was the most unfortunate of circumstances to meet him just when she thought to bury Helen forever and take up the life expected of her. Her heart had begun racing the moment she saw him, and now her whole frame suffered an agitation the more acute because she could not show it outwardly. She gripped the handles of her mother's chair and smiled and nodded at the duke's conversation. At last the duke's party moved on to the next group, and Helen and her mother were claimed by Lady Bannister, a friend of her mother's. Helen did her best to attend to that lady's kindness and her pleasure in seeing Helen's mother in London.

But the evening had become a trial as she tried not to watch the progress of Wellington's party around the room. Her body turned like some demented weather vane to Will Jones's direction. She shivered like an idiot bird huddled in misery leaning into a chill, indifferent wind.

Her unease deepened into intense alarm as Wellington's party joined her father's group. Will Jones was actually speaking with her father. She remembered imagining that he would not be intimidated. Of course he wasn't. Whatever he believed about himself, he would not bow and scrape and toady to men of mere birth and rank, and certainly not to the Right Reverend

Arthur Percival Rossdale, Bishop of Farnham, Visitor of Magadalen, New Trinity, and St. John's Oxford.

In that moment Will Jones turned from her father's party and caught her gaze and held it trapped by his own piercing look. For several moments she could not attend to the people around her until her mother's voice brought her back to the present.

"Who is that man in Wellington's party talking with your father?"

"You mean Captain Jones?"

"You'll shake me out of my chair, Marianne. Sit down."

"I'm sorry, Mother, I . . ."

"Who is he?"

"I . . . I don't know."

"My dear, he looked at you with a look that nearly ignited your hair ribbons."

She tried to laugh. "Isn't that what we wanted, Mamma? With Tibbs to dress my hair, the new me is going to attract non-clerical gentlemen."

"That man may be the most non-clerical of gentlemen in London." Her mother actually batted her fan as if heated.

"Mamma, he looks as elegant as any man in the room." She felt her cheeks burn at her own quick defense of him.

"But twenty times more dangerous."

"Mother, you saw all this from one glance?"

"My dear, why don't you take a moment to visit the ladies' retiring room."

"Yes, Mamma." Her mother was right. She needed to regain her composure.

WILL watched her make her escape. Good. He'd unsettled her. She had sure as hell unsettled him. His thinking about her had undergone no less than a revolution in the last five minutes. It was jarring to have everything one thought one understood undone in the midst of the ordinary, in the midst of the lightest of conversation. Now he understood the full cost she had paid for her mad imposture and for whom she had sacrificed everything. He had come to the bishop's dinner party because outside in the dark, desperate men waited to overthrow the government. Inside Will was overthrown.

He kept every movement slow and deliberate, conscious of his loss of balance. All along his plan had been to wait. He didn't trust his feelings for her. And first he had needed to heal the hole in his chest and his damned ribs. Then he had been recruited to face up to the nasty little conspiracy that March had helped to arm. Then, then, his plan had been less clear. He had meant to make Wilde show him where she had gone.

He wasn't going to interfere in her life. She had risked everything for those letters. The letters were his gift to her. The letters freed her from their brief partnership. With the letters she could go back in peace to her real life, where she was not Helen, but someone else, someone's daughter, she had said, not some bleeding bishop's daughter.

He had had some vague idea of making a morning call, of inquiring after an acquaintance, just to see that she was in good health, just to see her once more with all his senses clear. He had considered those letters a dozen times. In the end he could think of only a few possibilities of authorship. A woman with a substantial account at Evershot's Bank had written them. The letters had at one time likely enclosed a draft, which the bearer had taken to Evershot, which that toady Evershot had shared with March. What had made those letters so very dangerous to their author?

He watched for Helen's return and saw instead a shift in the guests that left her mother alone. He stepped away from Wellington and moved toward her before his mind had time to form the thought.

"Mrs. Rossdale."

"Captain Jones." She extended her hand, her gaze frankly curious. "So good of you to seek me out. You see that my condition keeps me rather fixed in place in a gathering such as this."

"Your condition, ma'am, explains a good deal." He took a seat beside her. She looked brittle, wasted with some disease that left her with limbs like twigs that might snap in a wind.

"Perhaps, Captain, you can explain to me how you know my daughter."

"Helen and I met earlier this winter when she was seeking to recover certain letters of great value to a good person who might be ruined."

"Helen?"

He saw the knowledge in her eyes. "She will always be Helen to me."

"I see. Your blood, then, stains certain letters."

It was his turn to look away. "A few drops only. You must not consider it too deeply, ma'am."

"Oh, I rather think I owe you everything, Captain, for your assistance in the recovery of those letters."

"Everything, ma'am, might lead me to make certain demands."

"Excuse me?"

"Are you willing to give me your daughter, ma'am? For that is what I want."

"I don't know you, Captain Jones."

"Sophie Rhys-Jones is my mother, ma'am. I am one of her 'Sons of Sin.'"

He meant to shock her, but his announcement only provoked a wry smile. She cast a measuring look at her husband.

"I am asking you, ma'am, not the good bishop."

"He will rage and storm and call her a strumpet and deny her return to her own home."

"Her home will be with me, ma'am."

She drew a deep breath then and leaned toward him, resting a thin, gloved hand on his. "Take her, Captain. Steal her, if you must."

He turned his hand over and took hers. "I will take her, ma'am. Tonight. Tell me where you are lodged and which room is hers. She'll be married by morning."

"I like your style, Captain Jones." Mrs. Rossdale smiled then, and Will thought he saw in that sweet, frank expression a faint echo of a look of which he was rather fond.

WHEN Helen returned to the drawing room, she did not see Will Jones anywhere. Her mother was talking with Lady North, the wife of the suffragan bishop from Bexley. As she came in sight of her mother's face, she was surprised to see her mother beaming, a wide, happy smile, so unlike her. She doubted that Lady North could say anything to make her mother so glad.

Puzzled, she slowed her steps, and an iron hand gripped her arm and pulled her to a stand next to a fluted white marble column. She faced into the room while he stood, shadowed by the column, but so near that she felt him in every fiber.

"I believe you owe me money." His breath stirred the curls over her ears.

"I said I'd repay you." She tried not to shake.

"I have yet to see a shilling."

"You are working for Wellington, now, Captain Jones? You are recovered?" She wanted to turn to look at him, just to get her fill, just to have some further memory to add to those she had collected. He looked so vital, his grip on her arm tight, unyielding.

"My ribs are excellent. And how is your situation, Miss Rossdale? You're back behind walls, aren't you? Living in a bishop's palace in Farnham Close."

"You can see that I'm restored to the heights of

respectability, accepted even here in the Bishop of York's drawing room."

"I don't think so."

"You can see."

"Hell, what were you thinking? That you could have an adventure and go back to sewing samplers?"

"You met my mother."

He took a deep shaky breath. "I did."

"What else could I do?"

"You could have told me you were the Bishop of Farnham's daughter. I could not have made love to you, Helen, no matter how much I wanted to."

"Don't call me Helen." Helen was dead. *How had she dared such a masquerade?*

"That's who you are, damn it, bleeding Helen of Troy, not meek Miss Rossdale, who's going to push a Bath chair and hang her head and wait for her father to dispose of her to some pious nonentity who wants a mitre someday."

"You're wrong. That's exactly who I am." She was working so hard to answer to her old name, to think of herself as Marianne Rossdale, to put aside that other life.

"Only if you choose to be her."

"I have chosen, you see."

"You think so? Well, unchoose, damn it. I'm in bleeding hell, and so are you."

"No."

"Deny it if you can. You forget, Helen, I stole you

out of a brothel. I can steal you out of a bishop's palace. You're leaving with me, sweetheart."

He released her and crossed the room as if there had been no interruption in his path. When she next ventured to look for him, he was deep in conversation in a group of young men of serious aspect and broad shoulders. He departed just as the dinner was announced. Wellington spoke to the group at the drawing room doors, and they were gone, and Helen was left to push three courses and two removes about her gold-rimmed plate with a variety of cutlery while she considered why that last sight of Will Jones bothered her.

It was, she decided over the apricot tart, the purposefulness of their leave-taking that was so unsettling; they left like men with a mission to fulfill, and they had been sent by the one man an old soldier like Will Jones would willingly follow into battle. In the crowd of dinner guests exclaiming over the delicacies on the bishop's table, she alone knew that not half a mile from where they sat radicals had stored a wagonload of guns.

Three hours later the gentlemen had just joined the ladies when a breathless young man sought Wellington. Helen watched as the man delivered his message, and Wellington's expression turned grim. The young man left, and the men with Wellington began to question him. When other gentlemen moved to swell the crowd and the noise of the questioning, Wellington spoke with the bishop, who silenced everyone for the great man to make an announcement to the whole party.

"Police have intervened and apprehended a group of conspirators who plotted to assassinate the cabinet at a dinner at Lord Harrowby's this evening. All of the would-be assassins are in custody."

Everyone swarmed the duke asking questions.

"Lord Harrowby lives next door," their hostess exclaimed. "Are we safe?"

"Perfectly safe, ma'am," the duke assured her, taking her hand. "And heroic. Your gathering deceived the conspirators into going ahead with their plans."

"You used us as a damned decoy, didn't you, Wellesley?" It was almost a rebuke from their red-faced host, but Wellington merely turned to the men pressing him with questions, all charm of manner wiped from his grim countenance.

"Where were they stopped?"

"In the upper room of a stable on Cato Street."

"How many were there?"

"Twenty-seven."

"Were they armed?"

"Small arms only. We were able to stop them from acquiring a substantial cache of arms."

Helen alone heard her mother's gasp. She reached down to squeeze her mother's shoulder.

"Any casualties?" asked the Bishop of Bexley.

"I regret to report that one officer died. I don't yet have his name." The noise in the room became a buzz in Helen's head in which no words were plain.

The party began to break up within minutes of the duke's startling announcement. None of the young men who had accompanied Wellington earlier returned. Helen wheeled her mother to the top of the stairs where a pair of servants took up her chair to carry her down to the door. Their carriage was summoned. Her father remained in conversation with the bishop and other gentlemen as the ladies departed.

Chapter Twenty-two

H OURS later the square was empty and silent. Helen stood in her nightgown at her window looking out on the bleak, wintry park in the center with its iron rail. She felt empty and shriveled and tried to rouse herself to feel otherwise. The unnamed officer could be anyone. She could not have lost Will Jones twice, not when she'd never really had him, but a little truth emerged as she stood there. She had planned to take him with her in her imagination into whatever life she ended up leading. The thought of him prowling London or lying in his great sultan's bed would remind her of what it was to be alive, to be Helen, to be herself.

But tonight his substantial, real presence had shown

her in an instant what a shadowy insubstantial substitute mere memory was in place of the man.

Now she stood on her own two feet and felt that she'd lost all connection to her body, that she was elsewhere. She wondered if that was what her mother felt, as if one's body were an object separate from oneself that one had to push about like a hawker's cart. Her limbs seemed to have no life of their own.

Across the square a late carriage came slowly along, the horses moving at a crawl, a faint jingle of harness muffled in the fog. Her gaze became fixed on the slow moving coach. It seemed familiar, the devil's own coach drawn by a pair of black horses, the mist parting and swirling about them as in a dream. She was sure she was dreaming when it pulled up before the house. The white-haired driver bent over under his greatcoat and hat, speaking softly to his team. The horses stamped gently, snorting white vapor in the cold air. The door opened, and an elegant gentleman all in black sprang down, the devil himself, except for a cascade of white silk over his shoulder that made no sense.

The gentleman strode directly below her window and cocked his head to look up at her. Helen's impulse was to step back into the shadows, but her frozen limbs did not obey the thought. And then she was shaking and sobbing. He wasn't dead. She put her cold palms to her face to brush away the icy tears, and when she took them away, he was gone. She couldn't see him.

The coach still stood in the street. She tore open the door to the little balcony and heard his real breath huffing from him as he climbed.

"Are you mad?" She leaned over the edge. Her breath, too, made a frosty puff of air.

He'd left his hat below, but he still had the white silk over his shoulder.

"I told you . . ." He caught his breath. ". . . I could steal you from a bishop's palace."

In another minute he had reached the railing and climbed over it. She couldn't move. The devil strode forward and closed her in his arms.

"Oh God, sweetheart, you are real. I thought I'd dreamed you."

"You made me, I think, made me Helen. I couldn't go back to Marianne. I thought I could, but she had no life."

"Do you choose to be Helen now and forever?"

She nodded against his shoulder.

"Then marry me. Tonight. I've a license in my pocket."

Her throat hurt from the joy of it. She clung to him, to his real solid self. When she didn't speak at once, he offered her a further inducement. "You'll have a lifetime to save the devil, you know."

She made her tight throat work, her cheek pressed to his shoulder. "I thought you died. I thought I had to go on in your absence. I couldn't feel my body tonight."

She felt his kiss on the top of her head, so slight a touch, but a sign that her body was real.

"You still haven't answered my proposal."

"Yes. Yes. Yes. I'll marry you tonight." She pressed closer against him, clinging to the fine wool of his coat.

"Good. I've brought you a gown. Let's get you in it." He turned her in his arms and nudged her toward her dressing room.

In the little room she fumbled to light a lamp with cold, stiff fingers, and he took over from her, his hands closing over her trembling ones, to still them briefly. "You are an icicle, aren't you?"

When lamp glow filled the room, his face grew intent. He reached for her and cupped her breasts in his hands, warming them with the stroking of his thumbs. She felt her body returning to her, becoming her own again, united to her will.

She stepped back from his touch and threw open her clothespress, momentarily forgetting her object, then laughing to recall that she wanted a shift and drawers and a corset. When she turned to him again, she stopped, caught by his gaze, which made her feel exquisitely alive. She dropped the garments in her hand on her dressing table bench and shed her nightrail to stand naked before him, his Helen, at last. He came to her then, taking her by her waist, kissing her fiercely, his hands, warm and strong, skimming over her back and shoulders and waist and hips, claiming her.

He stopped and held her tight, his heart beating fiercely against her breast. "I'm bleeding besotted."

Helen pulled on the lawn drawers, and he dropped the shift over her head. He stood behind her to lace the stays of her corset and steadied her as she stepped into the white silk gown.

Quiet laughter shook them both.

"Quick now. Don't make me wait for you any longer." He trimmed the lamp and tugged her hand. They passed back into her bedroom, and he led her to her balcony doors.

She resisted briefly at her balcony, about to make a protest, but he kissed her hard.

"You have to go out the window, love. Harding has the coach in place, and I've a warm cloak for you inside." He swung a leg over the balustrade, her hand still held in his.

She stepped forward and laughed. No sense in telling her impatient groom that she wore no stockings, had no slippers on her feet. Harding had pulled the coach up under her window. She could climb over the balcony rail and step directly onto the carriage roof. Harding tipped his hat at her.

"Where are we going?" she asked.

"To my mother's house. The whole family is waiting there."

Epilogue

❧

THEY had waked all the lost boys and gathered them in the drawing room. Sophie Jones gave Helen a bouquet of winter roses. Cleo Jones arranged a veil for her hair. With little Robin leading the way, Xander Jones walked her down an aisle arranged of a dozen gilt chairs. Kit Jones, still in that black velvet coat of his, stood at Will's side waiting for her. Though a distance of only twelve feet separated her from her groom, Helen knew that in traveling it, she left the walls of her old life behind forever.

The service was blessedly brief. A young curate from a church in Soho read the words. The guests smiled and yawned their way through it. No one commented on the bride's bare feet. Robin clung to her gown until she had to turn to meet a searing kiss from her groom. No danger that her toes would grow cold. Brief toasts were made and hugs exchanged all around.

Already the delay was too much for Will. He needed her now and saw his moment when Xan took Kit aside, and Cleo and his mother began herding the youngest boys toward their beds. Xan had his arm around Kit's shoulders, and the boy stood at ease under the touch. It was a sign that Kit would stay with them after all.

Will stretched, and his ribs felt just fine. Between stopping a radical conspiracy and arranging to steal himself a bride, he'd had no time to go back to his Greek books. Now he tried to remember what that idiot Paris had said to win his Helen.

She smiled at him just then, and he saw her bare toes peeping from under the hem of her ivory gown. They shared a silent laugh across his mother's drawing room. He probably didn't need to tell her that he was burning up with impatience, but his Helen deserved the words. He crossed the room and allowed himself the pleasure of circling her waist with his arm and pulling her to his side. Maybe his Greek lessons had faded but he knew the words he needed to say. He leaned down to his bride and whispered in her ear the words of love and irresistible longing and hunger that overwhelmed him.

She lifted her face to his and pressed a quick kiss to his cheek. "I understand you have a great sultan's bed."

"Oh, I do, and I want you in it, sweetheart."

Keep reading for a special preview of
Kit's story, told in the stunning conclusion to
the Sons of Sin Trilogy

To Seduce an Angel

Coming Fall 2011 from Berkley Sensation!

EMMA faced two gentlemen in front of the massive stone fireplace. A painting on the wall above the gray stones depicted a hunting dog pinning a spotted fawn in agony between his forepaws. Emma knew just how that spotted fawn felt.

They had her pinned, the duke and his nephew. The Duke of Wenlocke, tall, gaunt, and imperious, his face as unyielding as granite, leaned heavily on a black cane. His gnarled hand curved over its golden head like an eagle's talon. His other hand clutched a document.

"This is the girl?" His haughty gaze sent an icy wave of alarm over her. "She doesn't look like a murderess to me."

Emma willed her knees to remain steady. It took steady knees to run.

"Oh she's the one, uncle. Emma Portland." The other man, the duke's nephew the Earl of Aubrey, turned from prodding a great log with an iron poker. A shower of sparks vanished up the flue. *If only escape were that easy.*

"What's your age, girl?" the duke demanded.

"Twenty, Your Grace." Her voice came out thin and reedy, unrecognizable to her own ears over the pounding of her heart.

The duke's gaze fixed her to the spot. "Stuck a knife in some fellow's ribs, did you?"

Don't deny it, Emma. She clenched her fists in the folds of her shawl. Let them think her a murderess. Let them stare as if she were a beast in a menagerie to be baited.

"She's accused of the deed, Uncle, not convicted. I'm sure she'd rather do a favor for a pair of gentlemen than face the law." Aubrey had a smooth voice and a powerful body, his muscled thighs bulging in skintight riding breeches, his calves sheathed in gleaming black leather. Emma had seen him return his pretty mare to the stables with bloodied sides. She had not imagined that he noticed her.

The duke's stare pierced her. "She'd better. I'm done with the law and the courts. Hang all lawyers. I want that whore's get out of Daventry Hall and back in the gutter where he belongs."

He shook the paper in his fist at Emma. "You know what this is, girl? A request for the king's pardon. The duchess wants me to sign it. If I don't, you'll be had before the justices at the next assizes in Taunton."

Emma drew a sharp breath and blinked hard against a sudden sting in her eyes. Somehow, despite all their care, the law had connected her with the spy's death. She knew what that meant: once more, she and Tatty had been betrayed. Her thoughts raced back through the long chain of coins pressed into willing palms and hasty bargains made with low characters. Their enemies might have bought off anyone on sea or land in the thousand miles between home and England.

"You'll hang, you know." The duke handed the paper to Aubrey. "Read it to her."

Aubrey circled her, making a slow deliberate perusal of her person, the privilege of a man with power. A mad desire to pick up her skirts and run passed in an instant. She would not make it half the distance to the library door. She would never make the first set of stairs or the grand entrance or the drive, let alone the woods below Wenlocke House. Escape took care and planning and, above all, luck. No one knew that better than Emma. How many times had she and Tatty and Leo tried and failed in seven years until their jailers had hanged Leo?

Aubrey stopped so close to her she breathed his scent, a heavy male mix of musk and leather with a tang of sweat. "Not pleasant to contemplate, is it? Much better to hide here at Wenlocke, teaching servants' brats. That's what you do, isn't it, Miss Portland?"

She glanced at the flimsy paper in Aubrey's hand. A pardon meant the duchess, their mother's friend, still believed in her. When she and Tatty had reached Her Grace, all their difficulties had seemed to melt away.

Until now. Now the duchess had gone to London to visit her daughter. Tatty was on her way to Bristol. There was no one at Wenlocke to help Emma. Still the duchess's wish must count for something. "The duchess kindly gave me a position."

"Don't think to hide behind Her Grace, girl," the duke snapped.

"But she's done it for weeks, Uncle. Look at her. With her pink cheeks, golden curls, and round blue eyes, a man thinks butter won't melt in that sweet mouth, but that's a lie, isn't it?" Aubrey lifted her chin, the cutting edge of his nail against her throat. Her stomach roiled at the touch. "You're a lie, Emma Portland. There's a dead man in Reading whose reeking corpse says you're someone else."

His broad back was to his uncle. He let go of her chin and reached down and dealt her breast a swift, stinging blow with a flick of his middle finger.

Fear cramped her insides, but Emma knew better than to show it.

"Listen to Aubrey, girl." The duke's voice brought her gaze back to him. "If you don't want them to break your pretty neck and feed you to the crows, you'll do as he says."

Crows. She steadied her treacherous knees. *Don't think about crows, Emma.* Tatty and the babe must reach the coast and the awaiting messenger.

The fire crackled, and outside a March gale howled against the windows. The Englishness of the place, which had seemed so warm and comforting when she first arrived at Wenlocke, now seemed chillingly cold.

The baroque grandeur of the room dwarfed her. Its dark oak cases held thousands of morocco-bound tomes with gold-tooled spines, crushing slabs of history and law. The English liked their law to do the killing. They did not send assassins to kill babes in their cradles, but they would hang the merest child for stealing.

Aubrey and the duke had picked her for some ruthless business because they believed her to be a murderess. She could tell them what a joke that was. Tatty was the fearless one. Leo had always admired her for it, married her for it. Her older brother and her friend had been well-matched in courage. It had been Emma's duty to kill the flies and spiders in the cell she'd shared with Tatty. Once Emma had even been so bold as to kill a rat. But if these gentlemen knew the truth about her, if they saw that she would be of no use to them, they would simply give her over to the law. And the crows would get her.

Aubrey handed the duke the paper. His voice turned coaxing. "We want you to teach a different group of brats. That's all. Here, read this notice." Emma swung her gaze back to him. This time he offered her a newspaper, and she was pleased with the steadiness of her own hand as she took it. Inside her everything quaked as if she would shake apart.

The paper was folded open to a small notice inquiring after a schoolmaster.

Private instruction wanted in letters, mathematics, and geography. References required. Inquire at Daventry Hall for interview.

Emma handed the notice back. Asking a murderess to tutor children in a private gentleman's house was not the favor Aubrey meant. "What makes you think this person would hire me?"

She did not know where her boldness came from. Aubrey watched her with a twisted smile. A ridge of vein marred his smooth, broad forehead. "We will send impeccable credentials with you."

She waited for the trap to close.

"In return, you must do something for us. It's simple, really. I'll keep a man in the village. He'll tell you what to do, and you'll report to him everything you discover about your new employer's habits and plans."

"I must spy?" She tried not to betray any relief. They had not asked her to kill anyone. *Still she would have to report to a man, Aubrey's man. Aubrey would know where she was. Escape would be very, very hard.*

"Or hang if that's your preference."

"On whom must I spy?" Her mind raced. Let them think her agreeable. Let them think she could be bought with a piece of paper. While she spied for them, there would be time for Tatty to reach the coast and Emma to plan another escape. She was the planner, not Tatty.

"On the Marquess of Daventry."

"A lord?"

"A whore's get," the duke's cold voice insisted.

She turned to him. The lines cut deep in his harsh face. The hooded eyes were unreadable. "May I know why I am to spy on this lord?"

"He's an enemy of this house, Miss Portland."

"Is he dangerous, then?"

"He's damned hard to kill."

She stared at the duke, but his closed expression revealed nothing. Emma's brain could make no sense of it—to send a schoolmistress to spy on a dangerous lord. "For how long must I spy?"

"As long as it takes. And we may ask you to obtain certain items for us."

They wanted her to spy and steal. "You will sign the pardon request if I spy?"

In answer, the duke tossed the paper aside. The weary gesture told Emma all she needed to know about her predicament. The duke's unsteady leg buckled, and Aubrey took his arm to help him to a leather chair. Emma understood the gesture. The duke relied on Aubrey now, and Aubrey only waited to take power as it slipped from the duke's grip.

"When do I leave?"

"Today."

DAVENTRY Hall stood on a hill with a wide view of surrounding woods and fields, still bleak and bare in March. Composed of four stories of yellow stone in a mix of styles that spanned centuries, the hall had the look of a house aspiring to be a castle. Emma could not stroll away undetected in such an open setting.

When Emma explained that she was expected for an interview, a cheerful manservant in a plain brown suit led her to a stone chapel. Entering its small, vaulted nave, she experienced a moment of confusion. On Sundays, when their jailers took them to chapel, she and Tatty had counted the painted cherubs on the ceiling with their tiny fluttering wings, peeping around clouds or dangling their bare feet over the architecture. Here the angels seemed to have fallen from the vision of heaven painted on the ceiling to the floor. Sturdy fallen angels lay tangled on one another, round limbs protruding from snowy linen, rosy cheeks and tumbled curls in a jumble.

At her footfall on the stone, the heap of angels stirred.

A mid-sized angel opened one blue eye and peered up at her. "'Oo the devil are you?" he asked with a surprisingly earthly accent.

His words prompted other angels to stir and scramble to their feet in a row. Emma counted seven staring openly at her. They came in all sizes and shapes, dark and light, rough-hewn like carved figures, or rounded with curls about their rosy cheeks—not angels after all, but barefoot boys in white shirts and nankeen breeches. One last angel lay on the stone floor. He was no cherub.

A thin lawn shirt, open at the throat, clung to a powerful chest and shoulders. One sleeve was sheered off completely, exposing a gleaming muscled arm like living marble, and a lean hand gripping a great sword. The warrior angel rolled to his bare feet in a fluid move, tall and lithe and fierce. His shirt billowed about him. Charcoal wool trousers hugged his lean hips and legs. He took Emma's breath. Angels such as he had fought each other for the heavens with fiery swords when Lucifer revolted.

His bold gaze met Emma's and held.

"I came about the position," she told the angel. She had no idea what his place on the household staff was, but the boys around him must be her intended pupils.

He leaned his folded arms on the hilt of his great sword and regarded her with frank interest and a sardonic lift of one brow. "I don't remember advertising for anyone with your qualifications."

"I beg your pardon—*you* placed the notice in the paper?"

"*You* are hardly the expected result."

Emma blinked. "*You* are Daventry?"

"None other." He bowed slightly. "You are E. Portland?"

Emma tried to pull her wits together. *This was the man on whom she was to spy? The dangerous man who was hard to kill.* She found herself babbling her qualifications, real and false. "Emma Portland. I speak French, German, and Italian. I know Latin, maths, and geography. Do you wish to see my credentials?"

"Can you teach?"

"Of course."

"Let's find out." He brandished his sword. Emma retreated a step before she realized it was made of lath. "To the schoolroom, lads."

The ragged cherubs erupted into motion and noise, surging around Emma. In a blink they had snatched her reticule and letters of reference and whisked them away.

She could see her bag bobbing from hand to hand above their heads as they disappeared down a wide stair.

"After you, Miss Portland." The warlike angel lord, whatever he was, grinned at her discomposure. It was not a good start. Her escape plan was not in place. She could not go back to Aubrey's man at the inn. She needed this man to hire her, not to mock her.